DISCOVERING HANNAH

Jane felt someone bump her from behind and turned her head. It was Ernie, who was staring past her with a look of alarm.

"Ginny, what on earth is going on?" he demanded.

Ginny's face was white, almost green, and she looked as if she was trying hard not to pass out. She said nothing, instead pointing with her eyes to something deeper in the woods.

They could see only feet, grimy feet in sandals, dangling about a foot and a half off the ground. Foliage obstructed the rest, and Jane, followed by the others, moved slowly around.

Jane's hands flew to her face. It was a young woman, thin, in a simple pale blue cotton dress sprinkled with tiny white flowers. She hung by the neck from a noose at the end of a rope that had been thrown over a heavy branch; from the branch the rope extended straight and tight at a downward angle to where it was tied to the base of another tree's trunk. . . .

Books by Evan Marshall

MISSING MARLENE

HANGING HANNAH

STABBING STEPHANIE

Published by Kensington Publishing Corporation

Hanging Hannah

Evan Marshall

KENSINGTON BOOKS
KENSINGTON PUBLISHING CORP.
http://www.kensingtonbooks.com

KENSINGTON BOOKS are published by

Kensington Publishing Corp.
850 Third Avenue
New York, NY 10022

All Kensington titles, imprints and distributed lines are available at special quantity discounts for bulk purchases for sales promotion, premiums, fund-raising, educational or institutional use.

Special book excerpts or customized printings can also be created to fit specific needs. For details, write or phone the office of the Kensington Special Sales Manager: Kensington Publishing Corp., 850 Third Avenue, New York, NY 10022. Attn. Special Sales Department. Phone: 1-800-221-2647.

First Kensington Hardcover Printing: May, 2000
First Kensington Paperback Printing: April, 2001
10 9 8 7 6 5 4 3 2 1

Printed in the United States of America

To Justin and Warren

Though he slay me, yet will I trust in him.

—Job 13:15

ACKNOWLEDGMENTS

I would like to express my heartfelt thanks to my editor, John Scognamiglio; and to my agent, Maureen Walters of Curtis Brown, Ltd. Two brighter and more supportive colleagues a writer could not hope to find.

ACKNOWLEDGMENTS

One

There were marigolds in her salad, bright spiky orange petals among the radicchio. With a groan of disgust, Jane pushed the plate away.

Across the table, Bertha looked up from her own identical salad, crunching with gusto on a mouthful of greens. "You don't like it?" she asked, eyes wide with concern.

"No," Jane said petulantly, "and I don't like this restaurant, either." Why had she agreed to have lunch here? The establishment, called Dig, was, in Jane's opinion, one of the most pretentious of New York's expense-account lunch spots. Faux archaeological "finds" that looked like gargantuan stone bowls hung by massive chains from the ceiling of the cavernous room. There happened to be one of these bowls directly over Jane's head, and every so often she cast a wary glance upward at its grimy bottom, wondering how much it weighed. A ton? Two?

"I'm sorry, Jane," Bertha said. "I should have suggested something more . . . down-to-earth. Maybe Smith and Wollensky, or Gallagher's."

Jane forced a smile and shrugged. Where they ate, she realized, didn't really matter. It was self-centered Bertha she disliked more than she could dislike any restaurant. But Bertha was one of the most successful clients of Jane's literary agency, a writer of historical romances beloved by hundreds of thousands, and once in a while Jane was obliged to lunch with her because, unfortunately, Bertha lived here in New York City, no more than twenty-five miles east of Shady Hills, the village in northern New Jersey where Jane lived and worked.

Bertha was a pouter. That was what Jane disliked about her most. In fact, Bertha was pouting now, her lower lip pushed out like a child's, her pale blue eyes sullenly downcast. With her index finger she played with a lock of her badly dyed yellow hair—a yellow, Jane realized, that was uncannily close to that of the marigolds in their salads.

"Jane," Bertha said, "have I done something to offend you?"

"Offend me?" Jane feigned horror. "No, Bertha, of course not." *I just don't like you.* "What makes you ask that?"

"You're not yourself today."

"Oh, yeah? Who am I?"

Bertha looked impatient. "Come on, Jane, we've been working together too long for you not to be honest with me. We're *friends.* What's wrong?"

Yes, they'd been working together a long time—four years—and for the commissions she earned on Bertha's novels, written under the famous pseudonym of Rhonda Redmond, Jane was grateful. But Jane rarely allowed herself to become true friends with her clients. She'd tried that once, had become far more than just friends with one of her clients, and the result had been disastrous.

Besides, Jane wasn't sure herself what was making her so grouchy, other than having to take Bertha to lunch.

"Is it that you have a birthday coming up?" Bertha asked in a coy voice, watching Jane obliquely.

Jane looked at her sharply. "How did you know that?"

"I've always known your birthday. Don't you remember—when I first met you, I asked you your astrological sign and you told me your birthday."

"Oh, right." Yet another reason she disliked Bertha, who had made Jane's astrological sign an important criterion in her decision as to whether to hire Jane. Thank heavens Jane's moon had been in the seventh house, or whatever had happened to be right for Bertha to sign on.

But despite her irritating qualities, Bertha was perceptive, and she was right—Jane had been feeling depressed at the thought of her upcoming thirty-ninth birthday.

"It's May 26, right?" Bertha said.

"Right."

"Mm." Bertha nodded as if suddenly understanding everything. "You're already lonely without Kenneth, and this is an especially bad time for you in that respect."

"What respect?"

"Being with people. Your natural tendency right now is to avoid people, to be reclusive. But you have to fight that tendency."

"Or else what?"

"Or else stay lonely!"

"Bertha," Jane said with exasperation, "I haven't the

slightest idea what you're talking about." But to herself she admitted Bertha was right. She was lonelier these days than she could ever remember feeling in the two and a half years since Kenneth's death. She had told herself that time would make the loss easier to bear, but it had done the exact opposite. The longer he was gone, the more she missed him. He had, after all, been not only her husband, the father of Nicholas, but also her business partner, the other (and principal) literary agent at the Kenneth Stuart Agency. Thus he had been the person with whom she'd spent nearly all of her time. There would never be another Kenneth—of that she had been bitterly reminded half a year ago when she had hoped to take an intimate friendship with one of her clients to an even more intimate level. In the end she had lost him as both a friend and a client—and realized how faulty her judgment could be.

The waiter approached their table. "Are you ladies finished with your salads?"

"Quite," Jane said, watching him take Bertha's empty plate.

He frowned down at Jane's salad, barely touched. "You didn't care for it?"

"I like to keep my flowers in the garden, thanks," Jane said, but the young man didn't hear her because he had already stepped away to take plates off a tray held by a white-aproned young woman who had followed him from the kitchen.

"Now then," the young man said, placing a plate before Bertha, "for you we have the warm buffalo calzone with eggplant chutney."

Bertha smiled and eyed the plate eagerly, like a child. "Yum."

"And for the other lady, the free-range chicken with the yucca frittata."

"Ooh, doesn't that look nice," Bertha commented, leaning forward to study Jane's plate. "Jane, you *must* try this buffalo. It's simply heavenly. Have you ever had it?"

Jane had, once. It had tasted like liver. "No, thanks," she told Bertha with a smile, and cut into her chicken. She'd figured there wasn't much they could do to chicken. As for the yucca frittata, she had no intention of even touching it. With her knife she pushed it to the extreme edge of her plate.

When Jane looked up, Bertha was watching disapprovingly. "No sense of adventure."

"What do you mean, no sense of adventure? This chicken is *free-range*."

Bertha shrugged. "All that means is that it was allowed to forage."

And eat bugs and worms, Jane thought. *My goodness,* she told herself, *I am in a bad way.* Maybe Bertha was right. Maybe the cure for her funk was to do something new, get out more, see people.

"You know, I've been thinking," Bertha said, cutting her buffalo.

Good, Jane thought. *Keep it up and maybe someday you'll be a decent writer.* Then she felt ashamed at such a mean thought and made an effort to listen to Bertha.

"This year," Bertha said, "the annual convention of Romance Authors Together is in New York City. June 17 through 19—Thursday through Saturday. Why don't you come, circulate, maybe give a workshop?"

"A workshop? About what?"

"Since it *is* a romance convention, what about—romance!" This was Bertha being sarcastic.

"What about it?"

"I don't know, Jane, think of something! What your agency is looking for . . . the qualities you look for in the books you take on . . . what constitutes the perfect client!" Bertha threw back her head and laughed. "You and I should give that one together!"

Jane would have laughed, too, but there was a very good possibility Bertha was serious. Could she actually consider herself the perfect client?

"Nah," Jane said. "I'm not a convention person. Can't stand people swarming around me. And some of those romance writers—you know how catty and back-biting they can be."

Bertha seemed to take her remark as a personal affront. She looked on the verge of pouting again. "Present company excluded, of course."

"Of course."

"Oh, come on, Jane." Now Bertha was absolutely pleading. "It would be so good for you. A workshop is about fifty minutes long, with ten minutes for question-and-answer. An hour. What's the big deal?"

Jane had to smile. "You've been put up to this, haven't you? Someone asked you to recruit me?"

Bertha seemed about to protest, then to decide it was no use. She looked down, abashed. "Yes," she whispered. Then she seemed to fill with new courage. "You should be flattered. The people on the board really want you, Jane. You have no idea what an excellent reputation you have. Besides, after that piece in *People* . . ."

Not *that* again. Two months ago the magazine had

finally run its profile of Jane and her fellow inhabitants of Shady Hills, where last fall Jane—with the help of her tortoiseshell cat, Winky—had solved the mystery of Jane's missing nanny, Marlene.

Bertha had bent over to rummage around in her bag and now sat up brandishing the magazine, folded to display a half-page photo of Jane sitting on her sofa with her assistant, Daniel, and his fiancée, Laura. Above the photo ran a headline in bold capital letters: AGENT OF JUSTICE and below it: "Book peddler Jane Stuart is North Jersey's Miss Marple."

Jane rolled her eyes. The notion of being profiled in the magazine had sounded fun at first, and the whole village had gotten into the act: On the following page was a shot of hundreds of Shady Hills residents, all in matching detective-style trench coats, standing in a huge cluster on the green, the white Victorian bandstand behind them.

But now the idea of making her search for Marlene the subject of one of the magazine's lighthearted human-interest pieces seemed obscene to Jane, and she inwardly cringed whenever she thought of it.

Bertha giggled. "I still can't believe it. You can't *buy* this kind of publicity. Anybody who didn't know who you were certainly knows now! You owe it to yourself to cash in on this exposure."

"I don't want exposure," Jane said. "I want clients."

"That's what I'm trying to tell you. People who are considering approaching you to represent them will have a chance to meet you at the RAT convention. It's the largest writers' convention in the country! Think of the possibilities!"

It was true that Jane needed more clients. Her roster

of mostly B-level writers of genre novels barely provided her with a living and allowed her to pay Daniel and Florence, her son Nick's nanny. Jane realized now that she'd known she would eventually have to get out there and beat the bushes for new business. She supposed this was as good a time as any—a better time than any, if Bertha was right. But Jane did hate these things.

She sat pondering for a moment, while Bertha watched her, eyes wide.

"All right," Jane said at last, "but on one condition. That Daniel present my workshop with me."

"I'm sure that's fine," Bertha said. She smiled suggestively, wiggling her eyebrows. "He's dreamy."

"He's also half your age, Bertha Stumpf."

"Age!" Bertha dismissed the whole issue with a flip of her chubby hand. "I'm surprised you didn't point out that he's African-American."

"I think age matters more. But it's a moot point, because he's engaged. To a Caucasian woman!"

"Jane." Bertha leaned forward, her tone that of a parent trying to be patient while lecturing a child. "Love is love! Love is the answer! *C'est l'amour!* Love knows no color or age. Love doesn't even know time!"

Oh, brother. Jane remembered that Bertha's last novel had been a time-travel romance. Jane felt a wave of nausea coming on. Bertha was quickly sliding into Rhonda Redmond mode. Was it too soon to leave?

"Speaking of love"—Bertha leaned even farther forward, eyebrows rising—"who knows who you might meet at the convention?"

Jane looked at her aghast. "You mean a man? At the RAT convention?"

"Why not? There *are* male romance writers, you know.

And some of your fellow speakers are eligible male agents and editors. It's just one more reason you should attend."

"I've already said I would!"

"I know, I know," Bertha said, as if deciding to let up on Jane. "Now," she said briskly, "I'll need a brief bio on both you and Daniel, and also a nice photo of each of you for the convention program booklet. Oh, and a line or two describing your workshop."

Jane, who was fully aware of her own absentmindedness, pulled a small notebook from her purse and jotted these things down.

As their waiter appeared to remove their plates and take their coffee order, Bertha changed the subject to the plot of her current romance, a vintage Rhonda Redmond about a prim English heiress who is separated from her party during a tour of the Sahara and found wandering half-dazed by a darkly dangerous sheikh. Bertha was calling it *Casbah*.

It was a good forty-five minutes more before Jane felt comfortable looking at her watch and exclaiming that she'd better get back to the office.

Outside on the sidewalk, Bertha gave Jane a hug. "Happy birthday. Now don't forget those things I need. And thanks for lunch, sweetie. We really must do it more often."

Sweetie? Jane forced a big smile and waved as she backed toward Seventh Avenue, where she would hail a cab that would take her to the Port Authority Bus Terminal and her bus to New Jersey.

At the corner of Forty-eighth and Seventh, she turned her head sharply when she passed a man who for an instant she thought was Kenneth. Like Kenneth, he was tall and lanky, with sandy hair and light green eyes. She almost called out to him before catching herself.

It wasn't the first time that had happened. Bertha was right. Jane needed a man in her life.

Well, Jane reflected, at least she wouldn't have to see Bertha again until the RAT convention, which Jane was already regretting having agreed to. Beyond that, who knew when she would have to see Bertha again? Lunch with Bertha Stumpf was like jury duty: Get it over with and you're left alone for two years. Laughing at this thought, Jane stepped off the curb at Seventh Avenue and hailed a passing cab.

At the Port Authority she started for her bus's gate, then realized she was starving and veered toward a snack bar for a slice of pizza.

At the precise moment Jane entered the office, Daniel uttered a curse she had never heard him utter before. Hearing her come in, he turned to her from his computer, a sheepish smile on his handsome coffee-colored face. "Sorry. I'm having trouble with this database."

Recently Jane had bought a software program created specifically for literary agencies, and it had fallen to Daniel, whose knowledge of computers far surpassed Jane's, to supervise the entering of client and deal data into the program's database.

Jane plopped her bag on his desk and sat down in his visitor's chair. "What's the problem?"

"The problem is me. Instead of pressing Tab after entering information in a field, I keep pressing Enter, which saves the record and takes me to a fresh record."

"I haven't the slightest idea what you're talking about. Maybe we should just forget the whole thing."

He frowned at her as if she were crazy. "We paid a fortune for this program." He nodded with assurance. "We'll get it right. It's just a matter of getting used to it."

He was right; they *had* paid a fortune for it, and every time Jane thought about that, she felt a pang of money anxiety that tied her stomach in knots and kept her awake nights. But the representative from the software company had convinced her and Daniel that in the long run, the software would save them money—"more than pay for itself," as he had put it. So, trying to think like Kenneth, who had always been up for a risk, Jane had said yes and invested in the program.

Daniel had turned back to the computer and was typing something. He pressed Enter and immediately slammed his hand down on his knee. "Damn! I did it again."

"Why not take a break," Jane suggested. "How did the morning go?"

He swiveled away from the computer, his composure returning. "Pretty well. Quiet. Oh—Angela Nightenson called. She has some questions about her Harper contract." He referred to a small pile of pink slips on his desk. "Agnes Enright at Fawcett says it's too late to change the back cover copy on Joanna Fairman's mystery."

"What! Joanna's going to be livid. That copy gives away the whole solution!"

He gave her an indulgent smile. "Now, Jane, it doesn't really."

"Yes, it does! The caretaker did it, and the copy describes him as sinister."

Daniel opened his mouth to speak, then seemed to

think better of it and instead just shrugged. "It's too late."

She blew out her breath. "You know, sometimes I would like to march into these editors' offices and wring their necks. How the hell would they like it if someone just whipped out the cover copy for *their* books as if it mattered as much as a—shopping list!"

"My, my," Daniel said, pulling back in surprise. "And what kind of a day have *you* been having?"

"What kind do you think? I was having lunch with Bertha."

"Was it that bad?"

"You know I can barely stand her simpering face. But it gets worse." How should she tell him? She smiled her little-girl smile. "Daniel . . ."

"Uh-oh."

"Please don't be mad at me."

"Mad at you?" He frowned in puzzlement. "What have you done?"

"I . . . volunteered you."

"Volunteered me? For what?"

"Bertha begged me. The steering committee or whatever it's called put her up to asking me."

"To do what?"

She winced and forced the words out fast. "To present a workshop at the RAT convention."

"The RAT convention! But you hate conventions. And you hate giving workshops even more."

"That's true," she said reasonably. "But I agreed to it on one condition."

He sat back in his chair and exhaled in tired resignation. "Me?"

"Yes," she said meekly. "Please don't be angry. I'm

sorry, I shouldn't have done it, but Bertha begged me and said it would be good for the agency, especially after the *People* article. I knew she was right, that I should do it, but I . . . I didn't want to do it alone. You know how nervous I get speaking in public."

He smiled understandingly. "I'm not angry. I do know how scared you get—though I've never understood it. You're certainly not shy one-on-one."

"No, that's true," she said thoughtfully, "but it's a proven fact that some people fear public speaking more than they fear death."

"I see. Well, even without the statistic, I'm not mad. I know how hard it must have been for you to agree. I'm happy to help. What is our workshop about, if I may ask?"

"I thought about it on the bus. How about 'The Changing Face of Romance'?"

He shrugged. "We can do that."

She rose happily. "Thanks. Really. Guess I better return those calls." She started for her office.

"Jane?"

She turned.

"Is something else bothering you?"

"What do you mean?"

"You seem . . . down."

"X-ray vision!" she said, pointing at him. "I am down. It's silly, though. It's my birthday a week from Wednesday."

"That's not silly at all."

She cheered slightly that at twenty-six he could understand this. "You don't think so? After all, in nine days I'll be turning *thirty-nine.*"

He frowned slightly. "I understand being a little

depressed at growing older, but does thirty-nine have some special significance?"

"Of course! It's one year from forty!"

"Ah." He gave this some thought, then brightened. "Look at it this way. Kenneth was forty when he met you! You see—that's proof positive that wonderful things can happen even at that advanced age."

He was right; she had met Kenneth when he was forty. Suddenly, not for the first time, she could envision Kenneth emerging from the office at the far end of the reception room, a room she and Daniel now used for storage. In her vision he was giving her that huge white smile he had used so freely. He was as handsome as he'd been the last time she'd seen him, the day he'd left for a meeting in New York City, only to emerge from the Simon & Schuster building, step off the curb, and get killed by a careless truck driver.

She fought down the lump growing in her throat.

"Jane," Daniel said, sitting up, "I'm so sorry. That was thoughtless of me. I didn't mean to make things worse."

"I know, I know." She smiled. "It's not you. And I've already got a plan for dealing with this thirty-nine problem."

"Oh?"

"I'm going to do like Jack Benny and stay thirty-nine forever."

"That works."

She laughed and walked into her office, throwing her bag onto the top of the work heaped sloppily on her desk. She realized that the image of Kenneth was still with her. She sat at her desk and looked at the phone, thinking of the calls she had to make to Angela Nightenson and Joanna Fairman.

She had a better idea. She'd call Nick. He'd be home from school by now. She punched out her home number.

Florence answered in her lilting Trinidadian tones. "Ah, missus, and how has your day been going?"

"As well as can be expected, Florence. Is Nick there?"

"He sure is, sitting right here having Yodels and milk. Hold on."

Jane made a mental note to speak to Florence about giving Nick fruit for his after-school snacks.

"Hi, Mom."

Jane felt her face break into a smile. "Hello, darling. I love you."

"What? Why are you saying that?"

"Aren't mothers allowed to say that to almost ten-year-olds?" Nick had a birthday coming up too, three days before hers.

"Mom," Nick said impatiently, "why did you call?"

"Aside from telling you I love you? To ask how your day is going."

"Fine," he said. "Can I go now? Aaron will be here in a minute, and I promised I'd have my army men set up when he got here."

"Okay. I'll talk to you later." She hung up, feeling better.

Nick always made her feel better. He was all she had left of Kenneth. If only Kenneth had lived to see Nick now; he'd have been so proud. In six days Nick would be ten, only three years from being a teenager.

Jane supposed she would have thoughts like this at various times throughout her life. When Nick graduated from college. When he got married. When his first child was born. And perhaps by then the pain would have lessened. But now that pain was still raw. She glanced at the photo of her and Kenneth and Nick on her credenza, the picture of the three of them in life jackets in Cape May. Had Kenneth known how much she loved him? If she could just be sure that he had, perhaps it wouldn't hurt so bad.

With a deep sigh, she reached for the phone again, finally ready to call her clients.

Two

Was there anything as relaxing as knitting? Jane wondered, ensconced on one of the green-and-gold tapestry-print sofas in the living room of Hydrangea House. She yanked some more yarn out of the bag at her feet, then let her hands fly as she surveyed her friends, fellow members of the Defarge Club, sitting about her.

Next to Jane on the sofa sat Ginny Williams, her pixieish face scrunched up while she tried to untangle a network of different-colored yarns that traversed the back of the sweater she was knitting for Rob, her long-time boyfriend. Jane had lost count of the number of times she had tried to convince Ginny, a neophyte knitter, to attempt something simpler than this complicated sweater pattern she'd selected. More importantly, Jane had recently begun to try to convince Ginny that perhaps her relationship with Rob was never going to work out the way Ginny wanted it to.

Ginny wanted desperately to get married, to have children. Rob, though basically a decent man, was ethereal and free-spirited—not surprising in an artist (he designed silver jewelry)—and even after five years of living with Ginny, he refused to make the move from boyfriend to fiancé.

Jane saw Ginny frequently—more than she saw any of the other members of the Defarge Club—because Ginny worked as a waitress at Whipped Cream, the cozy café across the village green from Jane's office. Jane went there every morning for her muffin and coffee, and often lately she'd been going there for lunch as well. Terribly fond of Ginny, Jane wanted her friend to find happiness and knew she wouldn't find it with Rob. So, when the time seemed right, Jane planned to delicately broach to Ginny the idea of her and Rob separating—ceasing to live together. From there they could end their relationship, and Ginny would be psychologically available to other men, men who would appreciate her.

Jane had it all figured out, the perfect plan. Unfortunately, so far the perfect time had not presented itself for Jane to share this plan with Ginny.

"Oh, pooh!" Ginny exclaimed, almost as if reading Jane's thoughts. Poor Ginny had the colored strands of yarn in more of a tangle than before.

"Ginny, darling," Jane said gently, "why don't you just cut them and weave them into the back?"

"Because," Ginny replied, slamming the half-sweater into her lap, "that's not how it's supposed to be done. You told me yourself that I should carry over the yarns that aren't in use, and then pick them again when I need them."

Jane opened her mouth to speak, then closed it. Ginny was clearly in no mood to be reasoned with.

But old Doris, seated on the matching sofa directly

across from Jane and Ginny's, did not sense Ginny's mood—or if she did, she didn't care about it. She had lowered her own knitting—a magnificent magenta shawl she was making for a woman she had befriended at the Senior Center, where she volunteered two days a week.

"Oh, Ginny, for pity's sake!" she said, her wrinkled face growing even more wrinkled in an exasperated frown. "I've never seen such stubbornness. Give it up! You work at that sweater the way you work at Rob— and you should give him up, too!"

Jane, shocked, looked sharply from Doris to Ginny, who just gaped at the older woman. Tears appeared in Ginny's eyes.

"Doris Conway." Rhoda, in her chair at one end of the grouping, smiled a polite smile, clearly trying to keep things light, or bring them back to their former lightness. "You do speak your mind, don't you?"

The ever-unflappable Doris turned her attention to Rhoda. "You, of all people, should agree with me. Wasting all those years with that—dentist!"

Rhoda, who had been keeping the group up-to-date on the throes of her divorce from the philandering David, abruptly lost her smile. "I'm going to try to keep my temper, Doris, because you always have a big mouth. But I'll thank you not to decide for me that my years with David were wasted. I think that's something for me to decide, thank you. I do, after all, have two beautiful children to show for those years."

Doris shrugged, though whether it was in concession Jane couldn't be sure. Jane noticed that quiet little Penny Powell, seated only a few feet from Rhoda, was knitting furiously, eyes downcast, her neck-length brown hair shielding much of her face like a curtain. Everyone knew that Penny let her husband Alan, a chauvinist of the classic kind, walk all over her. For example, the reason Penny came to these meetings less often than anyone else was that if Alan suddenly announced he was going out with his buddies, Penny meekly agreed to stay home and take care of one-year-old Rebecca. But anyone who knew Penny knew nothing would ever change—unless Alan changed it.

An uncomfortable silence had descended. At the head of the group, in her customary armchair, bird-faced Louise sat like a statue, only her eyes moving, as if judging the temperament of each club member in turn.

Jane realized that Louise, though uninvolved in the conversation, was more upset than any of them. Poor Louise, so repressed, hated conflict of any sort. And Hydrangea House was, after all, hers—well, hers and Ernie's. It suddenly occurred to Jane that one day Louise, weary of conflict like this, might someday decide to stop hosting the club's every-other-Tuesday meetings in this beautiful old inn. That would be a shame.

"Louise," Jane said, breaking the silence.

"Yes!" Louise burst out, as if startled.

Jane laughed. "Sorry. I've been meaning to ask you . . . I'd like to have a little birthday party for Nick—he's turning ten next Sunday. Our backyard is so narrow and steep, but I was thinking the inn's backyard would be perfect. I'll pay you, of course. Do you think I could have the party here? I'm thinking there will be about fifteen kids from Nick's class, and maybe ten adults." Jane looked around the group. "You're all invited, of course."

Louise was smiling, obviously relieved at the subject change. "Of course, Jane, that would be lovely. But I wouldn't dream of letting you pay me. What day were you thinking? We have been very busy lately." The inn often hosted weddings, corporate parties, and other such events.

"How about this Sunday?" Jane asked. "That's his birthday."

"Hmm," Louise murmured, surprised. "Today's Tuesday—not much notice."

"I know. I'm ashamed to say I've been so busy with work I haven't taken a minute to think this through till now."

Louise thought for a moment. "That will work out fine. I'll tell Ernie. We'll set up one of the long tables for the kids and another for the adults. What kind of food were you thinking?"

"Nothing fancy. I'll pick up some pizzas from Giorgio's and a birthday cake from Calandra's." Calandra's, in nearby Fairfield on Route 46, made elaborate and delicious cakes and pastries.

"Lovely," Louise said. "We'll work out the rest of the details—balloons and such."

"Great. Thanks, Louise." Jane surveyed the group. Her subject change seemed to have worked just as well on the others, who were all smiling to themselves, apparently at the thought of a children's birthday party. For a few moments everyone knitted quietly, the silence broken only when someone leaned forward to retrieve her coffee from the coffee table, or to replace her cup in its saucer.

Jane worked a few more rows on the swimsuit cover-up she was making as a surprise for Florence. This summer

Florence would be taking Nick to the Fairfield town pool, and Jane had thought it would be a nice gesture to make Florence this cover-up as a gift. Jane had found the pattern in *Vogue Knitting* and planned to make one for herself as well.

Out of the corner of her eye, Jane saw Louise peering about the room. When Jane looked up, Louise's expression was troubled.

"Is something the matter, Louise?" Jane asked.

Louise shrugged. "It's the weirdest thing. Do you remember the antique quilt I used to keep on the back of that sofa?" She indicated the one on which Jane and Ginny were sitting. Jane leaned forward, looked behind her, and realized the quilt was missing.

"Are you having it cleaned?" Jane ventured. "Repaired?" Jane knew the quilt was quite old and had needed minor repairs in the past.

"No," Louise said, clearly baffled. "I'm not. It's just . . . disappeared!"

"Disappeared?" Rhoda said.

"Louise," Doris said impatiently, "quilts don't just disappear. Ginny, look on the floor behind you and see if it fell."

Louise threw Doris an irritated look. "I think I would have found it if it had fallen." She shook her head. "It's gone."

"Did you ask Ernie about it?" Ginny asked.

"Yes. He has no more idea than I do."

Rhoda, eyes wide, said, "Do you think one of your guests *stole* it?"

Louise looked sad at this thought. "It's the only answer I can come up with. It *is* a valuable old piece. But to just *take* it. Who would do such a thing?"

"You'd be surprised," Doris said. "My mother, whenever we stayed at a hotel, took everything that wasn't bolted down. Ashtrays, towels, blankets . . . even took a picture off the wall once." She laughed to herself. "Why, once, when she knew we'd be staying at a really nice old place, she brought an empty suitcase just for the booty!"

All the women stared at Doris in horror.

Doris surveyed the group. "Don't look at me like that. *I* didn't do it, my mother did." She turned to Louise. "I didn't take your quilt."

"Oh, Doris," Louise said with an embarrassed laugh, "of course you didn't."

At that moment Penny spoke, and Jane realized it was the first time tonight. "I know who could find it," Penny said in her near whisper, her eyes still fixed on her knitting. Everyone waited. Penny looked up smiling, clearly pleased with herself. "Jane! She's the detective!"

She was referring, of course, to Jane's having solved the Marlene mystery, and *People* magazine's subsequent coverage of the story.

Jane said, trying to keep her tone light, "I thought we agreed we weren't going to talk about that anymore." She immediately felt bad for having said it, because Penny, crestfallen, immediately looked down again at her knitting.

"Yes, ladies," Louise said, sounding like a schoolmarm, "we promised Jane. No more talk of—all that."

"Well, don't look at *me*," Doris muttered. "*I* didn't bring it up."

Now poor Penny looked positively ashamed. Her face red, her lower lip clenched between her teeth, she gave a rapid nod and retreated behind her hair curtain, knitting furiously.

Jane felt awful. "Penny, it's okay, really."

"Well!" Louise said. "I don't imagine we'll ever find out what happened to my quilt, and now I think perhaps I don't want to know." She looked at her watch. "Ooh, late."

Doris was practically hurling needles and yarn into her bag. "Sometimes we're here as late as midnight, Louise Zabriskie, and you know it as well as I do. You just don't feel comfortable when there's tension in the air, and there's plenty in the air right now. Wouldn't you say so, Penny?"

Penny gaped at Doris as if the older woman had just suggested murder. Then Penny turned back to her own knitting and began putting away her paraphernalia.

Jane looked at Louise, who sat perfectly composed, as if Doris had not even spoken. "Thank you for coming, ladies. We'll see you in two weeks."

"Oh for heaven's sakes," Doris muttered in disgust, and got up. So did everyone else, heading out of the living room into the foyer.

Ernie, looking plumper than ever in chinos and a too-tight mint green polo shirt, appeared at the end of the hallway that led to the kitchen. He gave a big gracious smile. "Evening, ladies. See you soon." Then he seemed to sense the tension Doris had cited. His smile vanished, and he darted a glance at Louise. Jane saw her give him a warning frown with pursed lips, telling him to be quiet.

Jane lagged behind. When everyone else had said good night and left, she approached Louise. "I'll give you a call about Nick's party. Thanks again."

"My pleasure," Louise said. Her face grew troubled. Jane could tell she wanted to say something, but Louise was watching Ernie retreat back down the hallway to the kitchen, and seemed to be waiting until he was out of earshot.

"Jane," Louise finally said, in a low voice, "could I talk to you for a minute?"

Jane frowned, puzzled. "Of course, Louise. Anytime."

"Come in here," Louise said, and led the way into the dining room. In the far wall, on the far side of Louise's magnificent Queen Anne dining room set, was an immense bow window hung with elaborate drapes and shears. "Over here," she said, walking to the window and opening them. The moon was out that night— Jane recalled that last night it had been full—and the inn's spacious backyard was bathed in eerie moonlight. White wrought-iron tables and chairs had been placed randomly on the grass. At the far end of the lawn stood the thick woods, massive oaks and maples, a high black wall. Just to the right of the window, Jane could make out the inn's large patio under its green-canvas awning attached to the back of the building.

Jane waited. She looked at Louise, who stood gazing out into the semidarkness.

"Jane," Louise said at last, "I saw the strangest thing last night. A young woman—a girl . . ."

"A girl?"

Louise gave a slight nod. "Walking in the woods. Right at the edge." She pointed to the left, toward where Jane knew Hadley Pond to lie. "I was ready for bed and came in here looking for a book I couldn't find anywhere. I thought maybe I'd left it on the sideboard. Well, I hadn't, but as I turned to leave, something

moving in the woods caught my eye. Something pale
. . . I left the room dark and watched from this window."

"Who was it?"

"I don't know. Of course, I couldn't see her very well,
but I don't think it was anyone we know."

"Could you make out *anything* about her? Features?
Hair? What she was wearing?"

"No." Louise looked at Jane searchingly. "Only that
she looked pale, as if she had on a light-colored dress.
I'm certain she was no hiker or camper, though I
couldn't say why. Something about the way she was
walking . . . What I want to know is, why would she—
why would anyone—be walking in the woods at night?
It must have been almost midnight."

"I have no idea. Did you go outside to see who it
was?"

"No, not right away. I just watched her. She was walking very slowly, and she kept to just inside the woods;
she never came out onto the lawn. It was almost as if
she was afraid to come out—I can't explain it. After a
few minutes I decided I'd better go out and see who
she was, so I hurried through to the kitchen and out
the back door. I could still see her. I ran across the lawn
and called out to her. She stopped short, as if she was
afraid, and then ran deeper into the woods."

"Jane, you're still here."

Both women jumped.

Ernie stood in the doorway. There was no telling how
long he'd been there. He was smiling his big easygoing
smile.

For some reason she wouldn't have been able to
explain, Jane felt uneasy. "Yes," she said, affecting light-
heartedness, also without knowing why. "I'd better get

going." She led the way out of the dining room, and they joined Ernie in the foyer. "Thank you both for a lovely evening."

"Oh, Jane," Louise said, "you know perfectly well there was nothing lovely about it. All we did was fight."

"Isn't that what we always do?" Jane laughed.

Louise just stood awkwardly. Her gaze darted from Jane to Ernie, then fixed on the foyer's tile floor.

"My bed is positively calling out to me," Ernie said. He gave Jane a peck on the cheek. "Night, love, thanks for coming. See you in a couple of weeks." They watched him climb the stairs and disappear down the upstairs hall. Jane noticed that Louise's gaze lingered on Ernie an odd moment longer than seemed natural, as if Louise were lost in some thought about him.

At that moment the front door opened and a man entered. Jane was immediately struck by how big he was—not overweight, but muscular. Easily six and a half feet tall, he had a chest like a barrel and thick arms and legs. He was also, Jane noticed, exceptionally attractive, with close-clipped black hair and a chiseled face set with bright blue eyes. He wore black-cotton slacks and, like Ernie, a polo shirt, except that this man's was black and he sure filled it out better.

Seeing Jane and Louise, he grinned amiably. "Good evening," he said, nodded once rather shyly, and headed up the stairs.

Jane waited until he was out of earshot, then turned avid eyes on Louise. "Who was *that?*"

Louise had to laugh. "That's Mr. Vernell. Mike Vernell. Now he *is* a hiker. That's why he's here. He's been here all week, on vacation, hiking in our woods."

"Doesn't look like he's been hiking tonight."

"No," Louise agreed, "I think he has friends in the area who join him for dinner. He's a very nice man."

"Nice isn't the word for it," said Jane, who hadn't responded to a man this way in—well, years. "*Ooh là là* Sasson! He looks like Clint Walker. Do you remember him? *The Night of the Grizzly?* He can lie on my bearskin rug any day." She growled.

"Jane! Such talk. Clint Walker, *The Night of the Grizzly* . . . Boy, are you dating yourself."

"At least someone is!"

"Funny. You know perfectly well that there are several nice men right here in Shady Hills who would jump at the chance to take you out."

"Like Mark Stapleton?"

Louise said nothing. She was the one who had introduced Jane to Mark. Mark was the principal at Shady Hills High School, a man who lived with his mother (to take care of her, he'd told Jane, though when Jane had met the woman, she'd been in perfect, bouncy health). Mark had never married. A month ago he had taken Jane to dinner and a show in New York City. Jane had found him . . . prissy.

"Not for me," she said, and gave Louise a wicked grin. "I'd rather have old Clint up there."

Louise blushed.

Jane burst into laughter. "I'm sorry, Louise, I've shocked you terribly, haven't I? I'd better go before I do something I'll regret in the morning." She walked to the door. "But I'm serious. If Mr. Vernell turns out to be single, he can hike on over to my house anytime he wants! Oh—I'll call you to work out the party details. Thanks again."

Before Louise could respond, Jane closed the door,

crossed the wide porch filled with white wicker furniture and hung with baskets of begonias and petunias, and went down the steps to her car, parked on the wide circle of gravel in front of the inn.

It was a lovely night, the air fragrant with pine and lilac and honeysuckle. She drove down the long drive and onto Plunkett Lane, which wound through the woods to the village.

She thought about Mr. Vernell and felt an old stirring deep within her. Perhaps silly old Bertha was right. Perhaps love was, indeed, the answer.

And a deep sadness washed over her, for thoughts of love brought thoughts of Kenneth. Of course love was the answer. She'd *had* the answer, but one day it had simply disappeared.

What she needed to do, she realized, was to learn again how to ask the *question.*

Three

"Jane, can you help me with these rocks?" Ginny scrambled around the long picnic table, placing rocks from the supply of them in her arms at each corner of the table and at intervals along the sides. "This wind is fierce!"

She was right—the wind was strong, and without the rocks the tablecloth would have blown away. But it was a glorious day nonetheless, a perfect Sunday afternoon in May. The sun shone brightly in a cloudless china blue sky, birds sang in the woods surrounding the inn's backyard, and the air carried that scent of honeysuckle Jane had picked up leaving the Defarge Club meeting Tuesday night.

Suddenly the wind rose, flapping the edges of the canvas awning that shaded the patio. The tablecloth lifted at the edges, as if it would fly away.

"You know," Jane said, grabbing some rocks from Ginny and placing them between the ones already there, "they make special clips to hold tablecloths down. They have them at Kmart. This rock thing is what my *mother* did.''

''I like the old-fashioned way,'' Ginny said defensively, though she was smiling as if she knew Jane was right.

''Me too,'' Louise chimed in, emerging from the inn with a tray of brightly colored napkins and plastic cups, plates, and forks. ''It's more fun this way. Like ants at a picnic.''

Jane shrugged. She gazed far across the lawn at Nick and his friends, who were playing a game Nick had made up called *Star Wars* tag. Nick shouted, ''Obi!'' and tore across the lawn, squealing with laughter. The dozen or so other boys and girls bolted after him.

''Aren't they sweet?'' Ginny was watching them wistfully. Jane and Louise exchanged a silent, sympathetic look.

Louise worked her way around the table, setting down plates. ''I'll leave the napkins in a pile over here,'' she said.

''Yes, under a rock,'' Ginny said, and plunked one down on the pile.

The door of the inn opened again and Doris appeared, barely visible behind a stack of pizza boxes.

''Doris!'' Jane ran to her. ''Let me help you with those.'' She relieved the older woman of half the boxes and set them down at one end of the table.

''Such a fuss,'' Doris said in her deep brisk voice, and set her boxes on top of Jane's. Doris, who was seventy-two, hated being treated like an old person. She put her hands on her hips and surveyed the table. ''Now what?''

''Nothing, really, for the moment,'' Louise said. ''The

children are having a wonderful time. How about some lemonade for us?"

"Sounds good to me," Ginny said.

"Me too," Doris said, sitting on a bench of the picnic table.

Ernie rounded the corner of the inn. "Did I hear 'lemonade'?" he asked brightly.

Louise's smile vanished. "I'll get it, dear." She was all business now. "And I'd better make sure the cake is ready. Twelve candles, right, Jane? Ten years, one for good luck, and one to grow on—that's how we've always done it."

"That sounds perfect," Jane said, and felt a rush of warmth for Louise, truly a good friend. Jane wondered why Louise seemed troubled about Ernie. Perhaps they were in the midst of some squabble.

Ernie dropped his ample form into an Adirondack chair near the door and smiled at the children, who were now piling all over Nick and screaming, "Darth! Darth!"

"I want to be a kid again," Ernie said dreamily. "Things were so simple then."

"Hello, all!" Penny appeared from around the side of the inn, carrying an enormous box wrapped in vivid Looney Tunes paper. She set the box at the corner of the patio.

"Penny," Jane said, "what on earth—?"

"You said Nick liked *Star Wars*. This is Boba Fett's spaceship, or whatever it's called."

"That's much too extravagant," Jane said.

"Like I said," Ernie called from across the patio, "things were simpler when I was a kid."

They all smiled.

"Penny," Jane said, "where are Alan and Rebecca?"

Penny looked down at the patio, her hair falling to each side of her face. "Alan . . . had some chores to do. He's sorry he couldn't make it."

Ginny and Jane exchanged a knowing look. Poor Penny was constantly making excuses for Alan.

"Then he's watching Rebecca?" Ginny asked.

"No, she's in the car. I'm going to get her now." Penny turned and walked back around the inn toward the front drive.

Ginny shrugged and came over to Jane. "Do I *really* want to get married and have children?"

"Yes, Ginny, you do. Not all men are like Alan."

"I guess you're right," Ginny said.

At that moment Nick ran up to Jane. His face was red and sweaty, and he was breathing hard. His shorts were covered with grass stains. "Mom, I'm hungry. Are we eating soon?" He eyed the stack of pizza boxes.

"Soon, honey. It would be rude to eat before everyone's here."

"Who's not here?"

"Daniel and Laura. And also Rhoda. I'm sure they'll be here any minute."

"I know!" Ginny said. "Let's have the scavenger hunt now."

"But that takes a long time," Nick whined, "and we're hungry."

"We can call a time-out when Daniel and Laura and Rhoda get here," Ginny said.

Nick thought for a moment. "Okay. How does this scavenger hunt work?"

Ginny grabbed her bag from the edge of the patio and peered into it, finally bringing out several stacks of cards held together with rubber bands. "First we separate into teams. I just happen to have a list of who's on what team." From her bag she whipped out a list of the children's names grouped into teams of four.

"So efficient!" Jane commented.

"It's the waitress in me." Ginny winked. "Kids!" she hollered. "Over here, please!"

She met them in the middle of the lawn and began explaining the scavenger hunt. How sweet their faces were as they listened in rapt attention, Jane thought.

"Coming through!"

Jane turned. Rhoda rounded the corner of the inn, arms full of cardboard boxes. "Hi, all," she said brightly. "My arms are numb. I'd better get this ice cream into the freezer. Where's Louise?"

Ernie got up. "She's inside, Rhoda. I'll stick that in the freezer for you. Thanks," he said, relieving her of the boxes, and he disappeared inside.

Rhoda, looking smashing in a culotte set, came over to Jane. "Hi, hon. Read any good books lately?"

Jane smiled. "No." She looked Rhoda up and down. "Pretty snazzy for a kids' party."

"I," Rhoda announced proudly, "have a date."

Penny, who had been fussing with the napkin pile, stopped and stared at Rhoda.

Doris sat up straight. "Way to go, girl."

"Yes, Rhoda, how wonderful," Jane said. "May I ask who?"

"You may," Rhoda said, beaming. "His name is Adam and I met him at an antique store in Chester."

"He works in a store?" Doris asked flatly.

"No, Doris," Rhoda said, rolling her eyes, "he was *looking*, like me." She smiled and wiggled her perfectly tweezed brows meaningfully. "He's terrific. This isn't our first date."

"Way to *go*," Doris repeated.

Somehow even Ginny in the middle of the lawn heard this, and suddenly turned toward Rhoda with a bright smile. "That's fantastic, Rhoda!" She turned back to the kids. "Now everybody got it? Ready . . . set . . . GO!"

"Thanks," Rhoda said to everyone, looking quite pleased with herself. "I'm meeting him for a movie and dinner later."

"Wonderful," Jane murmured. To her own surprise, she felt a pang of envy. Rhoda's divorce wasn't even final and she was already snagging terrific men in antique shops. Jane wondered if maybe she ought to develop an interest in that area.

"What's wonderful?" Daniel, dapper in a blue-and-white seersucker jacket over navy slacks and polo shirt, appeared bearing a small wrapped gift under his arm.

"My date," Rhoda said, coming up to Daniel and planting a kiss on his cheek. "Good to see you." She looked him up and down. "Damn, you're cute. If you're ever available, don't you forget old Rhoda!"

Jane looked at the easily embarrassed Daniel to see if this had flustered him, but he took Rhoda's comment with good grace.

"Where's Laura—your *fiancée?*" Jane asked, shooting a pointed look at Rhoda, who gave her a mischievous grin.

"She went in the front," Daniel said. "Needed to use the ladies'. Now," he said, producing a small camera from his jacket pocket, "before I forget, let's get shots of us for that convention you got us roped into."

"Wonderful think-of-everything Daniel," Jane said. "I forgot all about it."

"I knew that," Daniel said cheerfully, looking around. "How about right over here, in front of Louise's azaleas?"

"Sounds good to me," Jane said, feeling a flutter of nervousness in her stomach at the thought of the RAT convention and wishing he hadn't brought it up. She positioned herself in front of the vivid mass of fuchsia flowers while Daniel took her picture; then they traded places and she took his.

"Good, that's done," Jane said. "Thank you, Daniel."

At that moment Ernie emerged from the inn. He looked preoccupied, and suddenly put on a smile as he stepped out onto the patio.

Behind him came Laura, smiling innocently. "Hello, hello." She looked summer stylish in a short lavender dress and a matching wide-brimmed hat that sat at a perfect angle on her light brown hair and complemented her pretty heart-shaped face.

"Love it," Rhoda said, eyeing the hat.

"Thanks," Laura said. "I thought it might be too—"

But before she could finish, the wind picked up her hat and carried it high into the air. "Oh, my!" she cried.

Daniel darted off to fetch it, but before he had reached the middle of the lawn he stopped short because a long shrill cry tore the air, and as it did a flurry of small black birds rose from the edge of the woods into the sky.

For the briefest moment Jane, in the confusion, thought the piercing shriek came from the birds. Then she realized, with a sharp intake of breath and a painful pounding of her heart, that the high-pitched sound was the terrified scream of a child.

And that that child was Nick.

Four

"Nicholas!" Jane cried.

She ran across the grass toward the source of his scream, the other adults close behind her. She realized now that the children had been in the woods, presumably gathering items for their scavenger hunt. Jane could see neither Ginny nor any of the children through the trees, but as Jane neared them, she could hear children crying.

She was the first to enter the woods, by means of a path that bored into the shadows between two wide oak trunks. She had walked only a few feet when she nearly collided with Ginny, who stood on the path with her back toward Jane and was calling desperately to the children, whom Jane could see just beyond her.

"Kids, quickly! Come out, follow me!" Ginny, oblivious of Jane and the others behind her, moved quickly among the children, roughly shepherding them toward the path that led out of the woods. Jane spotted Nick. His face was sickly white and tears ran down his cheeks.

Ginny grabbed his shoulder and pushed him after the other children. At that moment Nick saw Jane and ran to her, hugging her hard.

Jane felt someone bump her from behind and turned her head. It was Ernie, who was looking past her with a look of alarm.

"Ginny, what on earth is going on?" he demanded.

Ginny, having gotten all of the children headed out of the woods, spun around to look at him. Jane had never seen her like this. Her face was white, almost green, and she looked as if she was trying hard not to pass out. She said nothing, instead pointing with her eyes to something deeper in the woods.

"Oh, good Lord . . ." Doris whispered.

They could see only feet, grimy feet in sandals, dangling about a foot and a half off the ground. Foliage obstructed the rest, and Jane, followed by the others, moved slowly around.

Jane's hands flew to her face. "My God." It was a young woman, thin, in a simple pale blue cotton dress sprinkled with tiny white flowers. She hung by the neck from a noose at the end of a rope that had been thrown over a heavy branch; from the branch the rope extended straight and tight at a downward angle to where it was tied to the base of another tree's trunk.

"Who is she?" Penny said softly.

Jane studied the woman. She didn't think it was anyone she knew but it was impossible to know for sure because even in the dappled shade of the trees it was clear that the woman's face was covered with garish makeup, almost like a clown: a red circle of blush, like old-fashioned rouge, on each cheek; scarlet lipstick applied so sloppily that it extended well past her lips to create a weird oval red mouth; deep blue eye shadow on her eyelids, which were, mercifully, closed. Her hair was an ordinary brown and shoulder length; it hung straight and limp—as if, it occurred to Jane, she'd had a bad haircut. Jane squinted, studying the woman's face harder. Could she be faintly smiling? It seemed so, but this, too, was impossible to say for sure because of the lipstick. If not for the unnatural angle of her head, she might have been peacefully asleep, so relaxed was her face, so gently closed were her eyes. But that was how death often looked, Jane told herself. That was what death was—a kind of sleep.

The wind rose, rustling the leaves on the trees, playing with the girl's hair. Goose bumps rose on Jane's arms, and she shivered.

"Does anybody know her?" Ernie asked softly, and Jane jumped at the sound of his voice.

No one answered.

"Come on, let's get away from her," Louise said, taking control, and like automatons everyone turned and started back along the path.

Nick held Jane's hand tightly. She realized now that she should have shepherded him out of the woods with the other children, that she'd allowed him to study the poor hanging woman along with the grown-ups.

"Mom?" Nick was crying. "Who is she?"

"I don't know, darling," was all Jane could say, wrapping her arm tightly around his shoulder. "I don't know."

They emerged into the bright sunshine. Ginny had the children on the patio in a cluster. A few feet from

Jane and Nick, Louise was speaking softly to Ernie. "Nothing like this has ever happened at Hydrangea House," Jane heard her say, an oddly accusatory note in her voice. Then, "I'll call the police," Louise said, and ran toward the inn.

Jane led Nick to the patio. Ginny was gone, Penny overseeing the children in her place. Jane gave her an inquiring look.

"Ginny's calling their parents," Penny explained.

Jane nodded.

"You should take Nick home," Doris said. She was only now arriving at the edge of the patio from the woods. "Apparently he discovered her."

Jane looked down at Nick in horror. He was no longer crying, but he was deathly white and very still, staring into nothingness, as if seeing an image of the hanging woman that was imprinted on his eyes.

"Yes, come on, Nick, we're going home now." She took his hand again and started for the inn.

Daniel and Laura stood together near the door. Daniel's face was set in a frown she seldom saw, a frown that signified he was deeply upset. Beside him, Laura dabbed at her eyes with a handkerchief.

"We're leaving," Jane told them.

They nodded.

Rhoda approached Jane, gently touched her shoulder, and leaned over to whisper in Jane's ear. "Jane, if Nick found her, the police may want to ask him some questions."

Jane hadn't thought of that. She felt a sudden surge of fierce protectiveness. She shook her head firmly. "No. He's been through enough already." She felt anger, though at whom she couldn't say. And then she realized she was angry at the dead girl herself, for killing herself that way, for being so selfish, for letting innocent children find her like that, children who should never see such things. *But I'm not being rational,* she told herself.

She and Nick entered the inn's cool back servants' pantry. Louise emerged from the kitchen. "The police are coming."

And at that moment they heard a siren. It grew louder and abruptly stopped with a yelp.

Jane wanted to speak with Louise. "Nick, darling, just wait here for a second. Mommy needs to speak to Mrs. Zabriskie for a minute."

Hearing this, Louise followed Jane into the kitchen.

"Louise," Jane said softly, "I don't want the police questioning Nick and upsetting him. Don't tell them he found the girl."

Louise's jaw dropped; her eyes widened. "How awful. I didn't know. I thought Ginny found her."

"No," Jane said, already back in the pantry and grabbing Nick's hand. "Come on, honey, this way."

She hurried with him to the end of the pantry and out into the hallway that led to the foyer. Louise had no doubt told the police a dead woman had been found in the woods behind the inn. The police would park and walk around the inn. Jane would hurry Nick out the front to her car, which she'd parked on the gravel drive, and they would slip away before anyone could find Nick and upset him.

Reaching the end of the hallway, she could see straight across the foyer and through the windows to the front, where two police cars were parked.

"Let's go," she said softly to Nick, and pulled him

briskly across the foyer as the dark outlines of three
men loomed up against the shirred ivory-lace curtain
on Louise's front door, on which one of the men now
knocked firmly.

Louise appeared from behind Jane, looking dis-
traught. She started toward the door to open it, then
stopped and looked helplessly at Jane. Thinking quickly,
Jane pulled Nick back toward the hallway. She glanced
over her shoulder at Louise, who was clearly waiting to
answer the door. But to Jane's horror, the doorknob
turned and the door swung open before Louise had
even reached it.

Jane froze, still holding Nick's hand. One of the men,
the one in front who had knocked, looked familiar to
Jane. He wore plain clothes, a blue blazer over gray
slacks, and was of medium height, with exceptionally
broad shoulders. He had dark brown eyes and fine,
straight sandy hair combed in a neat line across his
forehead. Behind him stood two uniformed officers.

They strode into the foyer, the officers keeping
respectfully back, the man in plain clothes approaching
Louise. "Take me to her, please."

Louise turned to lead him through the inn to the
back. The man started to follow her, then noticed Jane
and stopped. His lips curved in the tiniest, most professional of smiles.

"Mrs. Stuart," he said, his tone respectful. "You probably don't remember me."

So she was right that he looked familiar. He was with
the police, obviously, but when had she met him?

As if reading her thoughts, he said, "We met when
you were looking for your nanny last fall. Greenberg,"

he said, pointing to himself, "Detective Stanley Greenberg."

She realized she'd blocked him out with as many of the other memories of that episode as she'd been able to block out. But she remembered him as having been kind to her, respectful and deferential, the way he was acting toward her now.

"Yes, of course," she said, forcing a little smile of her own. "I'm sorry."

"Not a problem. You're leaving?"

"Yes .... My son is very upset. You'll see—" She glanced at Louise, who stood nearby, silently waiting.

"All right," Greenberg said to Jane. "I'll call you if I have any questions. First I'd better have a look." He gazed down at Nick and gave him a kind, almost sympathetic smile, though of course he couldn't have known Nick had more reason than the others to be upset.

Jane walked with Nick between the two officers and out the front door. They hurried across the porch, down the steps, and across the drive to Jane's car.

"Mommy," Nick said, strangely calm, as Jane drove through the gate onto Plunkett Lane, "who *was* that woman in the woods?"

"I—I don't know."

"Why was she there?" Tears crept into his voice. Jane found herself starting to cry, too.

"I don't know, honey," she said. "I just don't know."

And then, though of course she'd known it all along, she remembered that the reason they had been at Hydrangea House in the first place, the reason for the party, was that today was Nick's birthday. If only she could turn back time, make it that he hadn't seen that horror in the woods. But of course she couldn't. He'd seen it, couldn't unsee it, and it occurred to her that the image of that poor girl hanging in the woods was no doubt one that would remain with him for the rest of his life.

Five

Florence had weekends off, though she often remained at home with Jane and Nick. Now that spring had arrived, she spent the occasional weekend with a friend, a fellow nanny in Randolph, where she had worked before coming to Jane last fall. Jane hadn't expected Florence back until that night, but when Jane pulled into the driveway, Florence stood on the front steps of the dark chalet-style house, terror on her dark pretty face.

Jane and Nick got out of the car and walked up the path.

"Missus!" Florence cried. "Who was it, do they know?"

Jane stared at her. "How did you hear about it?"

"My friend Noni, the girl I told you about from Saint Kitts—she called me."

Noni was also a Shady Hills nanny. "But Noni lives at the north end of town," Jane said. "How did *she* know?"

"From Yolanda, her friend who works as a chambermaid at Hydrangea House. Yolanda told Noni the girl was dressed up like a clown!" Florence looked horrified as she contemplated this picture.

"Not in front of Nick," Jane murmured to Florence as she passed into the house.

"Right," Florence said.

Nick, looking on the verge of tears, walked quickly past her through the foyer and into the family room, where he switched on the TV and sat on the floor, legs crossed.

"Winky!" he called, and the small tortoiseshell cat appeared instantly, climbed into his lap, and curled into a ball. He slowly stroked her fur, staring at the TV screen but as if not seeing it. "Oh, Wink . . ." he said softly.

Jane turned to Florence and tilted her head toward the kitchen. Jane led the way in, and they both sat at the table.

"He's very upset," Florence observed.

"He found her," Jane said.

Florence's hands flew to her face and tears appeared instantly in her large dark eyes. "The poor boy."

"The kids were having a scavenger hunt. They went into the woods to find some of the things on their lists. And there she was, hanging from a tree."

"But who is she?"

Jane shook her head. "No one recognized her. And she wasn't dressed like a clown, by the way; she was wearing heavy makeup, very garish, like a clown."

"Ah." Florence frowned. "But why?"

"No idea."

"And whoever she was, why did she hang herself there?" Florence asked.

"Excellent question. The obvious answer is that she had something to do with Hydrangea House."

"You mean someone who worked there, like Yolanda?" Florence shook her head. "No, Mr. and Mrs. Zabriskie would have recognized her."

"True, but she could have been connected to the inn in some other way. Perhaps she knew someone staying there, or had been staying there herself."

"But Mr. and Mrs. Zabriskie—"

"Would have recognized her?" Jane pondered this. "I wonder. How well can they know all the people who come and go at the inn? I believe it could have been a guest. Louise said they've been busy lately."

Florence rose. "Would you like some tea?"

Jane had to laugh. "You're off today, Florence. I'd love some tea, but I'll make it. May I make you some?"

"Yes, you are very kind," Florence said, and sat down again while Jane worked at the counter.

"You know . . ." Florence said, and her tone was different, deeply thoughtful, so that Jane turned to look at her. "I remember now that Wednesday night I was talking to Noni, and she said Yolanda had talked about seeing someone walking in the woods behind the inn."

A cold shiver passed through Jane. "So did Louise."

"Yolanda told Noni it was a young woman, thin. Yolanda watched from the window of her bedroom on the third floor."

Jane recalled that a number of Louise and Ernie's employees lived on the inn's third floor, especially in the summer, when young college students came to Shady Hills for jobs.

Florence went on, "Yolanda watched her for quite some time. The girl never left the woods, but she kept right to the edge . . ." She stopped, closed her eyes as if remembering. " 'Like a stranger looking in,' was how Yolanda put it. How very odd. . . ."

"Odd indeed," Jane said, pouring tea into two cups and taking them to the table. "Well, whoever she was, whatever she was there for, I think it's a safe bet that she's our hanging woman."

"But *who* is she?"

"I know very little about such things, but I'm sure the police have ways of identifying people in cases like this. Sending out bulletins, trying to match the dead person's description with that of any missing persons . . ."

"Yes, I am sure you're right."

Nick walked into the room, Winky at his heels, and the two women put on smiles simultaneously as they turned to him.

"I never got any birthday cake," Nick said in a deadpan voice.

Jane pulled him over and squeezed him tight. "You poor thing," she said, though she was glad he'd gotten over the trauma of his discovery enough to realize he'd missed a piece of cake.

Winky jumped onto the table with her combination purr-and-rumble that said, "Pay attention to me!" Florence, happy to oblige, began stroking the cat's soft orange-and-black fur.

"I tell you what we'll do!" Florence said, her face brightly animated. "I will make you one of my special vanilla cakes from a recipe straight from my mother in Trinidad! You will love it—it is full of raisins and almonds. How about tonight? I will run down to the Village Shop for the ingredients. And I will get ice cream, too."

Nick considered this for a moment, looking at Florence with something close to suspicion. "Well . . . okay!"

"Yes," Jane said, "that will be wonderful, Florence. Thank you." She gave Florence a wink.

Florence responded with a tiny nod and looked at her watch. "My goodness, it's past three. I'd better get going. This cake needs time!" She jumped up and went to the sink, where she ran her hands under the faucet. "Soon this cat will have more fur on me than on her!" Shaking her head, she dried her hands on a dish towel, then took a dab of hand cream from a jar near the sink and smoothed it over her hands.

"Now," she said briskly, "who wants to come with Florence?"

"Me!" Nick cried.

Florence threw back her head and released a big rich laugh. "I had a feeling. Is your homework done?"

He thought for a moment. "Yup—except for my spelling words."

Florence looked at Jane.

"I think it's okay for him to work on his words while you're baking. In fact," Jane said, turning to Nick, "if you ask Florence nicely, maybe she'll take you to the inn to pick up your presents. We left them there in all the confusion."

"I think that is very possible," Florence said with a smile.

"Yes!" Nick bent down and scooped Winky into his arms. "You can have a piece of my birthday cake, too,

Wink! *And* you can play with my presents." He started toward Florence as if he intended to take the cat along.

"Well, let go of her, then!" Florence said, throwing her hands out toward Winky.

Suddenly, with a loud yowl, Winky sprang from Nick's arms to the floor. For an instant she stood still, the fur on her back standing up, her tail bristling like a brush; then she bolted across the kitchen so fast her paws slid on the tiles. When she reached the back hall, she abruptly turned around, shot back through the kitchen, raced across the family room, and disappeared into the foyer. They heard her thumping madly up the stairs.

"I swear that cat understands English," Jane said.

"No, missus," Florence said, looking perplexed. "She has been acting like this for several days. I have been meaning to tell you. She just—goes bananas! Racing around the house, up and down the stairs! A crazy cat! What do you think it is? Maybe spring fever? I've told you I thought you should let her go outside."

Jane shook her head firmly. "I don't know what's making her act like that, but I've told you, Florence, you're wrong about her going outside. She's an indoor cat."

"But she has her claws," Florence argued.

"True, but so did all the other cats that wandered into the woods and lost fights with dogs and foxes and possums and raccoons . . ."

"No way is she going outside!" Nick put in. "Who cares if she acts crazy? That's just Winky. Come on, Florence." He went out the back door into the garage.

"My orders," Florence said with an indulgent smile.

"Florence—" Jane put a hand on the other woman's shoulder. "Thank you."

"No problem!" Florence said. "It's what the poor thing needs." She started to turn, then stopped, her expression darkening. "I just can't stop thinking about that poor girl. Why would she do that to herself?"

"Why does anyone commit suicide?" Jane asked rhetorically.

"Who said it was suicide?"

Both women turned in surprise. Nick, who had apparently been listening on the small landing just outside the door to the garage, had poked his head back into the hall.

"What do you mean?" Florence asked him.

He shrugged. "How do you think she killed herself?"

"Well, it's obvious," Jane said, though not really wanting to talk about this. "She tied a rope around a tree trunk, threw it over a branch, made a noose, put it around her neck, and . . ."

"Yes?" he said.

"Well, she could have either jumped from another branch or stood on something and kicked it away."

But Nick shook his head. "Mom, you're always telling me that things are rarely as they seem and that I should look for things other people don't see."

Jane didn't remember telling him that, but she decided to play along. "And?"

"Well, I looked at everything very carefully, because I knew I'd never get to see it again. There were no branches she could have jumped from—the tree just wasn't shaped that way. And as for standing on something—there was nothing there!"

"A rock?" Florence hazarded. "A fallen log? Don't forget, she would have kicked it away. So it wouldn't have been right under her."

"I know that." Nick looked at Florence as if to ask, Do you think I'm an idiot? "So I looked *all* around her feet. There was nothing. No rock, no log, no stump, no nothing."

Jane was becoming upset. "But then—"

"Then either of two things could have happened. One, she did stand on something and kick it away, but afterward someone came along and took it away."

Jane gaped at him. "But why would anyone do that? It doesn't make sense."

"No, it doesn't, does it?" he agreed solemnly. "So I'm leaning more toward theory two."

"Which is?"

"Someone strung her up! She was murdered!" His face was positively fiendish. "And I found her!"

"Nicholas Stuart!" Jane was horrified. He had gone from being traumatized to actually enjoying this. "How awful to find it fun that someone has died, and like that! Besides, who would have wanted to kill her? And why?"

"*I* don't know, Mom. Why do you think *People* magazine called you North Jersey's Miss Marple?" He wiggled his eyebrows the way Kenneth used to when he was at his most devilish. "You're the detective! *You* figure it out. And while you're at it, figure out why whoever killed her smeared that makeup all over her face." And he vanished back into the garage.

"Oh, missus," Florence said ominously, looking at Jane in a whole new way, and she turned and followed Nick outside.

Jane stood in the middle of the kitchen, thinking about what Nick had just said. He was absolutely right. Why hadn't she seen it?

Someone had killed that poor girl, strung her up right there among the trees not six feet from the backyard of Hydrangea House.

Someone who, quite possibly, lived right here in Shady Hills.

Six

The next morning Jane stopped at Whipped Cream, as she did every morning before work, for coffee and an apple-raisin muffin. She took her usual table near the fireplace, which was now filled with a brass pot of dried flowers.

Ginny came over with the coffeepot.

"You okay?" Jane asked her.

"Yeah. I was mostly upset for the kids, that they had to see that. Me, I've seen that sort of thing before."

"You have?"

Ginny shot a glance over the tall counter to make sure George, the owner, wasn't around. When she was sure he wasn't, she dropped into the chair opposite Jane's.

"When I was twelve I found my Uncle Dave hanging in our attic."

"Ginny, how horrible! You never told me."

"It's one of those things you block out. But it sure came back yesterday."

Jane decided not to tell Ginny Nick's murder theory.

What would telling her accomplish other than upsetting her further? "I'm so sorry. Why did he kill himself?"

"Because he was gay and he didn't want to be."

"How sad."

Ginny's gaze was downcast. "I loved him like I can't tell you."

"It might have been different for him now."

"I often think that—which just makes me sadder." Ginny looked up sharply at a sound behind the counter. George's beady black eyes stared at her from just over the top.

"Oops," she whispered, "back to work."

"Hello, George!" Jane called cheerily.

George made a grunting sound and disappeared.

Ginny crossed the shop and poured coffee for a man who was reading the *Star Ledger*. He held the paper high as he read something inside, and Jane could read the front page headline from where she sat: CLOWN GIRL FOUND HANGING BEHIND AFFLUENT VILLAGE'S INN.

"What do you think of that?" Ginny asked on her way past Jane's table.

"Not much," Jane said. " 'Clown girl' ... That's awful."

"Heard anything more about it?" Ginny asked, on the lookout for George.

"No."

"Louise is very upset."

"Of course she is," Jane said. "You would be, too, if it had happened behind your inn."

"It's not just that," Ginny said. "I talked to Louise last night—called her to make sure she was okay. She sounded funny, like she knew more than she was telling."

"You mean, as if maybe she *did* know who that young woman was?"

"I don't know. . . ." Ginny looked bewildered. "All I can say for sure is that she wasn't upset only because it happened behind her inn. Better get Mr. Raymond's croissant." She hurried behind the counter.

Jane didn't feel like lingering that morning. She finished her coffee and left half her muffin. Leaving a nice tip for Ginny, she took her bill to the register.

"You were quick today," Ginny murmured as she rung up the amount and handed Jane her change.

"Mm, lots to do." Jane noticed a stack of placards lying faceup on the counter near the register. They were upside down but she could tell they were for the upcoming church bazaar, a major spring event in Shady Hills. George was always willing to post placards on the front of the counter under the register.

"You going?" Jane asked, indicating the placards.

"Of course! Who doesn't? Besides, I have to. Rob sells his jewelry there every year, remember?"

How could Jane forget? Every year, out of loyalty to Ginny, she bought a piece of Rob's jewelry, even though she disliked Rob's designs almost as much as she disliked Rob. "Nick loves the bazaar, and I enjoy it, too. But this"—she tilted her head toward the man's upraised newspaper—"should put a bit of a damper on the festivities."

"Can't be helped," Ginny said on a deep sigh, and slammed the register drawer shut. "See you around."

Jane gave Ginny a smile and left the shop. She crossed Center Street and started down one of the brick paths that crossed the village green. The massive ancient oaks, towering above the grass and the white Victorian bandstand, were in full leaf now, and a gentle breeze passed through them with a shooshing sound. It was another glorious day—brilliant blue sky with only a few puffy clouds, sun shining brightly, probably a perfect seventy degrees. But very bad things could happen on glorious days, Jane reminded herself, and a chill passed through her as she crossed Center Street again and entered her office.

Daniel had the *Star Ledger* open on his desk. He was reading the story under the clown headline. He shook his head. "This is reprehensible! They make us sound like some tawdry little cauldron of sin."

"Hey, I like that! Write it down for Bertha."

"I'm serious, Jane. You should read this. This reporter is absolutely salivating. But what is there to salivate about? A pathetic young woman decides to kill herself, and for whatever warped reason, she decides to do it behind the inn. Why is that so . . . salacious?"

Jane sat down in his visitor's chair. "Is that what they call it? A suicide?"

"Yes."

She considered. "Then I guess the angle is that she's a mystery woman. I really should read that, I suppose," she added.

"Laura's been crying off and on since it happened. This kind of story doesn't help. I still don't see why it's such big news."

"Neither does the newspaper, obviously."

He frowned. "What do you mean?"

Jane leaned forward. "Nick gets the credit for this one." And she told Daniel Nick's two theories.

"*Nick* said that?"

"Yup. Smart kid, huh? What do *you* think?"

Daniel thought for a moment. "I vote for theory number one. I still believe she killed herself. And I'm sorry, Jane, but just because Nick says he studied the way the tree was shaped doesn't mean he's right. She may in fact have found a way to put the noose around her neck and then jump from a branch, or she may have stood on something and then kicked it far enough away that Nick wouldn't have seen it. The police will determine exactly what happened, I'm sure."

The police ... Jane thought about Detective Greenberg as she entered her office and tossed her bag onto her desk. He had been quite pleasant to her, under the circumstances, and it was kind of him to have remembered her. She realized now that he was quite a good-looking man, something she hadn't noticed the first time she'd met him.

She spent the first half of the morning reading book proposals by her clients. Bill Haddad had written a synopsis and the first hundred pages of a new thriller for St. Martin's. It was really a very clever idea—that a woman would stage her own murder to shed her unhappy life, only to find out someone had taken her place—with her husband's complicity. The story's heroine—and her replacement—were avid tennis players, and Bill had called the book *Doubles*. Very clever.

Barbara Ianelli had sent Jane a proposal for a romance she hoped Silhouette would want for its Desire line, but the proposal had a lot of problems. For one thing, all of Barbara's previous novels had been for the Christian inspirational market, and though she was an excellent writer, she had carried that tone into this proposal intended for sexy, secular Desire. "Too inspirational," Jane jotted on the title page.

In need of a break from proposals, Jane picked up an advance reading copy of *Relevant Gods*, a novel by Carol Freund that she had sold for a high advance last fall to Holly Griffin, executive editor at Corsair Publishing. The book's official publication date was in two weeks, and Corsair would be throwing Carol a lavish publication party on Thursday. Jane remembered that she was scheduled to have lunch with Holly, whom Jane could barely tolerate, tomorrow, and that at this lunch Holly would give Jane details of the party.

Jane studied the front of the reading copy, which bore a less expensively printed version of the book's jacket. In the background was a detail from Michelangelo's *The Creation of Adam* panel on the ceiling of the Sistine Chapel—the hand of God not quite reaching Adam's. The novel's title ran across the top in lettering meant to look old like the painting, and Carol's name was at the bottom in the same type. Jane felt that this jacket was just all right, not especially imaginative—that hand image, in Jane's opinion, had become a visual cliché—but she didn't hate it, and Holly and her colleagues at Corsair *adored* it, so Jane hadn't made a fuss, especially since Carol herself liked it.

Shaking her head, Jane swiveled in her chair and tossed the reading copy onto the cluttered credenza behind her. As she turned back to her desk, there was a soft knock on her door and Daniel popped his head in. When he had ascertained that she was not on the phone, he slipped into the room and quietly closed the door.

"Jane," he said, a perplexed expression on his face, "*Doris* is here."

She frowned. "My knitting Doris? Doris Conway?"

He made a shushing gesture with one finger. "Yes."

Doris had never come to Jane's office before. "Why is she here?" Jane whispered.

"No idea. She wants to talk to you."

Jane shrugged. "Okay." She got up and went to the door, following Daniel into the reception area. Doris stood near Daniel's desk. It seemed to Jane that she looked more stooped than usual, more frail.

"Hello, Doris," Jane said brightly. "This is a pleasant surprise."

Doris didn't return Jane's smile—not that Doris smiled much anyway. She looked quite serious; Jane even wondered if she was upset about something. Perhaps what had happened at the inn.

"Jane, can I talk to you?"

"Of course. Come on in. Coffee?"

"No."

Jane showed the older woman into her office and shot Daniel a baffled look before closing the door. "Have a seat," she said, indicating her visitor's chair, and sat behind the desk. What could Doris possibly need to talk to her about that couldn't wait until their next knitting club meeting? Jane noticed that Doris was pale and that her hands were shaking ever so slightly. Jane had never seen her like this. "Doris, what's wrong? Is it about what happened at Louise's yesterday?"

"Yes."

"We're all upset about that, of course."

"It's more than that." Doris met Jane's gaze. She seemed to be trying to decide where to begin. "Jane," she said at last, "you know I volunteer at the Senior Center on Mondays and Wednesdays."

Jane nodded. The Shady Hills Senior Center was an upscale nursing home on Cranmore Avenue, on the west side of town. What could this possibly have to do with the girl found hanging behind Hydrangea House? "Yes . . ."

"Did you know that my nephew Arthur works there, too?"

Jane shook her head, frowning slightly. "I didn't even know you had a nephew, Doris."

"Well, I do. He's my younger sister Marge's boy. I've told you about Marge, I'm sure I have. She passed away six years ago. Pancreatic cancer."

Jane nodded sympathetically.

"Arthur—Arthur Sullivan is his name—he works at the Center full-time. He's been there about two and a half years. I helped him get the job there."

"Is he . . . a doctor?" Jane asked.

"No," Doris scoffed. "Arthur . . . he's mildly retarded. He's thirty-eight. He can pretty much take care of himself, lives in a group home here in the village, but there are only certain jobs he's qualified to do. He works as an orderly at the Center."

"I see. But I don't see how this relates to what happened at the inn."

"Lemme finish. This morning when I got to the Center, Arthur came to talk to me. He was very upset. I'd never seen him so upset. He asked to talk to me privately. He said he had 'a secret.' "

"A secret?"

"That's right. I took him into an empty TV room and he told me what was on his mind." Doris paused, clearly reluctant to reveal Arthur's secret. At last she continued. "A week ago Friday—that would be ten days ago now—Arthur was walking along Cranmore Avenue. It was lunchtime, and he was on his way into the village to buy a sandwich at the Village Shop. He does that every day.

"As he was walking, he heard a sound behind him. He turned and saw a young woman come out of the woods. When she saw him, she started to run back into the trees, but he called after her, and she came back. She walked with him."

Jane stared at Doris intently. "Who was she?"

Doris shook her head. "She wouldn't tell him. Wouldn't tell him where she'd come from, either. Arthur grew up in Shady Hills. He knows everybody. He knew she wasn't from here in town. He said she was pretty, with brown hair. She was wearing a pale blue dress with little white flowers."

"Like the hanging woman," Jane said quietly.

"Yes, like the hanging woman."

"Why was she here?"

"She wouldn't tell him that, either. But the strangest thing was that when he asked her where she was going, she told him she was on her way to Shady Hills! He told her she was *in* Shady Hills, and when she heard this she was—overjoyed! Arthur tried again to get her to tell him what she was doing here, but she refused. All she would tell him was that she had a 'wonderful surprise'—that was how she put it. Then, after they'd walked a little more, she told him she had come to meet someone here in town. She couldn't say who because she didn't want to ruin the surprise for that person—and she wasn't ready to approach that person yet. She told Arthur that in the meantime, she needed a map of the village and was looking for a place to stay where no one would find her."

Doris's hands shook nervously as she fingered the collar of her fluffy white cardigan—a sweater Jane remembered seeing Doris knitting at the club.

"As I told you, Arthur grew up here," Doris went on. "He knew a place to show her. He walked with her into town, then took her down Plunkett Lane all the way to Hadley Pond. From there he led her into the woods beside the pond to a cave where he used to play when he was a little boy. He said she was delighted. He told her to wait there while he went into town for the map she wanted and some food. He walked back into town and bought a map and some sandwiches and soda, and brought it all back to her. She thanked him, and he asked her if she needed anything else. She said no, so Arthur left her there and returned to work."

"Didn't he think all this was strange?" Jane asked. "Why didn't he say anything to anyone?"

"Because she had told him it was her 'secret,' " Doris reminded Jane. "He wanted to honor that. Arthur's a good boy. He just doesn't . . . question things like that."

Jane waited, watching the older woman.

"That was the last he saw of her," Doris said. "He knows she was the same woman we found behind the inn yesterday. He recognized the newspapers' description of her dress and also of the girl herself. Who else could it be?

"Arthur's in a panic. He's terrified. Jane," Doris said, leaning forward on the desk, her wrinkled face pleading, "Arthur didn't kill that woman. Arthur couldn't hurt another person; it's simply not in his nature. But he's afraid the police will think he did it. And he *was* in the cave with her for a moment, while he showed it to her, and the police—well, these days they seem to have all kinds of ways of knowing who's been where." She frowned, as if she disapproved of such methods. "Also, Arthur isn't certain he wasn't seen walking with her on Cranmore. A lot of cars do pass by."

"Doris," Jane said, remembering Nick's theories, "what makes you think the woman was killed by another person?"

Doris sat up, shocked at this question. "What are you talking about? We *found* her hanging there. Jane, what the devil are you talking about?"

"To me it looked like simple suicide," Jane said innocently. "She hanged herself."

Doris gave her a look of amused disdain. "For someone *People* magazine called North Jersey's Miss Marple, you're not very observant. There was nothing under that poor girl's feet—no rock, no nothing. Jane, that girl was strung up! And the sicko who did it smeared that makeup all over her face."

Jane, taken aback, sat up straight in her chair. "All right. Makeup aside, how do we know she didn't put the noose around her neck and jump from a branch of the tree?"

Doris shook her head firmly. "Something else you didn't look at very closely. There were no branches she could have jumped from—all the other branches were much too high on the tree."

"Doris," Jane asked searchingly, "why . . . how could you have studied all of this closely, and in so little time? We couldn't have been there more than half a minute before we got the children out of there."

Doris was unruffled by this question. "You forget I was

a schoolteacher for forty-five years, Jane. When you're a teacher you have to notice everything or you're lost." She gave a little chuckle. "I think you're the one who has to work on her observation skills."

Jane forced a smile. "North Jersey's Miss Marple was *People* magazine's name for me, not mine. I have no interest in detective work."

Doris shrugged indifferently. "Be that as it may, anyone with eyes and half a brain could see that girl was murdered."

Jane knew Doris too well to be insulted. "Well, here's a question from my half brain: Couldn't the girl have used something to stand on, which someone else later took away?"

Doris stared at her. "*If* she had, why would anyone have taken it away? You mean someone who found her before we did?"

"Possibly."

"But *why?*" Doris repeated. "To make a suicide look like murder—what reason could anyone have to do such a thing?"

"I don't know. I'm just putting forward all theories."

Doris waved this all away with a flip of her hand. "I think you *do* have an interest in detective work, Jane. But you're lousy at it. The important point is that it's clear someone killed that girl, and it wasn't my Arthur."

"So he says."

"I told you," Doris blurted out, "he could never do such a thing. Besides, why would he have told me about it in the first place if he'd hurt her?"

"To cover himself! *That*'s pretty obvious." A thought occurred to Jane. "Doris, why have you told me all this?"

Doris looked down at her hands. "Because, believe it or not, Jane, you're the most sensible friend I have."

Jane bit her tongue at this backhanded compliment.

Doris went on, "I need advice about what to do now—*if* I should do anything. And I have to admit you did a pretty good job of putting two and two together when your Marlene disappeared."

Jane had to smile. "Despite my being lousy at detective work, eh? But that involved a murder case, Doris, and you've just insisted that Arthur is incapable of hurting anyone."

Again Doris looked down. She mumbled something.

"Excuse me? I didn't hear you."

Doris met Jane's gaze. "Maybe . . . maybe I'm not so sure."

Jane gaped at Doris. "Then you think Arthur *could* have done it?"

"I don't really think that, Jane, not really. I think he's an innocent man who may be blamed for this. But if there's any chance that he might have done it, then he would have to be . . . dealt with, wouldn't he? He would have to be stopped from hurting other people."

"Yes, he would," Jane said. Doris had tears in her eyes now, and Jane's heart went out to her. "Doris, whatever really happened, you have to go to the police. They'll want to question Arthur. Especially if someone driving on Cranmore did see him with that girl, wouldn't it be better for Arthur to come forward than for them to find out and go after him? I'm sure that, as you say, he's not capable of hurting anyone, but he can no doubt provide some clues to her identity."

"You're right, Jane. I'm going to tell Arthur we have to go to the police. I suppose I knew all along that that was what we had to do. I just needed to hear it from someone whose judgment I respect. Jane," Doris said, her eyes beseeching, "will you go to the police with us? You know that Detective Greenberg. I saw him speaking to you at the inn."

"Of course I'll go with you. But you must be aware that the police will want to question Arthur alone."

"I know, but until that moment, he—and I—could use your . . . moral support."

"Maybe I can give you more than that," Jane said. "If you like, I'll speak to Detective Greenberg first about Arthur and his story."

"Oh, yes, I'd like you to do that," Doris said eagerly.

Jane rose and Doris followed suit, Jane leading the older woman toward the office door. Before opening it, Jane said, "I'll call him this afternoon. And I'll meet you at the police station whenever you and Arthur go."

"Thank you, Jane. If Detective Greenberg gives you a time, you just let me know and we'll be there."

"All right. I'll call you right after I speak to him." She opened the door and Doris preceded her into the reception room. Daniel looked up, his face composed, but Jane saw the consternation in his dark eyes.

"Good-bye, Daniel," Doris murmured to him, then looked back at Jane. "Good-bye, Jane. Thank you." And looking older and more frail than Jane had ever seen her look, she walked slowly to the door and let herself out.

Seven

Jane watched two of the lights on her phone flash, heard Daniel answer one, put the call on hold, and take the other. Her intercom beeped.

"Bill Haddad on one," came Daniel's mellow voice, "and Bertha Stumpf on two."

Though Jane had liked Bill's proposal quite a bit, she just couldn't deal with Bill right now. Extremely insecure despite his considerable talent, he needed a lot of stroking—something Jane was in no mood to do. "I'll call Bill back," she told Daniel. "What does Bertha want?"

"She says it's about the RAT convention."

Jane rolled her eyes. "Ask her what about it, and tell her we're sending the photos and bios, if that's what she's calling about."

"Will do," Daniel replied cheerfully, and the intercom light went out.

She stared at the pile of work on her desk, but it soon blurred, to be replaced by a collage of haunting images.

A pretty young woman walking along a country road, excited about a "wonderful surprise."

A young woman waiting in a cave for a kind stranger to return with food and drink.

A young woman walking at the edge of the deep woods behind Hydrangea House, peering out at the trees . . . an outsider looking in. . . .

A young woman hanging by her neck from a tree, her face garishly made up. *CLOWN GIRL* . . .

Jane shook herself. It was all too awful to contemplate. She thought about poor Doris, so worried about Arthur, whom she had never mentioned in all the years Jane had known her, in all the meetings of the Defarge Club they had attended together. Surely she couldn't be ashamed of or embarrassed by Arthur because he was retarded. No, Doris was too enlightened to feel that way. Then why *had* she never mentioned him? Was it perhaps because he wasn't at all the kind, easygoing sort Doris had just painted a picture of? Did he have some history of violence that made Doris now think he *could* have hurt that poor girl? As Nick had reminded Jane, it was she herself who had said never to trust the way things appear—a sad way to have to live, but especially necessary nowadays.

There was a soft knock, and Daniel came in with the mail. He walked to Jane's desk, searched for a clear spot, and placed the stack at the extreme right edge. Then he scrutinized Jane, his eyes narrowed.

She looked up and met his gaze. "What?"

"Anything you'd like to talk about?"

Jane smiled. Now that Kenneth was gone, Daniel knew her better than anyone. Or was she simply that transparent? Doris's visit alone would have made Daniel wonder what was going on.

Jane did confide most everything to Daniel, and he never betrayed her confidence. She nodded, and he sat down facing her. Slowly, trying to recall every detail, she told him what Doris had said. When she was finished, he sat looking more shocked than she would have expected.

"Wow," he said slowly. "Doris's nephew might have done that to that poor girl."

"Doris doesn't think so," Jane said. "Or at least she says she doesn't think so. I've never met this Arthur, have you?"

"No, but I've seen him."

"Really? Where?"

He thought for a moment, rising. "The last time would have been about a year ago. He was at the church bazaar with Doris. That's coming up soon, you know. You going?"

"Of course! Who in Shady Hills misses the church bazaar?"

"Laura loves it," Daniel said at the door.

"Tell her to buy jewelry from Rob."

"I've seen his jewelry," Daniel said with a smile. "Even in friendship, there's a limit." He was laughing to himself as he went out.

She had to laugh, too. Rob's stuff was pretty awful. She kept to her work, called Bill Haddad, duly stroked him, vetted two contracts, rejected some manuscripts, and when she wasn't thinking about work, she tried to force herself to think about the church bazaar instead of Arthur. But she knew she was just procrastinating, and remembering one of Kenneth's favorite sayings,

"Do the worst first!" she picked up the phone, called the police station, and asked to speak to Detective Greenberg.

"Mrs. Stuart," he said brightly. "What can I do for you?"

"This is very awkward. I don't know quite how to say it. It's about that poor girl we found in the woods on Sunday. I have something to speak to you about, but I'd really rather do it in person. May I come over to your office and see you?"

"I have a better idea. Why don't I meet you at Whipped Cream. That would be more convenient for you, wouldn't it?"

"Yes—it would," she said, surprised, "but I really don't mind—"

"No, let's meet there. What time is good for you? It's four-thirty now. Shall we say five?"

"Yes, that will be fine. I'll see you there."

Bewildered, she hung up and then called home.

"Florence, I have to do something on my way home from work, so I'll be about an hour late. Is that all right?"

"Yes, missus, not a problem at all," Florence replied. "But, missus, I don't know what to do with this crazy cat!"

"Winky? What is she doing?"

"What is she doing! She is still running around this house like a ball in a pinball machine, that's what! And when I go near her to pick her up and pet her, she goes even crazier! I think you really should take her to the veterinarian."

"All right." Jane heaved a great sigh. A visit to the veterinarian was the last thing she needed right now.

But she did love Winky, who was, after all, a member of their small family, and something was definitely wrong with her. "Florence, let's watch her for one more day. If she's still bouncing around tomorrow, I'll make an appointment at the vet."

"Okay, missus, you're the boss," Florence said, but it was clear from the tone of her voice that she disapproved. "We'll see you about six, six-thirty, then?"

"Yes. How's Nick? Doing his homework?"

"Yes, he is right here at the kitchen table. For language arts he must write an ad, and I helped him decide what it will be for."

"Really?"

" 'Trinidad!' " Florence recited. " 'Treasure of the blue Caribbean!' "

Jane heard Nick giggle in the background. "That's very good, Florence. I especially like the alliteration."

"Exactly!"

"Just make sure *he* writes it, okay?"

"Got it, missus," Florence said cheerfully, and hung up.

Twenty minutes later, Jane was at her table at Whipped Cream. The shop was always quiet at the end of the workday, and since George was always gone by four, Ginny poured them both big mugs of coffee and sat down with Jane.

"Ginny, you don't look so hot today," Jane said. "Long day?"

"Thanks a lot," Ginny said.

"Ginny!" Jane chided her. "You know what I mean. Is something bothering you?"

Ginny lowered her gaze. "Actually, I've been crying off and on all day."

"About that girl?"

"No, though I am sad and creeped out about that. It's Rob. Yesterday we drove to a craft show in Flemington, and on the way back we had a heart-to-heart."

"Ah. Whose idea was that?"

"Mine, of course."

"And what came out of his heart that upset you?"

"He doesn't want to get married, doesn't see the point." Ginny's eyes welled with tears.

"Doesn't see the point! How about love, children . . ."

"That's just it. He doesn't want children. So if we're not going to have children, and we know we love each other, why get married?"

"Says Rob?"

"Says Rob."

"But you *do* want children, Ginny. And—forgive me—but *do* you love him?"

Ginny was quiet for a long time. Then, "I don't know, Jane," she said, meeting Jane's gaze. "I don't know."

"Sweetie, if you don't know, something's wrong."

"That's true," Ginny said, gaze lowered. A tear rolled down her cheek and plopped into her coffee. "Ick." She laughed, wiped at her eyes with the heels of her hands. "I know, Jane, it's what you've been telling me for some time now: Something's gotta give. Rob and I, we—have problems. We're always fighting. We want different things. He seems to want only to be left alone. I don't know if he even wants me around anymore. It's not like you and Kenneth—" She caught herself. "Oh, Jane, I'm sorry."

"Don't be silly, Ginny. That was very sweet of you to

say. *You* didn't kill Kenneth. And you're right, what we had was special. I want that for you."

Ginny gave her a grateful smile and pressed her hand down on top of Jane's.

"Now let's talk about you," Ginny said. "Since when do you hang around here at a quarter to five?"

Jane couldn't suppress a giggle. "Since I've started meeting with police detectives!"

"What?"

"It's the oddest thing. I needed to speak to Detective Greenberg about—about what happened at Louise's on Sunday, and when I asked if I could come see him, he suggested we meet here instead."

"Oh, Jane!" Ginny said, her eyes aglow.

"Oh, Jane, what?" Jane said, feigning innocence.

"This is so romantic. I know all about him."

"You do?"

Ginny nodded eagerly. "He's never been married. He lives here in town. He had a girlfriend he used to bring by here once in a while—that was maybe two years ago. It was that woman who used to work as a hostess at Eleanor's. But they must have broken up. One day they just stopped coming. And she must have moved away, because around that time she left her job at Eleanor's, too."

Eleanor's was the nicest restaurant in town, a converted gristmill on the Morris River, not far from the village center. Jane remembered the woman Ginny was talking about, a lovely woman about Jane's age who had always been friendly and gracious to Jane when she'd gone there for lunch or dinner.

"Very promising," Ginny said, neatening the table. "Why?"

Ginny leaned forward. "Why do you *think*, Jane? Why do you think he wants to meet you here?"

"Because it's so romantic?" Jane said in a deadpan voice.

Ginny frowned defensively. "It's more romantic than the police station. What time is he coming?"

"Five."

Ginny checked her watch. "That's in five minutes. Fix your hair."

"What's wrong with it?"

"It's"—Ginny fumbled for words—"squashed. Fluff it up or something."

"For goodness' sake!" Jane said, but she did throw back her head and fluff her hair by running her fingers up through it. "Such foolishness. Is that better? How's my lipstick?"

"Fine. Yipes, here he is!" Ginny shot up from the table and stood to one side like a soldier with a coffeepot.

Jane looked up just as Greenberg entered the shop. He really was quite attractive. He looked around the shop and when he saw Jane he broke into a smile. It occurred to Jane that he was like a little boy, knowing he shouldn't smile because this was serious business, but unable to stop himself.

"Mrs. Stuart," he said, shaking her hand, and dropped into the chair Ginny had just vacated. Ginny, with a wink at Jane over Greenberg's head, approached the table. "Can I get you something?" she asked sweetly.

"Uh, tea, please," he said, and with a nod Ginny went off to get it.

Jane didn't know quite how to begin, but she didn't have to, because he looked at her with a devilish grin and said, "You're probably wondering why I've called you here today."

She laughed. "Well . . . yes."

"I know it's not very professional. I don't even know what it is you want to tell me. But I have a confession to make—a personal one."

She waited, frowning slightly in surprise.

"When you came to see me last October, I was . . . very impressed with you. I didn't know if you—I want to—"

Jane, delighted, burst into her own big smile. "You wanted to ask me out?"

He blushed. "Well, yeah."

"Then why didn't you?"

"Because this big bad old police detective is a coward!" He laughed.

She shook her head. "Consider this our first date."

He actually blushed, looking as happy as a child with a new toy. Jane realized that Ginny had emerged from the kitchen just in time to hear what Jane had said. Ginny's mouth was open, her eyes wide, in an expression of amazed delight.

"Here we are," Ginny said, now the total professional, and set down Greenberg's tea. "Would you like anything with that? A piece of cake? Some cookies? We also have salads and sandwiches if you like."

"No, thanks," he said, smiling up at her. "I'm having dinner at my sister's tonight."

Ginny left them alone.

Greenberg turned to Jane. "You may remember I mentioned my sister to you last fall. You spoke to her reading group."

"I most certainly do remember. I also recall that you had a novel you wanted me to look at. Well?"

"Well . . . what?"

"Where is it?"

He blushed again. "It's in my desk drawer in my apartment." He shook his head. "It's no good, not good enough to show."

"Have you finished it?"

"No," he admitted.

"Well, I guarantee you'll never get anywhere with it unless you finish it. Publishers—at least the ones I sell to—aren't interested in half-finished books. Unless, of course, you're Jane Austen or Louisa May Alcott or Charles Dickens."

"You're right. I should get that thing out and just get it done!" He looked at her searchingly. "I bet you're great with your writers, or authors—or whatever you call the people you represent."

" 'Writers' and 'authors' are fine; also 'clients.' " She shook her head. "It's just common sense. To be a player, you gotta get it finished. I don't care if it's a book or a screenplay or a piece of music. A half-finished masterpiece sitting in someone's desk drawer doesn't do anybody any good."

"So true," he said, clearly inspired. "Tonight I'm getting out that manuscript—provided your promise is still good."

"I brought it up! Of course it's still good. Though I must caution you, I can't guarantee that even if I like it I'll be your agent."

He looked crestfallen. "Why not?"

"Because I've made myself a promise—never to mix

business with pleasure. I've tried it, and believe me, it doesn't work."

He nodded. "You mean that Haines guy you were seeing. I used to see you in here with him once in a while. One time you seemed to be . . . having an argument, and he walked out on you."

"My, my, you *were* watching closely, weren't you?"

"Yes, I was. And because I saw you with him, I didn't call you when I wanted to."

"You should have," Jane said ruefully. "You would have saved us all a lot of trouble. Anyway," she went on, her voice cheerful, "that's all over now. He's back in New York where he belongs."

"And you think my business with you might turn into pleasure?"

Now it was Jane's turn to blush. "Yes," she said, looking him straight in the eye in a way she knew would make Ginny proud of her, "I do."

"So," he said, playing along, "just supposing you liked my manuscript, if you became my agent, I couldn't ask you out. And if I asked you out, you couldn't be my agent."

"That's right."

"And if you don't like my manuscript?"

"Well, then there wouldn't be any conflict, and you could ask me out."

He pondered this. "I see. . . . Of course, in order to find out whether you liked my manuscript, you'd need to read it first."

"That generally helps."

"But it's not finished, as I've just told you. So . . . let's not wait to find out if you like it. Let me just ask you out now. Then I won't even show you my manuscript."

"Except as an interested friend."

"Right. So . . . will you go out with me?"

She felt herself flush. "Yes," she said, barely able to contain her delight. Out of the corner of her eye, over Greenberg's shoulder, Jane saw Ginny behind the counter, silently jumping up and down.

"Great!" he said. "What shall we do?"

"I know. This Thursday is a publication party in New York for a book by one of my clients. Would you like to come as my date?"

"Sure! Rub elbows with the literati and all that!"

Jane made a doubtful face. She had never thought of anyone at Corsair as belonging to the literati. But she thought he would have fun. "Then that will be our second date."

"Good," he said, looking truly pleased. "Now that we've got the important stuff out of the way, what was it you wanted to see me about?"

Jane felt a sinking in her stomach at the thought of poor stooped Doris and her Arthur. Hesitantly, she told Greenberg what Doris had told her about Arthur's encounter with the strange young girl who fit the description of the woman found hanging in the woods. She left out Doris's slight doubt about Arthur's innocence.

Greenberg was all business. "Of course you're right— I'll have to have him in for questioning."

"Would it be all right if I came along—for moral support? As I told you, he's quite scared. So is Doris, for that matter."

"You can come along with them to the station, sure, but I'll have to see him alone. I'd like him at my office at eight-thirty tomorrow. If for some reason he doesn't show up, I'll have to send someone to pick him up at the Senior Center or at his house."

"I understand. Thank you."

He simply gazed at her; she could tell he was lost in thoughts of the story she'd just told him.

"You know," Jane said, watching him closely, "Doris—and . . . other people—feel pretty certain that poor girl didn't kill herself."

He looked at her, his expression giving away nothing.

"The reason they think so," she went on, "is that apparently the tree had no branches from which she could have jumped after putting the noose around her neck." She watched him for a reaction.

He seemed to hesitate. Then, with a guarded look, he said, "That's correct."

"And if she'd put something on the ground to stand on, it wasn't there when we found her. A rock, a log . . . Unless someone had taken it away."

He allowed a small smile. "Doris is sharp. We—the police, I mean—came to the same conclusions. But let me ask you this: Why would anyone have taken it away? That suggests someone wanted to make a suicide *look* like murder."

Jane shook her head to signify she had no idea. "This is where you come in."

"Sounds as if you and Doris have *already* come in. And why not?" he asked with a devilish grin. "You are North Jersey's Miss Marple."

She gave a great groan. "Not that again, please." Agreeing to that interview was turning out to be the worst mistake she'd ever made.

He shook his head. "We can't imagine why anyone would want to make a suicide look like murder, so . . .

we're treating this as a homicide. In which case, this Arthur could be a vital clue. His story may be a cover-up."

Jane sat up at this implication.

Greenberg sipped his tea. "I really should pick him up now, but I'll stick with what I agreed to and wait for him to show up in the morning."

Jane found herself growing increasingly alarmed at what she knew he must be thinking. "If Arthur *had* killed this poor girl, why would he have volunteered all that information—about showing her the cave, for instance?"

"Because he knew we'd find the cave anyway. Like I said, he could be covering himself."

"And have you found the cave?"

"Sure," he said matter-of-factly. "We found that late Sunday afternoon. It was obvious the young woman had been living there."

"Why didn't you tell me this sooner?"

He sat back and looked at her, laughing. "I don't suppose you've thought of this, but I really shouldn't be telling you anything at all, ever!"

She shot him a mischievous grin. "But you are. Why is that?"

He gave a little shrug. "Because I know I can trust you. But I'm breaking rules here."

She waved the word away. "Rules!" She laughed. "We're on a date, for goodness' sake! You're ... *confiding* in me."

"You twist words around."

"I'm a book person—that's my job." Suddenly she had an idea. "Will you show me the cave?"

He looked at her askance. "Why?"

"I'm curious, that's all. Maybe there's a clue there to who this woman was."

"Has it occurred to you we've already searched it with that in mind?"

She grinned. "Sure, but they don't call me North Jersey's Miss Marple for nothing."

He paused for a moment, considering. "All right," he said finally, "I don't suppose there's any harm in it. It's not the crime scene. But you can't touch anything— and you can't tell anyone I showed it to you."

"I could have found it on my own," she pointed out.

"Would you have looked for it?"

"Maybe."

"Why are you so interested in this?"

An image of Doris, lonely and defeated, flashed before Jane's eyes. "Because," she answered honestly, "if Doris says her nephew isn't capable of hurting any-one, I believe her. Which means that if this young woman was murdered, someone other than Arthur mur-dered her. There may be a clue in the cave to who that person is."

"A clue we haven't found," Greenberg said.

"Perhaps," Jane said, rising, and grabbed the check Ginny had left on the table.

"Please, let me," he said.

"You can get the next one," she told him. She paid the bill, said good night to Ginny, and borrowed the phone to let Florence know she'd be home a little later than she'd originally planned.

"I've never been in a police car," Jane said, and got into Greenberg's cruiser, which he'd parked right in front of Whipped Cream. Later he would drive her back to her car, parked behind her office.

Greenberg drove around the green, tawny gold in the light of the setting sun. The trees that towered over the lush grass and the white bandstand were perfectly still, and suddenly Jane remembered the whipping of the wind in the trees when they had found the hanging girl, the stirring of her hair. She forced the image from her mind.

Greenberg started down Plunkett Lane, negotiating its twists through the thick woods. "This isn't exactly what I had in mind for our first date," he joked.

"Our first date is over. This is just . . . business."

He shot her a frown and slowed to a stop. The road ended there. Before them stood a wall of thick trees and bushes, behind which lay Hadley Pond. Several times Kenneth had taken Jane and Nick fishing there. They had caught perch and sunfish. That image, too, Jane forced from her mind.

Greenberg grabbed a flashlight from the glove compartment. They got out and Jane followed him into the woods by way of a path that began between two pines. Fortunately, there was still plenty of daylight, for rocks and low bushes were plentiful, even on the crude path, and walking was difficult.

"Is it much farther?" Jane asked, struggling not to stumble in her medium heels.

"Just a little."

A few moments later they reached what appeared to be a solid wall of rock, the lower part of its face obscured by bushes. Jane frowned in puzzlement, then watched as Greenberg bent slightly and ducked between two of the bushes, seeming to disappear. "It's in here," he called back to her.

She followed him through the bushes and saw that he had squeezed between two outcroppings of rock that formed the cave's entrance. She stooped to enter. Inside she found Greenberg standing against the right wall, aiming his flashlight at the cave's center. The ceiling was high enough that Greenberg had to stoop only a little to stand up straight. Jane, at five-foot-nine, rose to her full height and slowly surveyed the space.

It was narrow, about seven feet long by four feet wide. The still, cold air had a dank, mushroomy smell.

On the cave's dirt floor lay a grimy blanket of indiscriminate color. Scattered all about were bits of waxed paper, plastic wrap, aluminum foil, crumpled-up napkins, empty Coke cans. "Who was she?" Jane wondered aloud. "What was she doing here?" She crouched to get a closer look.

"Remember, don't touch anything," Greenberg said.

"I remember," she said, and let her gaze travel from one end of the cave to the other.

Something odd caught her eye. Near the head of the blanket lay a folded piece of paper that was neither wax paper nor napkin, but appeared to be a page torn from a magazine.

"That," Jane said, pointing. "Have you looked at it?"

Greenberg crouched beside her and shined his flashlight on it. "That?" he said. "It's garbage—wrappings from her food."

Jane shook her head. "I don't think so. It's got printing on it. May I look at it?"

With a little exhalation of annoyance, he leaned forward and gingerly picked up the piece of paper between two fingers.

Oh, she thought, *you can touch.*

Carefully he unfolded the piece of paper. Jane watched closely. The folds in it were sharp, as if the paper had been folded many times along the same lines. Finally, he had it fully open. Jane drew in her breath sharply, for she had seen this page before.

It was the story *People* magazine had run about Jane and her detective work. In the middle of the page was the close-up photo of Jane, Daniel, and Laura with Winky on Jane's sofa. The reporter had insisted that Winky wear a deerstalker cap, and the poor thing looked truly ridiculous trying to peer out from under its brim. Jane was grinning widely.

Greenberg turned over the page. Here was the remainder of the story and more photos: the members of the Defarge Club during one of their Tuesday night meetings (minus Penny, because Alan had gone bowling in Boonton that night and demanded that Penny watch Rebecca); Florence and Nick standing in front of Jane's house; and the group shot of other Shady Hills residents, all dressed in detective-style trench coats, standing together on the village green in front of the bandstand.

Jane stared at the page in complete bewilderment. "Why on earth is this here?" she asked softly.

Greenberg shrugged, and out of the corner of her eye she saw him shoot her a suspicious look. "Good question," he said, refolding the page and putting it back where they'd found it. Then he rose, clearly signaling that it was time to leave. Jane sensed that he now regretted having agreed to show her the cave.

Jane rose, too. Starting to follow Greenberg out, she

cast a final glance at the cave's contents, still visible in the reflected glow of his flashlight. Something else caught her eye and she stopped short.

"May I borrow your flashlight for a second?"

He shrugged. "Sure." He handed it to her, waited.

Jane shined the light onto the floor and crouched again. She held the light close to the blanket and involuntarily drew in her breath. She hoped Greenberg hadn't heard her.

The portion of the blanket within the flashlight's beam displayed a diagonal lattice pattern of small squares of apricot and peach. It was, in fact, not a blanket at all, but a quilt. Louise's missing Irish Chain quilt. She couldn't imagine how it could have gotten there, yet without knowing why, she decided not to mention her discovery to Greenberg.

"What is it?" he asked behind her.

She rose. "Nothing. I thought I saw something else. It was nothing." She handed back the flashlight.

He turned and started out, and Jane followed. They made their way back through the woods, now deep in cool shadow. They rode in silence back to the village center, where Greenberg drove to the parking lot behind Jane's office building and pulled up alongside her car.

He glanced at his watch. "I'd better get over to my sister's or I'll catch hell."

She nodded. "Well, thanks for the look." She felt awkward now, wished she'd never asked him to show her the cave in the first place.

He looked preoccupied, elsewhere. Then he smiled. "Don't forget—"

"I know, don't tell anyone you showed it to me."

"Right. I guess I'll see you in the morning, with Arthur and Doris." His face brightened. "And I'll look forward to our next date."

She gave him a warm smile. "Me too."

"Missus . . . yoo hoo!"

Jane jumped. Across the kitchen table, Florence was looking at her, her smile wide but her eyes concerned. "You don't like my sweet-and-sour pork? My mother made up this recipe. It's one of my favorites."

"Yeah, Mom." Nick sat next to Florence, digging into the sauce-drenched meat with gusto. With his free hand he stroked Winky, who sat on the chair next to him— once Kenneth's chair—purring loudly.

"I'm sorry, Florence, it isn't that. It's been a long day."

Florence shook her head. "All those crazy writers. I don't know how you put up with them."

Jane laughed. "They're not all crazy. Some of them are actually quite sane. But it's not my writers. I've got something on my mind."

"What?" Nick asked. "The dead woman?"

Jane had considered asking that they not speak of her again, but then had decided that that wouldn't be wise. She *was* thinking about the dead woman, about the cave deep in the woods with its pathetic litter scraps. About the *People* magazine page . . . About Louise's quilt.

Why had the young woman come to Shady Hills? What had her "wonderful secret" been? Why had she needed to hide until she was ready to approach someone—someone here in town? But who? Someone pictured in the *People* article? If so, it could be anyone:

More than a hundred people had appeared in that piece.

"Mom, you *are* thinking about that dead girl," Nick said, and took another bite of pork. "Who was she, do you think?" He turned to Winky, who sat up straight, no doubt thinking she was about to get a handout. "Wink, you know who she was, don't you?"

"How silly," Florence said.

Nick turned to her. "She's smarter than you think. Cats know things we can't even imagine."

"Such foolishness," Florence scoffed. She shivered violently. "I don't think we should talk about that woman anymore. We should leave all that to the police."

But mention of the police made Jane think of Greenberg, of visiting the cave, of meeting Doris and Arthur at the station in the morning.

While Nick turned back to Winky, Florence shot Jane a look that said, "Let's change the subject."

"Yes," Jane said. "We have many other things to worry about. Like homework."

Nick slumped in his chair. "Blech."

"Never mind blech," Jane said. "You still have to finish that report on Sussex County. Have you finished gathering your information?"

Nick shrugged indifferently. "No. I'll get it tonight off the Internet."

"All right. I'll help you."

"And what about the New Jersey cake?" Florence asked. "Aren't we supposed to *bake* Sussex County?"

Nick slammed down his fork. "Have you ever heard of anything so stupid?" he said, his eyes bulging so that he looked the way Kenneth always looked when he was exasperated. "What's the point of baking a cake in the shape of Sussex County? What do we *learn* from that?"

"You learn the counties of New Jersey, obviously," Jane said. "The cake makes it fun. And when you have fun learning something, you're more likely to really learn it and remember it."

Nick gave her a distasteful look. "Mom, you sound like some kind of textbook or something. Well," he said with a sigh, "I'm not baking any counties."

"No one asked you to," Florence said. "I will bake Sussex. I have the mix and everything." She looked slightly embarrassed. "Normally I would not use a mix"—she spoke as if doing so were a sacrilege—"but for this project I think it is okay, and besides we are in a hurry." Nick hadn't told Florence and Jane he needed a cake in the shape of Sussex County until that morning. "But I'll need that template Mrs. Arnold gave you," Florence went on.

"Yeah, yeah," Nick said. "It's with my stuff in my backpack." He put down his fork and got up, heading for the green backpack leaning against the kitchen wall near the back hall.

Florence smiled at Jane and shook her head.

In actuality, Jane had wondered more than once why Mrs. Arnold couldn't have simply had the children color a map of New Jersey's counties, but one never undermined the teacher. So she jumped up, full of enthusiasm. "I'll clear the table and load the dishwasher, Florence. You and Nick can start on Sussex."

"Thanks, missus. This will be fun." But as soon as Nick had left the kitchen in search of scissors for cutting out the template, Florence's face grew troubled again, and Jane had no doubt as to the subject of her thoughts.

* * *

Later that night, as Jane lay in bed, eyes shut as she waited for sleep, the Irish Chain pattern of Louise's quilt appeared before her. *How had the quilt gotten into the cave?* She didn't want to know. In fact, she wished she had never recognized it. But it was her own fault; she'd asked Greenberg to take her to the cave.

She drifted closer to sleep, then remembered something, and her eyes popped open. She'd forgotten to call Doris. She checked her bedside clock. It was a little after eleven. She grabbed the phone and dialed Doris's number. Doris answered on the first ring.

"Doris, I'm sorry to call you so late. I did speak with Greenberg. He said he'd like to ask Arthur some questions. He wants Arthur at the station at eight-thirty tomorrow morning. I'll meet you both there at twenty past."

"All right," Doris said.

"Oh, and Doris—" Jane said uneasily. "He said that if Arthur doesn't show up, he'll have to have him picked up and brought in."

"He'll show up," Doris said.

Eight

At 8:15 the next morning Jane pulled into the parking lot of the Shady Hills Police Station, a one-story glass-and-brick building about a mile from the village center on Packer Road. Doris was already there; Jane recognized her tan Buick. Doris and Arthur got out of the car as soon as they saw Jane arrive. Jane got out and approached them.

Arthur was of medium height and of average build. He was a pleasant-looking man, with dark brown hair neatly trimmed and parted on the side, and large hazel eyes. He wore chinos and an olive-colored nylon windbreaker. Doris introduced him to Jane and she took his hand.

"Thank you for coming," he said.

"My pleasure, Arthur. I'm sure it will be fine."

Doris looked at her watch. "It's almost time. Should we go in?"

"Yes, all right." Jane forced a reassuring smile and led the way to the station entrance. Inside she told the desk sergeant that Arthur was there to see Detective Greenberg.

While they waited, Doris turned to Jane. "Thanks, Jane. You don't have to wait with us. We'll be fine."

"That's all right," Jane said, but at that moment Greenberg appeared, smiling a small official-looking smile.

Jane introduced Doris and Arthur.

"Thank you, Mrs. Stuart," Greenberg said. "Arthur, will you come with me, please?"

Arthur shot Doris an apprehensive glance. She smiled and nodded quickly to reassure him, but her smile disappeared as soon as Arthur had turned to follow Greenberg.

Jane took Doris's arm and walked with her out of the building to the parking lot.

"Thank you, Jane."

"My pleasure, Doris. Would you like to get a cup of coffee or something?"

"No." Doris glanced at the police station. "I'll wait out here until they're finished. Then I have to drive Arthur to the Senior Center."

"There's a place to wait inside," Jane suggested.

"No, I'll wait in my car."

Jane watched Doris walk slowly to the Buick and get in. Doris raised a hand in a halfhearted wave. Jane waved back, got into her own car, and pulled back onto Packer Road, turning left toward the village center and her office.

When she arrived, Daniel was cursing at the new database again. She dropped some manuscripts she had read last night onto the reject pile on the credenza by the window, then turned to poor Daniel and couldn't help laughing.

"I'm glad *you* think this is funny," he said. "I'm beginning to think you were right. Maybe we should go back to the way things were."

She gaped at him. "I wasn't *serious!* We spent thousands of dollars on that program. It will more than—"

"More than pay for itself, I remember."

"Why don't you let me input some data, or whatever you call what you're doing?"

"I call what I'm doing getting frustrated."

"Well, please don't. It's not worth it. I can always get the money back."

He considered this for a moment, then shook his head. "No, we just need to get comfortable with it."

"Suit yourself," she said with a shrug. "Any calls?"

He smiled slyly. "Holly Griffin about lunch today."

Jane groaned. Daniel knew how much Jane disliked Holly, the embodiment of everything Jane hated in an editor. Holly was arrogant yet dumb, far more interested in office politics than in books, completely untrustworthy, and a master brown-noser. But editors weren't what they once were, Jane often had to remind herself, and if she submitted books only to the editors she respected, she'd be out of business fast. So Jane did submit manuscripts to Holly, manuscripts like Carol Freund's *Relevant Gods.* Jane had squeezed a hundred thousand dollars out of Holly—quite a coup for Jane, and for Carol, a former schoolteacher from Northampton, Massachusetts.

Though Holly didn't like to admit it, she was excited about *Relevant Gods,* truly a remarkable novel, and had rushed it for publication in June. That was next month.

Corsair was throwing its publication party for Carol this Thursday, in two days. That party, Jane remembered, would be her next date with Stanley Greenberg. Today Jane and Holly were supposed to have lunch so Holly could give Jane the final party details.

Lunch with Holly was the last thing Jane needed now, but she was curious about Corsair's party plans, and she knew that if she canceled, Holly would just doggedly pursue Jane until she agreed to make a new lunch date.

"Please call her and tell her I'll meet her wherever she wants, and to let me know the time."

"She's already left all that in her message. Twelve-thirty at the Russian Palace."

Jane groaned again. She should have known Holly would choose that restaurant, which Jane disliked almost as much as she disliked Holly. The Russian Palace was a pretentious, overpriced, overcrowded, noisy tourist trap. But at least Holly would be paying; the editor always paid.

Jane realized she wasn't liking many people or places lately. With a deep sigh, she headed into her office, where she jotted down answers to a list of questions Daniel had left her about a contract he was vetting for one of his own clients. At 10:45, when she could put it off no longer, she rose heavily from her chair and headed out of the office for the bus that would take her into New York City.

"Jane! Jane!"

Jane squinted into the crowd of people who filled the narrow red-and-gold expanse of the Russian Palace's dining room. Finally, she spotted Holly at a table near the back and told the maître d' she saw her party and would make her own way.

Holly was half standing at the tiny table, waving furiously and wearing a big grin. Jane forced a grin of her own. The two women exchanged air kisses, and Jane set down her bag and dropped into the empty chair, careful not to bang into the man in the chair just behind her.

"Why don't they just stack us up," she said dryly, "like a totem pole."

"Ooh," Holly said, "in a bad mood today, aren't we?"

Jane stared at Holly. Something was different. A lot was different. Then Jane realized it was her hair, which, the last time Jane had seen it—at their last lunch here, actually—had been curly, shoulder-length, and medium brown. Now it was straight and a shiny darker brown, almost black, cut in a severe sort of sharp pageboy that reminded Jane of Claudette Colbert in *Cleopatra*.

Without realizing it, Jane must have been staring, because Holly stroked one shiny wing. "Like it?" she purred.

"It's very different from last time," was all Jane could think to say. She wasn't going to lie and say she liked it, because she didn't, any more than she liked Holly. She was here, she reminded herself, for Carol Freund. She simply had to get through it.

"Know who did it?" Holly said, leaning forward.

"No."

"Hec-tor," Holly said, with exaggerated pronunciation, "at Snip Snip."

Jane had to laugh. She tossed back her own shoulder-length auburn mass of hair. "Joanie. At Selma's Cut 'n Curl."

Holly frowned, pushing out her lower lip. "Are you making fun of me?"

"*Moi?* Never. Now," Jane said, ready to change the subject, "how are things at Corsair?"

"Totally fabu!" Holly cried. Suddenly her head turned as if someone had snapped it with a rubber band. She gasped. "That's Mort Janklow." She slitted her eyes and made an angry pouting mouth. "He's having lunch with Ham Kiels."

"So?"

"So," Holly said, turning back to Jane, "Hamilton Kiels works at Corsair, like me, and he's only a senior editor. I'm *executive* editor." She looked thoughtful. "I wonder why he wouldn't have lunch with *me.* He said he didn't have anything for me."

Jane shrugged. "Maybe he was being honest—he doesn't have any projects right for you."

"Oh, yeah, but he has some that are right for Ham Sandwich over there." Holly sneered in Ham's direction. "We all work for the same company. What's right for Ham is right for me." She looked at Jane as if she'd had an epiphany. "He just didn't want to have lunch with *me!* What am I, chopped liver?" She cocked an eyebrow. "That's very shortsighted of Mort. One day I'll be running Corsair. Then he'll be sorry."

"I'm sure he will, Holly. But in the meantime, you're here with me."

"Mm, right." Holly shrugged petulantly, heaved a great sigh, and gazed despondently down at her menu.

"You were telling me that things at Corsair are, um, fabu," Jane coaxed.

"Right," Holly said, mustering some of her former enthusiasm. She smiled. "And the reason they're so fabu is the party we're throwing for *your* Carol Freund. Jane, I'm telling you, it's going to be the biggest event of the year. And I take all the credit for that."

"Thank you, Holly," Jane said, because she knew that's what she was supposed to say.

"You're welcome. You're gonna love it. My decision to have it at our offices was a touch of genius. The media people think it's brilliant. Did you see Liz Smith? She called it 'intellectual chic.' "

"Did she?" *Please, time, pass quickly. This is worse than lunch with Bertha.*

"Mmmm-hmmmm," Holly said with gusto. "And it will be." Her eyes grew widely innocent. "I do hope Carol likes what we're doing for her book."

"She's *thrilled*," Jane said. "She never dreamed she'd receive such treatment."

"Have you seen the reviews? I had Jilly send them to you."

"Yes, they're—fabu!" Jane said. "*Publishers Weekly* gave it—"

"A *starred* review," Holly finished for her. "Which I like to think is due in large part to my editing. And the *Kirkus*! They weren't nasty at all!" Her face grew pensive. "I wonder if my affair with—Never mind." Her head snapped to the left again as a tall, thin woman with skunk-striped hair sauntered past their table. Holly fairly jumped out of her seat. "Jana! Jana!" The skunk-striped woman turned to look at Holly, her face registering absolutely nothing. "Holly Griffin!" Holly chirped brightly, and the woman just turned and walked on.

Jane could stand it no more. She'd manufacture a headache in a few minutes, even ask Holly if she had any Tylenol. She waited, taking a sip of her water.

A waitress appeared and asked if they wanted something from the bar. Holly asked for Perrier and lime, and Jane said she'd have the same. When the waitress was gone, Holly turned to Jane, eyes gleaming. She looked like a crazed tiger.

"Holly, what is it?"

"I swear I'll burst if I don't tell you."

"Tell me what?"

"I have a wonderful surprise for you, Jane Stuart."

Jane waited. The waitress arrived with their Perrier, and Jane took a sip, watching Holly.

"Well," Holly said, "don't you want to know what it is?"

"Of course! What is it?" It probably had something to do with someone else Holly had slept with to get a good review for Carol's book.

"Okay," Holly said, wiggling in her chair. "Okay. I'm bringing a very special guest to Carol's party. Someone who wants to do a book and needs an agent. This . . . person asked me who she should consider, and I told her the *only* agent to even consider is Jane Stuart."

Jane frowned at Holly skeptically.

Holly waited, watching Jane carefully.

"Well?" Holly finally blurted out. "Aren't you going to ask me who it is?"

Jane set down her drink. "All right. Who is it?"

Holly's eyes grew even wider and she leaned closer to Jane. "Goddess!"

A woman at the next table turned at the sound of the name. Jane could only stare at Holly. Jane must have misheard her. "Goddess?" Jane repeated.

Holly's head bobbed up and down. She was positively gleeful.

Jane continued to stare. This couldn't be true.

Goddess was one of America's—indeed, the world's—hottest stars. *Newsweek* had called her "Madonna and then some."

Everyone knew who Goddess was. Goddess was a phenomenon. No one was exactly sure how old she was, but she couldn't have been more than twenty-five. She had burst into the public consciousness two years ago when she starred in an underground sleeper of a film called *Doing It*, in which she played herself—the daughter of Viveca and Carl Hamner. Carl Hamner was the founder and chairman of Hamner Global, makers of the world's best-selling running shoe, the Hammer. Goddess, whose real name Jane had read was Katherine, had publicly stated that she hated and rejected her parents, and in *Doing It* she ridiculed them by having brutal sex with a man inside a gigantic scale model of the Hammer. Even the movie's title was a parody of Hamner Global's slogan, "Go ahead and do it!"

Since *Doing It*, the multitalented Goddess had starred in several more hit films, recorded a number of international hit songs (and sexually graphic videos to go with them), and appeared on Broadway in a one-woman show called *Goddess of Love*. It was still running, one of the city's most popular shows. Tickets were virtually impossible to get. It seemed anything Goddess did, the world wanted to see.

Holly stared at Jane, waiting for a reaction. Jane didn't know what to say. Could this be true?

"Well?" Holly said at last. "What do you think of *that?*"

"*The* Goddess?"

"Yes! Goddess!"

A strange sensation washed over Jane—the feeling one gets when it appears possible that one might make quite a bit of money. But Jane and Holly's relationship over the years had been strained, to say the least. Why would Holly have done this for her?

"What's the catch?" Jane asked.

Holly made her pouty mouth. She tilted her head a little to one side, her Cleopatra hair swinging. "No *catch*, Jane. Really, I'm *très* insulted. I really felt you would be the right agent for her. Look what you've done for Carol."

Jane felt a wave of guilt about all the bad things she'd thought about Holly all these years. "Holly, I . . . I don't know what to say. Except—well—thank you!"

Holly smoothed her hair, smiling as if to say, Now you've got it.

"How do you know her?" Jane asked.

"My parents have been friends with her parents for years. Goddess and I—we haven't been that close, but when she decided to do a book, she naturally came to me for advice. I'm her friend in publishing!"

Jane tilted her head in the direction of Mort Janklow, agent to the stars. "I'd have thought someone like that would have been more suitable."

"No no no, Jane. If you think that, you don't understand the phenomenon that is Goddess. Goddess never does what's expected. Goddess never does what you'd *think*. That's what makes her—Goddess!"

Jane still wasn't convinced. "If she wants to do a book, and you, an editor at a major publishing house, are her 'friend in publishing,' why don't you just sign her up? Why steer her to an agent when you could just buy her book?"

"Jane," Holly said, her tone indicating that Jane should know better, "Goddess may be eccentric and outrageous, but she's a sophisticated businesswoman. Don't let the tender age fool you. She knew that even if she published with us, she'd need a killer agent, and she asked me to recommend one. And I did. You! Of course . . ." Her smile grew coy.

Here, at last, was the catch.

". . . Of course, I would expect you—just as a courtesy, of course—to offer Goddess's book to me first and exclusively."

"Of course," Jane promised solemnly. She thought she understood the situation now. Holly knew Goddess wouldn't be satisfied until she had an agent, so Holly steered Goddess to Jane, whom she considered not a tiger but a pushover who would sell the book to Holly for a relatively low advance. This would be just like the scheming Holly. On the other hand, Jane *had* sold Carol Freund's book to Holly for big money, six figures . . . though for Goddess's book, that kind of money would be considered paltry. Yes, Jane's theory made sense. But if Jane really did sign Goddess as a client, really did handle her book, she'd prove Holly wrong. Jane *could* be a tiger.

"Holly, I don't know what to say. I'm stunned. She's the biggest star—"

"In the world!" Holly grabbed a rye bread stick from a basket on the table and crunched on it. "Where the hell is that waitress," she muttered. "I'm *starving.*" She looked around, spotted the waitress, and summoned her with an upraised hand. They ordered quickly, and the waitress hurried away.

Holly leaned forward again, touching Jane's hand.

"And Goddess," she said, "is my big surprise for Carol's party! Dontcha just love it?"

Jane didn't think she just loved it. Carol's novel was a quiet story about people on a farm in Indiana during the Korean War. She didn't see how the outrageous avant-garde Goddess fit in.

"Do you think she's quite—appropriate?"

"Appropriate! Jane, as you just said, she's the biggest star in the world right now. Who *wouldn't* want her at their party? And she's agreed to do something *very* special for us—but I'll keep that a surprise. Besides, I intend to introduce you to Goddess at the party."

Jane remembered that Stanley Greenberg would be with her. What would he make of all this? she wondered, not knowing him well enough even to guess.

During the remainder of the lunch, Jane toyed with her blinis and watched Holly carefully, trying to figure her out. By the end of the meal, Jane had decided her pushover theory made the most sense. Nevertheless, signing Goddess would be an incredible coup for Jane as an agent.

When they were out on the sidewalk, Holly suddenly grabbed Jane in a hug. "I'm so excited, Jane. This party is going to be a triumph for me—I mean for all of us. Remember, our offices, eight o'clock."

"Got it." Jane watched Holly hurry away down Fifty-second Street toward Fifth Avenue. It was a beautiful warm day and Jane decided to walk to the Port Authority. On Broadway in the mid-Forties she passed the Minskoff Theatre and stopped short. Mounted to the building was an enormous billboard. It was Botticelli's *The Birth of Venus*, except that it wasn't Venus rising from the sea on the half shell; it was Goddess, nude, stray locks of her famous waist-length light brown hair floating before her perfect body in strategic places. Draped around her waist and shoulder was a sash like a beauty queen's, and on it were the words *Goddess of Love*.

Jane stared up at the image for a long time. Goddess's eyes seemed to gaze down on her, as if she were about to tell Jane something.

Finally, Jane pulled her gaze away and continued west, shaking her head at thoughts of how Carol Freund's publication party might turn out.

Nine

The next morning, Jane stopped just outside the back door of her office building and took off her crown. Nick had made it for her. He had cut it from yellow construction paper, written "Happy Birthday!" across the front in black marker, and sprinkled gold glitter all over it. With a little chuckle, she shrugged, placed it back on her head at a jaunty angle, and entered the office.

"Mrs. Jack Benny has arrived!" she announced to Daniel as she burst from the back corridor into the reception room. She'd resolved this morning not to sulk on her birthday, and this was part of her plan.

Daniel looked up from his desk, where he appeared to have been drafting a letter in longhand. He looked gloomier than Jane could remember seeing him look. "Oh, hi, Jane." He summoned a wan smile. "Happy birthday."

"Boy," she said, dropping dispiritedly into his visitor's chair. She removed her crown and tossed it on the desk.

"You look as bad as I promised myself I wouldn't feel. Software got you down again?"

He allowed a little laugh. "No."

"Do you want to talk about it?"

He met her gaze gratefully, thought a moment, and nodded. She led him into her office and closed the door. They both sat, Jane behind her desk, Daniel in front of it.

"So," she said, "my birthday's got you down, too, huh?"

"No." He looked at her. He seemed not to know where to start.

"Something at home?" she ventured.

"Definitely. Last night," he began, "when I got home from work, Laura was unusually cheerful. I thought she was even acting kind of strange."

Jane waited. She had a feeling she knew what he was about to tell her, yet she hoped she was wrong. "She's not—"

He nodded as if reading her mind. "Pregnant."

"Oh, Daniel." Jane knew that Daniel and Laura had expressly agreed not to have a child yet—not this early in their careers, not before they were married, not when they each made so little money that they still couldn't afford to buy a house.

"How could this happen?" Jane said, then realized exactly what she was saying. "I mean, I know how it happened, but why?"

"That's what I asked Laura." He looked down, embarrassed. "I tell you everything, Jane." He met her gaze. "Laura reminded me of a night when she and I made love without using any precautions. It was just . . . one of those things. I was sound asleep; she woke me up . . ."

He shook his head, as if unable to explain it any better than that. "The next morning, when I suddenly realized what we'd done—or not done, I should say—she told me not to worry. She said it was the wrong time of the month for her to get pregnant. Last night, when I reminded her of what she'd said, she just shrugged and held up one of those home pregnancy test things. She looked so happy. She said she guessed she'd been wrong and threw her arms around me. She said she felt wonderful."

"And you don't, clearly."

"I feel anything but wonderful. Jane, you know I didn't want a child yet. Neither did Laura, or so I thought. But I was wrong. When I even started to bring up the possibility of—well—stopping the pregnancy, she looked at me as if I'd committed the ultimate betrayal. I don't want to hurt her, Jane. So I said to myself, 'I guess I'll just have to get used to the idea of a baby coming much sooner than I'd planned.' And of course I want the baby. So I put on my happiest face, hugged her back, and told her I guessed it was time to plan that wedding she's always wanted."

Jane nodded. "Somehow I knew you'd feel that way."

"Laura says I'm an old-fashioned boy, which is why she loves me so much. She says it's about time our engagement ended anyway, that she was starting to get embarrassed when her friends at Unimed asked her when our wedding date was and she had to say she didn't know."

"And when *is* it?" Jane asked.

"We talked about that this morning over breakfast. Laura pointed out that neither of us has any family, so almost all the people we'd invite to our wedding would be our friends here in Shady Hills."

"I never knew Laura had no family," Jane said. "What happened to them?"

"Laura doesn't know. She was raised in a foster home. She no longer has any relationship with her foster parents and doesn't even like to talk about them. I'm not sure she even remembers much about them."

"That's sad."

"Laura sees no reason to put off the wedding any longer than necessary, especially under the circumstances. She suggested two weeks from Saturday. June 12. She's always dreamed of a June wedding. As far as I'm concerned, one date's as good as another, so I said fine, but I pointed out we'd better start inviting people—there isn't much time. Laura agreed."

"Where are you having this wedding?"

"Laura wants it at Eleanor's."

Jane was surprised. Eleanor's *was* the nicest restaurant in Shady Hills, but virtually all the wedding receptions in town took place at Hydrangea House.

"Not at Louise and Ernie's?" she asked.

"That would be the logical choice, of course. But Laura says in light of the recent—event there, that's out of the question. She says it's too grisly, bad luck, too grim." He shrugged.

"I understand," Jane said, feeling bad for Louise. She looked at poor forlorn Daniel, and her heart went out to him. She got up and went to him, taking him in her arms. "Congratulations. I know you'll be very happy. You already are!" She thought of the joy Nick had brought her, the comfort since Kenneth had been gone.

She perched on the edge of her desk. "Know what I think?"

"What?" he asked sadly.

"I think you'll make a wonderful father. You'll wonder how you ever got along without that baby."

He smiled wanly. "You think?"

Suddenly Jane sensed that something was still wrong, something more than what he'd told her. "You love her, don't you?"

He looked surprised. "I'm marrying her, aren't I?"

"You're not answering my question."

The phone rang. Daniel reached across her desk and grabbed it.

Saved by the bell.

He put the call on hold. "It's Pam Gainor."

She was about to ask him if he'd like her to call Pam back so that they could talk some more, but he held the receiver out toward her, which answered her question. Clearly he'd said all he wanted to say. He left the office as she took the call.

After Jane had hung up from Pam, Daniel reappeared. "I wanted to show you the pictures from Nick's party." He spread out the snapshots before her. She chose a decent shot of herself. Daniel studied the shots of himself before selecting one, though to Jane's mind he looked great in all of them.

"I'll send these on to Bertha," he said. "Now, are we decided on our workshop topic?"

"Yes, 'The Changing Face of Romance,'" she said, already bored with the subject.

"All right. I'll write up a brief description, and also bios of you and me, and I'll send them to Bertha with the pictures." When she expected him to turn and leave, he reached to his back pocket and brought out a small rectangular gift-wrapped box and a card. "Happy birthday, Jane."

"You shouldn't have," she said, and opened the card, whose front read *For My Dear Friend.* "Thank you, my dear friend," she said, her eyes filling, and opened the gift. It was a fountain pen made of jade, slim and sleek. "It's beautiful. Thank you."

He smiled and kissed her cheek. "You have those jade earrings. Now you have a matching pen!"

"What a great idea." She placed the pen and card at the corner of her desk where she could see them all day, and surveyed the pile of work in front of her, trying to figure out what to do first. Before Daniel had reached her doorway, she looked up and watched him, her eyes narrowing, then shook her head in puzzlement.

Near closing time, Daniel invited Jane to dinner for her birthday.

"That's lovely of you, Daniel, but you've already given me a gift."

"But I'd like to do more," he said, and Jane could tell he really wanted to do this.

She smiled. "All right."

"Great. We'll go to Eleanor's."

Jane called Florence and told her she'd be late because a handsome young man was taking her to dinner. Then she and Daniel drove in his car to Eleanor's and were shown to a table in the back room, which overlooked the mill wheel and millpond.

"I hope I didn't shock you with my news this morning," he said. "I mean, my getting so personal."

"Personal! We're practically family, you and I. We *are*

personal. No, you didn't shock me. Though I have had a few shocks lately." Yesterday, when she'd returned from her lunch with Holly, she'd told him about Goddess.

"Yes, your new client," he said.

"No, not just that," she said coyly. "Your Jane has got a . . . date!"

"A date!" He looked truly pleased. "Jane, that's wonderful. With whom?"

"Stanley Greenberg," she said proudly.

He frowned. "The cop? *Detective* Greenberg?"

"Yes," she replied, now frowning, too. "What's wrong with that?"

"Nothing, nothing at all. I'm just surprised."

"Why?"

"He's not the kind of man I imagined you with . . . after Kenneth, I mean."

"And what kind of man did you imagine me with?"

"Someone like Kenneth!"

She nodded. "I see what you mean. Kenneth was so literary, so urbane. And Stanley, as you so eloquently put it, is a cop." She wagged a finger at him. "But you've got to understand something about women, Daniel. It's not qualities like being bookish and sophisticated that necessarily attract a woman to a man."

"Are you saying you're attracted to Greenberg?"

She pondered. "Perhaps, yes." Suddenly, at hearing her own words, she felt a wave of sadness wash over her. She'd never thought she'd say such a thing after losing her beloved Kenneth. She looked down at her water glass, trying to hide her feelings from Daniel.

"Jane," he said gently, "I knew Kenneth, too. And I think it's pretty safe to say he would want you to have someone, someone new. Don't shut out happiness because of him."

She felt a tear roll out of her eye and down her cheek. She wiped it away with her hand. "I haven't. Not consciously. Now that I think I *could* have a relationship with another man, I feel so . . . guilty."

"You hoped for a relationship with Roger Haines," Daniel pointed out, referring to Jane's ex-client on whom she'd had romantic designs.

"True, but it never got anywhere, and I think deep in my heart I knew it wouldn't. But this . . . This could be something real. He's a good man, Daniel, I can tell that."

"If you like him, I'm sure he is."

She smiled gratefully.

"You've been so lonely, Jane. You *should* have someone." He laughed. "Watch out, though. If your mystery-writing clients find out about him, they'll be all over you for inside information."

"You're right! I never thought of that." She shook her head. "I'm keeping all of that for myself. And for you, of course."

"What do you mean?" he said, suddenly serious. "That girl?"

"In the woods. Yes." Now she told him what Doris had said to her Monday morning, and about meeting Doris and Arthur at the station yesterday so Greenberg could question Arthur. But she'd promised Greenberg she wouldn't tell anyone he'd shown her the cave, so she kept silent about that now.

Daniel seemed eager to change the subject. They spoke of the agency, of imminent sales and recent rejections. At ten minutes to eight, Daniel slapped himself in the forehead.

"I completely forgot! Laura asked me to pick up a sweater she left at Louise and Ernie's on Sunday. You know, in all the confusion. Would you mind if we stopped there on the way back to the office to get your car?"

"Of course not," Jane said, and after Daniel paid the check, they walked out into the mild night.

Daniel drove right on Cranmore. They passed the Senior Center on the left, low and landscaped, and Jane thought of Doris and Arthur. From the village center, Daniel took Plunkett Lane, turning in at the inn's gate.

"It looks so pretty tonight," Jane remarked as they pulled up in front of the porch. "Lit up like a Christmas tree."

He led the way up the porch steps and knocked. Louise opened the door.

"Evening, Louise. Laura left her sweater here on Sunday and asked me to pick it up for her."

"Yes, I have it. Come in. Oh, Jane, hello. Come in, dear."

Jane followed Daniel into the foyer. She frowned. Daniel, instead of following Louise to wherever she'd put Laura's sweater, just stood in the center of the floor, Louise beside him. Jane opened her mouth to speak, but before she could, a mass of people burst from the living room on the right and cried in booming cheerful voices, "Surprise!"

There was Laura, and Ginny, and Penny, and Doris, and Rhoda, and Ernie—and Greenberg, who was smiling and carrying an armful of red roses. He came forward, handed them to her, and planted a chaste kiss on her cheek.

"Happy birthday," he said.

Beaming with pleasure, Jane looked around at her friends. "I believe I'm going to cry."

"Jane," Greenberg said softly, leaning forward, "you already are."

Ten

Jane stepped farther into the foyer, and as she did, Nick and Florence appeared from the dining room, faces bright.

"Happy birthday, Mom!"

"Yes, many happy returns, missus."

"Why, you devils," Jane said. "When I called and said I'd be late, you knew all about this."

"Of course we did, Mom." Nick looked extremely pleased with himself. "Winky wanted to come, too, but I told her she couldn't."

"I see," Jane said solemnly. "Well, we'll have to make sure we don't stay too late. It *is* a school night."

"Oh, *Mom.* It's a party. Lighten up!"

Before she could respond, the doorbell rang. Jane turned and saw Louise hurrying to answer it. When Louise opened the door, Audrey Fairchild stood framed in the doorway, tall and blond and elegant in an ivory silk pants suit, and behind her hovered darkly handsome Elliott, looking uncomfortable. The Fairchilds lived across the street from Jane. Jane was fond of them but was surprised to see them here because she knew they'd been having marital problems. In fact, Audrey had confided to Jane that they were seeing a marriage counselor.

Audrey looked over Louise's head and waved at Jane. "Whoo-ooo! Happy birthday, doll!"

Elliott visibly winced. "Louise, I'm sorry we're late. I know you said to come at seven-thirty so we could surprise Jane, but . . . we ran into some difficulties."

Audrey, hearing this, rolled her eyes and swept into the foyer, leaving Elliott standing in the doorway with Louise.

"No problem," Louise told him softly. "It's just nice to have you here."

Audrey hurried up to Jane.

"So? Were you surprised?"

"Totally," Jane said. "This really is wonderful."

Audrey stroked her sleek honey blond head. "I have a little something for you," she said softly. "But I felt I should give it to you privately."

"Oh?"

"Yes. I didn't want to embarrass anyone."

Jane knew exactly what Audrey meant. The Fairchilds were quite wealthy—Elliott, a cardiovascular surgeon, had recently been named director of the New Jersey Rehabilitation Institute—and Audrey's gift to Jane was no doubt excessively lavish.

"Thank you, Audrey," Jane said graciously. "It was sweet of you to get me something."

"Well, of course, doll! You're my neighbor! You're my pal!"

Neighbor, yes. Pal? Jane wasn't so sure about that. She thought not, but just smiled.

Greenberg stepped up to Jane and Audrey. Audrey

immediately turned, as if she had a built-in man detector that had activated, and quite unabashedly looked him up and down.

"Hello," she said brightly.

"Audrey," Jane said, "I would like you to meet my friend, Detective Stanley Greenberg."

Audrey raised her perfectly tweezed blond brows. "I knew you looked familiar. You're with the police here in the village."

"That's right," Greenberg said. "Nice to meet you, Mrs. Fairchild. I've seen you around town."

"Have you now?" Audrey said, moving closer to him.

Jane realized that Audrey wouldn't have seen Greenberg here on Sunday, because Jane hadn't invited Audrey and Elliott to Nick's birthday party. She hadn't felt they would have been interested. Now she felt a pang of guilt about that. Audrey did, after all, consider Jane her pal.

Audrey's face grew serious, and she said to Greenberg, "I'll bet you've got your hands full these days." She cocked her head in the direction of the dining room and the inn's backyard beyond.

"Uh . . . yes," he replied, looking uncomfortable.

"A cake!" Jane exclaimed, happy to rescue Greenberg. She walked to the dining-room table, where a large white sheet cake covered with pink-and-yellow frosting roses sat beside plates, forks, and napkins. On the sideboard Louise had set out a selection of sodas and mineral waters, along with coffee and tea.

"Isn't this lovely?" Jane said to Nick, who had followed her. Behind him came Louise.

"Louise, you've outdone yourself." Jane gave her a hug. "Thank you so much."

Louise waved the thanks away. "Thank Ginny," she said, looking out to the foyer, and Ginny, hearing her name, turned. She excused herself from Laura and Daniel and came into the dining room.

"What did I do now?"

"Was this your idea?" Jane asked.

"I confess," Ginny said.

Jane kissed her on the cheek. "Thank you."

Ginny looked pleased with herself. "When you were in New York having lunch a week ago Monday, I went to see Daniel at your office and asked him to help us plan this party. It was really all of us in the club who thought of it. We felt you needed a boost."

"So Daniel was in on it from the beginning," Jane said.

"Absolutely. He loved the idea. He said he'd find some way to get you here at the right time without your suspecting."

"Ah," Jane said. "Laura's sweater."

"Ginny!" Laura called from the foyer. "You didn't finish that joke!"

Ginny laughed. "Be right back." And she hurried away.

"Feel better now?" Daniel asked.

Jane turned to him; she hadn't heard him come up behind her.

"You sneak," Jane said. "I didn't think it was in your nature to lie."

"It is, for the right reasons," he replied, and winked at her. "But all I did was get you here. Your club friends planned it all."

"So I heard."

"Ginny and I planned it while you were having lunch

with Bertha. Then on my way home after work I stopped at Whipped Cream to help her with the guest list." His brow creased and he looked thoughtful. "You know, I really like Ginny. I never knew her very well. There's something about her—something very straightforward. And she's always so—upbeat."

"Who's that?" Laura asked, appearing beside Daniel. "Talking about me again?"

Daniel grabbed her by the waist and pulled her close. "No, honey, for once I'm not."

Jane smiled at the couple. It occurred to her that Daniel might not have told Laura he had confided in Jane about the pregnancy and upcoming wedding, so Jane decided to say nothing, and just kept grinning.

"Over here, everyone!" Louise called out. She stood over the cake, lighting candles—too many of them for Jane's liking.

Everyone moved into the dining room and crowded around the table. Louise finished lighting the candles and turned to Jane. "Now don't forget to make a wish, and promise never to tell it to anyone or it won't come true."

"I promise." *I wish for someone in my life who will take away my loneliness* . . . Melancholy swept through her at this thought, but she kept smiling, took a deep breath, and, with some effort, managed to extinguish all the candles. Everyone cheered and then broke out into a loud rendition of "Happy Birthday."

Gazing about the large table at all her friends, Jane felt her eyes well with tears and chastised herself for thinking she was lonely.

"Now the birthday girl gets to cut the cake," Ernie said, and handed Jane a knife and plate.

"I want the first piece, Mom!" Nick cried, and everyone laughed.

"How can I say no to that?" Jane cut him a nice corner piece piled high with frosting roses. She cut more pieces and people dispersed again to chat in scattered groups.

"Lovely, just lovely," Jane said, putting down the knife when she was sure everyone had cake.

"Jane—" Louise said softly.

Jane turned to her. She looked troubled, her brow wrinkled, her lips pursed.

"Yes, Louise?"

Louise licked her lips nervously and took Jane's arm, leading her over to the window where they could speak quietly. "Jane," she said in a low voice, looking around to make sure no one overheard. She appeared to be close to tears. "I truly hate to bother you with this now— at your own birthday party—but I need your help with something. There's no one else I feel I can turn to."

"Of course you can turn to me, Louise, anytime," Jane said, concerned.

Louise let a tiny smile of gratitude appear on her face, but it quickly disappeared. "I want to show you something. Come with me."

Louise, clearly trying to look casual, walked slowly out of the dining room and wove her way through the clusters of guests chattering in the foyer. She walked to the corridor at the back of the foyer that led to the kitchen, and Jane followed.

"In here?" Jane asked softly.

"No." Louise opened a drawer, took out a flashlight, and headed for the servants' staircase at the back of the kitchen. She flipped a switch on the wall next to the stairway's entrance. "Up here."

Jane, puzzled, followed Louise up the stairs. They were narrow and steep. Single bare bulbs at intervals in the low ceiling cast a weak light. The air was still and had an atticky smell of old wood and dust.

The staircase turned on itself twice before a door to the inn's second floor came into view. Louise walked right past it.

"Is this a stress test for my birthday?" Jane joked, but Louise, clearly not in a joking mood, turned and quickly shushed her. Where on earth were they going?

The stairway ended at a door to the third floor, and Louise pushed it open, holding it so Jane could walk through.

Louise switched off the flashlight. More bare bulbs at intervals in the ceiling illuminated a narrow corridor that appeared to run the length of the inn. The walls were plain, and a number of doors opened off it on each side.

"Don't make any noise," Louise whispered. "Some of the help live up here."

Jane, remembering Yolanda, followed Louise to the end of the corridor, where Louise opened a door on the left. They entered a small room, bare of furniture. Elaborate wainscoting ran around the lower half of the room, carved square panels within panels.

"Louise, what was it you—"

"Sh-h-h!" Louise walked to the room's right wall and switched on the flashlight. Abruptly she dropped to her knees and, with her free hand, pushed on one of the panels of the wainscoting.

"Louise Zabriskie," Jane whispered, "what the devil are you doing?"

"Jane, shush! Just wait a minute." Louise pushed some more, and to Jane's amazement, the panel swung inward. Jane watched in stunned silence as Louise pushed the panel all the way in. It was an honest-to-goodness secret door. Now Louise dropped onto all fours and started crawling through the square space. "Follow me," she whispered.

Jane did, crawling after her. Beyond the door, Louise was already standing, shining the flashlight around a small space, a tiny room about eight feet square. Jane got up. "All right, now will you tell me what we're doing? What *is* this place?"

Louise walked to the secret door and pushed it almost completely shut. Then she turned to Jane.

"Have you ever heard of the Underground Railroad?"

"Yes, of course. Nick studied it in social studies last year. It was a network of places where people opposed to slavery hid escaped slaves on their way to the north or Canada."

"Right. William Hadley, the man who originally built this house, was a staunch abolitionist and became part of the Underground Railroad. He had this secret room built to hide slaves. The only people who know it exists are Ernie and me . . . or so I thought."

Jane frowned. "This is very interesting, Louise, and I appreciate your showing it to me. But *why* are you showing it to me?"

Wordlessly Louise pointed the flashlight at the far right corner of the room. There, a rumpled sleeping bag lay rolled out on the floor.

"Whose is that?" Jane asked.

"Ernie's."

"Ernie's? But why would Ernie bring his sleeping bag in *here*?"

"So no one would know who he's sleeping with," Louise said, and watched Jane.

Suddenly Jane got it. Her jaw fell, and she closed it. "You mean Ernie— He's been having— In this room? How did you find out?"

"I don't know if you've noticed, but Ernie's been acting strange lately, kind of nervous and secretive." Louise laughed ruefully. "I know him so well. One day a couple of weeks ago I was outside hanging our clothes on the line, when Ernie came outside for no apparent reason. He could see I had a big basket of clothes to hang, and he remarked that I'd probably be at it for a while. I said that was true, and he nodded and went back inside. I waited a few seconds. Then I secretly followed him up here."

"But who was the woman?" Jane asked with trepidation.

"I don't *know*," Louise said, frustrated. "I followed Ernie to the outer room and watched him through the door from the corridor. I watched him crawl in here, and suddenly I realized the woman was already here! I . . . heard them." Her face contorted pitifully and she started to cry.

"Oh, Louise," Jane said. "I'm so sorry. That . . . rat!"

"And I have absolutely no idea who it could be." Louise took a handkerchief from her skirt pocket and wiped her eyes and nose.

"I know how much it must hurt," Jane said.

Louise gave a couple of quick nods. "I've suspected

Ernie of fooling around for some time, but I'd never had any proof. I'd even begun to tell myself I was imagining things."

Jane was still unsure why Louise had shown her all this. "So you wanted to confide in someone?"

Louise turned to Jane with an odd expression of puzzlement. "Don't you get it, Jane? The woman Ernie was seeing—I think she was the woman hanging in the woods."

A chill ran down Jane's spine. "Louise! Everyone is pretty much in agreement that that woman was murdered. You're not saying that Ernie could have done something like that?"

"No, I'm not, Jane. That's just it! But if the police find out that Ernie was seeing this woman—and they seem to have ways of finding out anything these days, with that awful DNA testing and all that—they'll immediately suspect him." Louise's eyes pleaded with Jane. "But you're right—he wouldn't do that. He *couldn't* do that. I know Ernie."

"Would you have thought he'd do *that*?" Jane asked, tilting her head toward the sleeping bag.

"No. But he's not a killer, Jane. And despite what he's been doing, I love Ernie. I don't want him blamed for what happened to that poor girl."

"But what can I do?" Jane asked. "What does it have to do with me?"

"You're seeing that Detective Greenberg. I want you to tell him Ernie would never do such a thing."

"Louise," Jane said, surprised, "you're asking me to influence the police?" She shook her head. "You're giving me far more credit than I deserve. Nothing I say about my opinion of Ernie will change the police's investigation. Besides, I hardly know Detective Greenberg."

"Then you won't do it?"

"I didn't say that. I agree with you about Ernie; I don't think he could ever kill anyone. I'll say as much to Detective Greenberg, sure. I doubt it'll make much difference, but sure, I'll do what I can."

"Thank you, Jane," Louise squeaked, dropped to her knees, and began crawling out through the secret door. While the flashlight in Louise's hand still illuminated the room, Jane took a last look around. She let her gaze linger on the rumpled sleeping bag and grimaced in disgust.

Then she noticed something lying on top of the sleeping bag, nearly concealed by its camouflage pattern. She knelt for a closer look. It was a sweater. It lay rumpled in the middle of the sleeping bag. In the dim light, Jane squinted to see it more clearly. It looked familiar somehow. . . . She decided to say nothing about it to Louise.

"Jane," came Louise's whisper through the door, "are you coming?"

"Yes." Jane pulled her gaze from the sweater and crawled out. Louise led the way back down the servants' staircase, and Jane followed in silence.

Downstairs, the party was in full swing. Only Daniel seemed to have noticed Jane and Louise's absence; he approached Jane as she emerged into the foyer from the kitchen corridor. "Everything all right?" he asked.

"Fine, wonderful," she said brightly. "I've just got a bit of a headache—all this excitement, I guess. Louise was getting me some aspirin."

"I see," Daniel said, though he looked unconvinced. Over the next hour, during which Jane had to force herself to be pleasant to Ernie, some of the guests departed. Florence, wishing Jane a happy birthday, said she would take Nick home and put him to bed. Finally, only Daniel, Laura, Jane, Greenberg, and of course Louise and Ernie remained. Seizing her moment, Jane excused herself to powder her nose.

She hurried through the corridor to the kitchen and grabbed the flashlight Louise had put back in the drawer. Then she hurried back up the servants' stairs to the third floor, and down the corridor to the room that opened onto the site of Ernie's trysts. Setting down her handbag, she knelt, pushed open the secret panel, and crawled into the tiny space. She made her way over to the sleeping bag, grabbed the sweater, and examined it carefully in the flashlight's glow.

The sweater was a well-knitted Fair Isle, in an especially intricate pattern of cinnamon, amethyst, and gold that looked disturbingly familiar. Jane pondered—and suddenly knew why.

It had been on display for months at the Yarn Basket, the needlework shop on the village green where Jane bought all her knitting supplies. The shop was owned by Dara Nielsen, an odious woman who was jealous of the Defarge Club because she hadn't started it and had never been invited to join. Jane was the only member of the club who bought her supplies at Dara's shop, and she did so only out of convenience. The other women all bought their supplies elsewhere, so strong was their dislike of Dara. Dara herself had knitted this sweater as a store sample.

Ernie and Dara . . . Jane shook her head in something close to horror. It was a difficult image to conjure. But Jane knew there was no accounting for taste, especially in matters like these. She folded the sweater tightly, carried it with her as she crawled back through the secret door, and stuffed the sweater into her bag. Then she hurried back downstairs, replaced the flashlight in the kitchen drawer, and walked back through the corridor to the foyer, all smiles and thanks for a wonderful birthday party.

Greenberg approached Jane. "I'll be happy to give you a ride to your car. That way, Daniel and Laura can go right home."

"Thank you, that would be lovely," Jane said, and thanked Louise and Ernie again for the party. As Jane passed the entrance to the living room, her gaze lighted on the sofa on which Louise had once displayed the Irish Chain quilt Jane had seen in the cave. On impulse Jane turned to Louise.

"Louise, what happened to that Mike Vernell, the hiker who was staying here?"

"He checked out Sunday night," Louise replied. "Why?"

The day the girl was found hanging . . .

Jane nodded thoughtfully, then shrugged. "Just wondering." She said good night, thanking Louise again for the wonderful birthday party, and got into Greenberg's car. He started back toward town.

"I was delighted when Ginny invited me to your party," he said, breaking the silence.

"I'm delighted, too," Jane said.

When he reached the village center, he drove around Center Street and through the alley to the parking lot behind Jane's building, pulling up beside her car.

"Well," he said, and for a moment they just sat in the near darkness.

Then he was drawing near her, and she felt herself moving toward him, and they were kissing—a soft, hesitant kiss. His lips were soft. She reached up and touched his face, smooth at the cheek, slightly beard-roughened at the chin. Gently they pulled apart.

"Well," Jane said this time, and smiled. "Good night."

"Good night, Jane."

She hadn't felt this flustered since her first middle-school dance. Hitching her bag higher on her shoulder, she got out and gave Greenberg a wave. Then she turned toward her car, knowing he wouldn't leave until she had gotten in and driven away first.

As Jane left the parking lot, it occurred to her that, as it turned out, she'd had a very nice birthday indeed.

Eleven

The Yarn Basket was everything Dara Nielsen wasn't: fun, warm, and cozy. Entering the shop the next morning, Jane breathed in the familiar smell of the yarns that filled the cubbyholes on two entire walls—row upon row of rich, vibrant scarlets and golds and sapphires and eggplants and goldenrods. Then there were the hand-dyed skeins, carefully hung from pegs on a third wall. The remaining wall displayed supplies of all sorts, from needles to crochet hooks to buttons and zippers, as did the three tables that ran lengthwise down the middle of the store.

At first Dara was nowhere in sight. Then out of the corner of her eye Jane saw movement at the counter and the top of Dara's graying head as she stooped to do something on the shelves under the cash register. She rose and saw Jane, her weaselly face barely breaking a smile. "Hello," she said coolly.

"Good morning," Jane said airily, pretending to admire the hand-dyed yarns. In reality, she *did* admire them—in fact, she intended to buy some in silk for a sweater pattern she had in mind to try—but yarn wasn't what she'd come for today, and she certainly had no intention of ever buying yarn here again.

"Anything I can help you with?" Dara asked.

"No, thanks," Jane called back. She waited a few moments, then approached the counter with feigned nonchalance.

Dara was watching her. Jane could tell she had noticed that Jane hadn't carried any merchandise to the counter.

"How's your husband, Dara?" Jane asked.

Dara looked surprised. She and Jane never exchanged small talk. "Fine," she replied, staring at Jane. She looked Jane up and down. "Nothing you need today?"

"Me?" Jane smiled. "No, thank you. But I do have something to show you."

Dara looked baffled.

Jane made a business of digging around in her bag. Then she grabbed the Fair Isle sweater, yanked it out, and tossed it onto the counter. Dara stared at it for a brief second; then her eyes widened, and she positively glared at it as if it were a scorpion ready to strike.

"Where—whose is that?" she said.

Jane put her hands on the counter and leaned forward. "Don't even try it, Dara."

Dara swallowed. "Where'd you find it?"

Jane gave her a look of pure loathing. "You know where I found it. And so does Louise Zabriskie."

Dara glared at Jane, saying nothing.

"You're in luck, though, Dara. Louise doesn't know who the sweater belongs to because she's smart enough not to shop here and never saw it on display. But I did." Jane narrowed her eyes. "Now you listen to me, and listen good. If you ever set foot in Hydrangea House again, or go anywhere near Ernie Zabriskie, I *will* tell Louise—and everyone else in Shady Hills, including your husband—who this sweater belongs to and where I found it. You got me?"

Dara gave one sharp nod, her face the very picture of terror, and gulped.

With a flick of her wrist Jane knocked the sweater off the counter. It landed in a heap at Dara's feet.

Jane then turned on her heel and walked through the shop door, vowing never to enter the Yarn Basket again.

Daniel spun around in his chair as soon as she entered the office.

"Florence has been calling," he said. "She's frantic."

Jane's heart skipped a beat. "Why? What's wrong?"

"It's something about Winky."

Jane went to her desk and dialed Florence.

"Oh, missus, thank goodness you called. I don't know what to do!"

"What's the matter, Florence?"

"It's Winky, missus. All morning long she has been shooting around the house like a rocket ship! I think she must be scared of something, but every time I try to pick her up and pat her, she just runs away and ping-pongs some more! She knocked the cookie jar off the counter and it smashed. What a mess! What should I do?"

"I'll be right home," Jane said, and immediately looked up the number of Winky's veterinarian, Dr. Singh. Jane called her, explained the situation as best she could, and was instructed to bring Winky right over.

Forty-five minutes later, Jane and Dr. Singh, a gentle Indian woman in her forties, stood gazing down at Winky as she roamed around the examining table. Calm and seemingly untroubled, she showed no signs of her morning behavior.

Jane scratched Winky between the ears. Winky rubbed up against Jane, purring like an engine. "What's going on, Wink?" Jane said.

"Now you say she ping-pongs about?" Dr. Singh asked.

"Yes. Florence—she's our nanny—says she does it more and more every day. She won't even let Florence near her."

Dr. Singh looked thoughtful and reached out to stroke Winky's back. "Hmm . . . I have an idea," she said. "Excuse me. I will be right back."

"Certainly," Jane said, frowning in puzzlement.

Dr. Singh left the room. A few moments later she returned. Jane had expected her to have some medicine for Winky to try, but Dr. Singh's hands were empty.

"Now," Dr. Singh said, approaching the table. "What do you think of this, Miss Winky?" She reached out to pat Winky's head.

Suddenly Winky leaped to the floor, scampered madly to the corner of the room, then shot like a bullet to the opposite corner.

Dr. Singh began to laugh. "But it is amazing!"

"What's amazing? What just happened?"

Dr. Singh reached into the pocket of her white coat and withdrew a small tube of what appeared to be hand cream.

"You see, Mrs. Stuart, many creams such as this for the hands contain a chemical called methylparaben.

Methylparaben smells just like a female cat in heat, and so male cats, when they smell it, go crazy. I put some of this cream on my hands when I left the room. What is amazing is that it affects a *female* cat this way. It is something new to me."

Jane shook her head. "Leave it to Winky to come up with something new."

"Yes, leave it to Winky," Dr. Singh said, nodding. "After all, isn't this the famous Winky who solved the mystery of your missing nanny?"

Not that again.

"Yes," Jane admitted.

"You have nothing to worry about. Winky is fine. But when you get home, have a look at the products your Florence is using. I'll bet you'll find methylparaben listed in the ingredients of at least one of them."

Winky wouldn't come anywhere near Jane until Dr. Singh had left the room. Then Jane was able to scoop her up and place her in the carrier.

Arriving home, Jane told Florence what Dr. Singh had said.

"My goodness!" Florence said with a laugh. "I will go check immediately." She went to the cabinet under the sink, where she kept her kitchen products, and rummaged among them until she found a white glass jar. She held it up to the light, squinted at the tiny print, and said, "Aha! Wouldn't you know it! It is here—methylparaben." She turned to Winky, who was eyeing the jar warily. "Winky, I am so terribly sorry. I will never use this again."

"Well, *that* mystery is solved," Jane said. "I'm going to work now. I'll be home around five, but then I'm going out again."

"Oh, yes," Florence said, eyebrows rising, "the party for your novel writer." She giggled. "Your date."

Jane rolled her eyes. "I should never have told you."

"Oh, no, missus, I'm sorry. I am delighted for you. I can tell that Detective Greenberg is a nice man—I have a good sense of these things. And you need a man, if you'll pardon me for saying it, missus."

"You're right, Florence, I do." Now Jane giggled. "And I have to confess I'm really looking forward to this. Having Detective Greenberg with me might even make Holly Griffin bearable."

"Who is Holly Griffin?"

"Never mind," Jane said. "See you later."

She drove back down into town, but instead of taking Packer Road into the village, she took Highland to Cranmore. She passed the Senior Center on the right and, just beyond it, pulled up in front of a black wrought-iron fence that ran along this section of the quiet road. She got out, walked through a gate in the fence, and made her way up a paved path that wound gently across perfectly manicured grass dotted with gravestones in neat rows. The path rose, and at the top of a hill she left the path and crossed the grass to stand before one of the stones.

KENNETH ADAM STUART
Beloved Husband and Father

"Hello, Kenneth," she said softly. A bird sang in a nearby tree.

"Kenneth, I need to talk to you. This . . . this is very

difficult for me. I've been putting off coming to see you." She paused, concentrated on what she would say. "Kenneth, I love you very much; you know that. I always will. But I have to let go of you now. I have to get on with my life. I have to try to find someone new.

"I didn't want you to go. If I'd had my way, you'd still be here. But things didn't work out that way, and Kenneth, honey, I'm so lonely."

The stone stared up at her, mute.

"I may have found someone, Kenneth. He's not you—no one will ever be you. But he's a nice man, different from you, but a nice man. And, well, I need to know that this is okay with you, that you're okay with my . . . going on."

Again she waited, staring at the stone. It was so quiet here. A squirrel chattered in the nearby woods. Below, on the road, a car whooshed softly by, like a whisper.

Jane shifted her weight to her other leg. "I want you to think about it, Kenneth, that's all I ask." She took a tissue from her bag and dabbed at her eyes. "Nicholas—who's fine, by the way; you'd be so proud of the little man he's turning into—he needs someone new. He loves you, he always will, too; but he needs to get on, too, Kenneth. Okay?"

She waited, then went on. "I guess I just needed to know you understand. I . . . I think you do."

She stepped closer to the stone, flicked off a few blades of grass thrown by the caretaker's lawnmower. "By the way, we're fine, darling—I mean with money. You know I've always worried about that. The agency is still going, and though it's not always easy, I'm getting the mortgage paid, buying groceries, paying Florence.

Oh, you don't know about Florence—she's our nanny. You'd like her. I'm paying Daniel, too, Kenneth. Yup, Daniel is still with us. I don't know what I'd do without him. He misses you, too.

"Well, I guess that's all I wanted to say. I love you, darling. Please remember that. I love you, and I didn't want you to go." On the last word her voice broke and she turned quickly, making her way to the path and back down the hill toward her car.

When she was about halfway to the space in the fence, a movement to her right caught her eye. Moving slowly down another of the cemetery's paths was Doris. She saw Jane and came up to her.

"Hello, Doris. What are you doing here?"

"Visiting my son."

"Your son? Doris, I—I never knew you had a son."

"Yes. I don't talk about him much. His name was James. He was six when he died. Cancer."

"I'm so sorry."

"That was almost fifty years ago," Doris said, looking as if she could scarcely believe it herself.

"Did you and Frank have any other children?"

"No. We tried, but we never could. Then Frank died."

Jane recalled that Frank had died of a stroke when Doris was in her forties. "I've never seen you here before. Do you come often?"

"No, not anymore. When I think of it. But when James first died, I used to come here a lot, like you. I've seen you here, talking to Kenneth."

Jane began to feel embarrassed, then realized that Doris felt this the most natural thing in the world.

"I used to talk to James, too. Now?" Doris shook her

head, her eyes distant. "Now, I just tell him I love him. That's the most important thing, you know—that they know you love them."

Jane took Doris's arm. Silently the two women walked down the path toward the road.

Twelve

"Eureka!" Greenberg cried, pulling his car into an empty parking spot on the right side of East Twenty-second Street.

"A good omen," Jane said with a laugh from the seat beside him. "I know this is going to be a fabulous night—Holly Griffin notwithstanding."

"I've never met this Holly." Daniel, in the backseat, sounded thoughtful.

Jane turned in her seat to look at him. "Take my advice. Meet it and beat it. Otherwise, she'll spoil your evening, I promise you that."

"Oh, Jane." Laura, next to Daniel, scoffed. "How bad could she be? She bought this novel of Carol Freund's for a hundred thousand dollars, she's throwing this big bash for her, and she's introducing you to Goddess, who will probably become your client!"

"True," Jane conceded. "But whose side are you on?"

They all laughed and got out of the car.

"Corsair's in that building." Jane pointed across the

street to a six-story building that, according to Holly, had once been a factory but had been converted into an elegant office building. Corsair occupied all but the first floor, which it rented to an advertising agency.

Jane checked her watch. It was a few minutes after eight. People were already streaming in through the building's wide glass double front doors. Jane, Greenberg, Daniel, and Laura joined the crowd and were directed by a security guard to the fourth floor.

They took the elevator and emerged into a corridor. At the left stood a young woman—Jane presumed she was an assistant at Corsair—who informed them that the party was being held in the library, down the corridor in the opposite direction, on the left.

Following these directions, they entered a vast, high-ceilinged room that appeared to be a combination library and conference room. There was already quite a crowd of men and women, most in trendy black, chattering as they sipped drinks and munched hors d'oeuvres.

Jane scanned the room. A bar had been set up on the far left, and the line was already long. At the opposite end of the room, in front of a wall of bookcases with a door in the middle, sat a dais, on which a microphone and an immense white projection screen had been set up. Jane wondered what all that was for. Against the wall directly opposite the room's entrance, several tables bore tiered trays of finger food.

"I've got to find Carol," Jane told Daniel.

"I'll look, too. Can I get you something to drink?"

"No, thanks." Jane moved to one side, out of the stream of people pouring into the room, and squinted as she searched for Carol Freund. Knowing shy Carol, she'd be on the sidelines somewhere, so Jane let her gaze skim the room's perimeter.

"There she is," she said to Greenberg, pointing. Carol, in a black cocktail dress that didn't look quite right on her stocky frame, stood alone near a door on the far left side of the room. Jane took Greenberg by the hand and led him over to her.

"Jane!" Carol's face lit up. "Thank goodness you're here!"

"Why? What's wrong?"

"Nothing. It's just that this is so . . . overwhelming!"

"It's all for you, my dear," Jane said. "Enjoy it." She introduced Greenberg, and they shook hands.

"Are all publication parties like this?" Carol asked Greenberg.

He shrugged exaggeratedly. "It's my first, too. Ask the expert."

Jane smiled. "I have a feeling this one will be different from most. Holly says she's got something special planned."

"Have you seen Holly?" Carol asked.

"I have," Daniel said, appearing with Laura at his side. "She was over there talking up some agent who looked familiar but whose name I can't remember."

"That sounds like Holly," Jane said, and shot Carol a knowing look. They both giggled.

Carol said, "Now, Jane, you must admit she's been very good to me." Throwing out her hands, she indicated the teeming party.

"True, she has," Jane hated to admit.

"Janey, Janey, Janey!"

Jane jumped. Holly had appeared as if from nowhere

and stood, positively beaming, in the circle that Jane, Greenberg, Carol, Daniel, and Laura had formed.

Jane blinked. Holly had once again changed her look and could have been a different person from the one Jane had had lunch with only two days ago. The Cleopatra look was gone. Holly had had her hair shorn to crewcut length and dyed a deep red, almost magenta, and she wore sandals and a sheath of what looked like crushed velvet in the exact same shade.

"Hello, Holly," Jane said, stepping forward for the obligatory air-kiss exchange. "You look—different."

"You like the look?" Holly asked eagerly. "*I* love it! I had help with it." She winked at Jane conspiratorially, and it occurred to Jane that Holly meant she'd had help from Goddess, who was known for her fashion eccentricity.

Since Holly had already said she loved her own look, Jane felt no need to comment on it, especially since she thought Holly looked awful. She just smiled.

"Isn't it just a scream?" Holly rattled on. She giggled. "Jane, we're both redheads now!"

Jane, alarmed at this thought, shook her head vehemently. "My hair is auburn, Holly, not red."

"Ooh, right, sorry," Holly said sarcastically.

Is it considered good manners to strangle an editor in the middle of a publication party?

Holly turned to Carol. "Well, Big Author, how do you like all this? Pretty cool, huh?"

Carol opened her mouth to speak, but Carol always weighed her words carefully, and there was a pause as she considered.

Jane interjected, "It's . . . fabu!"

"Sure is," Holly said. She looked around the circle

and smiled with feigned demureness. "So introduce me, Jane."

"Of course, I'm sorry," Jane said. "Holly Griffin, I'd like you to meet Laura Dennison, and this is Daniel, my assistant, whom you've spoken to, of course."

"Ah!" Holly screamed. "That velvet voice on the phone! Whoa, Jane, my girl, he's *gorg*eous. You never told me."

Daniel, embarrassed, looked down. Jane shot a quick glance at Laura, who seemed to be struggling to maintain even a tiny smile.

"And this is Stanley Greenberg," Jane said.

Greenberg put out his hand rather shyly. "Pleasure to meet you, Ms. Griffin."

Holly opened her mouth wide. "I love it. Call me Holly—please."

"All right," Greenberg said, smiling. "Holly."

Holly turned to Jane. "One of your authors?"

"No, a police detective," Jane said proudly.

"Yikes!" Holly said, and made an exaggerated I'd-better-watch-out face. "Guess I'll have to behave myself, huh?"

Greenberg laughed politely.

"And now," Holly said, "I want you to meet someone. I see her over there. Don't move." She darted away, leaving the others looking at one another. She returned a moment later with a woman in tow.

Jane heard Laura gasp when she saw Goddess, who stood next to Holly, surveying the group with a perfectly deadpan expression.

"Everyone," Holly announced, "I would like you to meet the one and only, the worldwide sensation—Goddess!"

They all smiled and stared at her, and Jane realized that Laura had gasped not only because she'd seen Goddess, but because of what Goddess wore: lavender hot pants straight out of the seventies, and her bra! She was as tiny as she appeared in her movies and music videos. This tininess accentuated the length and volume of her hair, that famous light brown mass that hung to below her waist, silky and straight, a curtain around her. Her features, in that legendary heart-shaped face, were perfect, like those of a tiny beautiful doll.

Holly introduced everyone in turn. No one extended a hand, because it was immediately clear that Goddess had no intention of shaking hands with anyone. She acknowledged each introduction with a mere small nod of her head.

"We're so unbelievably lucky to have Goddess with us tonight," Holly gushed, looking as if she would bubble over. "I don't know how many of you are aware that Goddess plans to write her life story."

All twentysomething years of it, Jane thought.

"Goddess, needless to say, has lived quite a colorful life," Holly went on. "I should know. I've known her since she was a little girl, and anything about her life that I *didn't* know, Goddess has now told me, and believe me, it's an *amazing* story!" She cast a meaningful look all around the little circle. "Goddess is putting it *all* in her book—and letting the chips fall where they may!"

Goddess, who still had not spoken a word, just nodded.

Jane decided to pick up on what Holly had just said. "I would be very interested in discussing your book with you," she said to Goddess. "Holly tells me you're looking for an agent."

"Yes, I am," Goddess said in that voice familiar the

world over, high and slightly nasal. "Let's go get a drink," she said to Jane. "I want to talk to you about it."

Jane, surprised, smiled. "All right."

Goddess led the way through the crowd to the bar, and Jane followed. Along the way, she made note of a number of other luminaries. She recognized Neil Sedaka at the hors d'oeuvres table, grabbing a piece of cheese-stuffed celery. A few feet away, Ben Gazzara was laughing it up with Adnan Khashoggi, at whose side stood a breathtakingly exquisite brunette. Jane almost collided with teetering old Dinah Calhoun, the legendary Broadway star who had once been married to Jane and Kenneth's ex-boss, agent Henry Silver. And then she spotted the loathsome Henry himself, who looked more than ever like a liver-spotted frog. Beside him stood a black-haired, pale-skinned young woman who Jane guessed was his latest wife, his fourth. Henry himself was in his eighties, and had had the industry buzzing recently when he married this former editor less than half his age. Jane had called it a Viagra marriage. Jane wondered if Beryl Patrice, who ran Henry's agency, was there. Perhaps she was, and had popped into the ladies' room with her flask of vodka.

Henry and his wife were chatting with Dina Merrill, at whose side stood Jack Layton, Corsair's editor in chief.

"How many publishers does it take to screw in a lightbulb?" Jack was saying.

Henry, his child bride, and Dina just stared at him.

"Three!" Jack cried. "One to screw it in, and two to hold down the author!"

Jane turned away too quickly to catch their reaction. She didn't want Henry to see her. She knew that if he did, he would be perfectly charming, even though she knew he disliked her as much as she disliked him. In Henry's eyes, Jane had, after all, taken away and married Kenneth Stuart, one of the most successful agents that Henry's agency, Silver and Payne, had ever employed. For her part, Jane had her own bone to pick with Henry: Last fall Henry and Beryl had tried to hire Daniel, who thankfully had remained loyal to Jane and declined their offer.

Jane reached the bar.

Goddess was waiting for her. "What'll it be?"

"Just some mineral water, please," Jane said.

Goddess shrugged and got Jane her water. For herself she requested a gin and tonic.

At that moment Laura arrived at the bar, next to Jane.

"Isn't this something?" Laura said, her eyes fixed on Goddess on Jane's other side.

Jane realized that Daniel was standing at Laura's other side, two drinks in hand. "Laura," he said, but she was so intent on watching Goddess that she didn't hear him. "Laura."

She turned to him. "Sorry." She took her cola. "Thanks. Jane, I had no idea the world you and Daniel work in was so . . . glamorous!"

"Believe me, Laura, most of the time it's just—"

But Jane couldn't complete her sentence, because at that moment there came the ear-piercing squeal of a loudspeaker. Jane looked up and saw Holly standing on the dais at the far opposite end of the room, before the white screen.

"Ladies and gentlemen," Holly said, and waited a moment for everyone to quiet down before continuing.

Then she beckoned animatedly to Carol Freund, who stepped reluctantly onto the dais to stand beside Holly.

"Ladies and gentlemen," Holly continued, putting one arm around Carol, "I would like to propose a toast to one of the most talented novelists I have ever had the privilege to publish." She raised her glass. "To Carol Freund and *Relevant Gods*, the most exciting new novel to come along in *decades*."

This is so Holly, Jane thought with a roll of her eyes as she and the rest of the crowd raised their glasses. Everything with Holly was "the most." Besides which, Holly, who was probably around thirty-four, had barely worked in publishing for one decade, so she really didn't even know what she was talking about. But that, Jane reflected, could have been said about many editors.

"May this be the beginning of a long and sparkling career!" Holly finished the toast, while Carol looked down, embarrassed. Holly said something to her, and she stepped off the dais.

"And *now*," Holly went on, looking as if she would explode, "I have a very special treat for all of you. With us tonight is someone who needs no introduction, a worldwide phenomenon who continues to stun us with her talent and versatility. You've seen her act, you've heard her sing, you've watched her dance. And tonight you will watch her in person. Ladies and gentlemen, here to perform one of the numbers from her record-breaking Broadway show, *Goddess of Love*, is the inimitable, the amazing . . . Goddess!"

A gasp of delight rose from the crowd, which broke into hearty applause. Jane glanced around and realized Goddess was no longer beside her. When Jane looked up again, Goddess was stepping onto the dais and taking the microphone from Holly.

A strange music began to play, loud and electronic, with a fast, driving, primal beat.

Daniel came up beside Jane. "Laura and I saw this show. We even have the CD. This is 'Alone With Me.' It's my favorite."

Goddess began to sing. Unlike her speaking voice, her singing voice was deep and throaty. The song began not with words but with a series of sharp "Oohs" in time to the music's beat. Then came the song itself, and Goddess crooned low: "I know a place . . . my darkest world. . . . Come to this place . . . *alone with me* . . ."

"Isn't she fabulous?" Daniel said.

Jane looked at him. He was truly enthralled. Was she missing something? She didn't find the music much more than just loud, but she'd promised to be polite. "Fabu!" she said, and he gave her a funny look.

At this point in the song there was a pause in the lyrics, which were replaced by high-pitched computerized squeaking. Now Goddess began to dance as Jane had to admit only Goddess danced—the swaying spin she'd made famous in her second film, a film even Jane had seen, *Slick Monkey*. Faster and faster Goddess twirled, bent at the waist, then straightening, her amazing hair flying straight out around her.

"Unbelievable."

Jane turned. This had come from Laura, who was watching Goddess and shaking her head. Then she turned to Daniel and Jane. "I'm feeling a little woozy," she said. "I'll be right back." She edged her way through the crowd.

"Her condition," Daniel said in Jane's ear, and Jane nodded understandingly.

On the dais, Goddess suddenly stopped dancing. At the moment she did, the screen behind her came to life with projected clips of her in her various movies, the images changing with the rhythm of the music. Goddess stepped off the dais and behind the bookcase at the end of the room. Jane hadn't realized there was space behind it. She figured it must have led to another entrance to the room.

"At this point in the actual show," Daniel explained in Jane's ear, "she steps behind a waterfall."

"I see," Jane said, nodding. Then she was aware that Greenberg was beside her, and she looked up at him. He was staring at the projected film clips, in many of which Goddess was either nude or almost nude, with a look of abject horror. Clearly this wasn't for him.

She leaned close to speak in his ear. "Would you like to step out to the corridor for some air?"

"Good idea!" he said gratefully, and they worked their way to the door through which they had entered the room.

The corridor was mercifully cool and quiet, though they could still faintly hear the thumping of the music. They moved a little farther down the corridor.

"Let me ask you something," Greenberg said, "and please be honest."

"Shoot," Jane said. "Oh, sorry. Guess that's not a good expression to use with a cop."

He smiled; then his face took on a look of sincere inquisitiveness. "Do you really *like* what she's doing in there?"

Jane laughed. "I have to confess it's growing on me.

I find it oddly fascinating—like driving past a car accident."

"Hmm," Greenberg murmured, pondering her words.

"And millions of people around the world like what Goddess does, too," Jane said.

Greenberg shrugged. "Guess it's me, then."

"Guess so," Jane said mischievously. "It's fortunate for me that I'm beginning to like what Goddess does, because it looks as if she's going to be my client."

Greenberg looked truly pleased for her. "Really? That's great, Jane. I don't know much about your business, but I would think a publisher would pay a lot of money for a book by her."

"Yes, and believe me, I could use a big commission."

"I hear you."

She tilted her head in the direction of the party room. "Think you can stand going back in?"

"Sure," he said good-naturedly.

Goddess was back on the dais, dancing again. Greenberg watched her for a moment and just shook his head.

"I'm going to get something to eat," Jane said. "Want anything?"

"Why not?" he said, and they squeezed through to the hors d'oeuvres table.

Jane spotted a tray of mushrooms stuffed with what looked like crabmeat. "Ooh, yum." As she reached for one, she heard a little squeal, and turned toward the sound.

About ten feet away, at the bar, Laura was blotting at her blouse with a thick wad of napkins. Jane hurried over to her. "What happened?"

Laura gave a little laugh. "It's nothing."

One of the bartenders was hovering solicitously nearby. "I'm so sorry, miss."

"It's okay, really," Laura said, and leaned to speak softly to Jane. "He spilled some tomato juice on me. Here I am trying to be so virtuous, drinking only tomato juice instead of my usual martini, and I get it spilled on me."

"Here, let me see," Jane said, and Laura lifted the napkins. The tomato juice had left a dark stain on the pale green silk. "Doesn't look so good."

"It's only a blouse!" Laura said. "Forget about it." She looked around and said to no one in particular, "Where's Martha Stewart when you need her?"

Jane laughed. "Or Heloise!"

At that moment, from the corridor, there came the sound of a woman's hysterical screams.

Thirteen

The screaming went on and on, like a siren.

Everyone froze, exchanging looks of terror.

Greenberg bolted toward the door to the corridor, and Jane followed, vaguely aware that others were, too.

In the corridor, Greenberg, ever the cop, turned to the crowd. "Everybody wait here." He ran down the corridor, and Jane unthinkingly ran after him.

There was no one in the corridor, on each side of which were office doors with assistants' cubicles outside them. At the corner of the building, the corridor turned, and following it, they found themselves looking down a similar expanse of office doors and cubicles. Near one of the office doors, a young woman in a short black dress leaned against the wall, screaming.

Greenberg approached her and touched her gently. The woman, who appeared to be in her early twenties, began to cry, her hands shaking violently.

"What is it?" Greenberg asked. "What happened?"

She looked up at him in terror. "I just went in," she managed to get out. "I went in and saw her."

"Saw who? Where?"

She pointed to the nearest office. Greenberg dashed in and Jane followed, stopping in the doorway to peer in.

It looked like any office at a publishing house. Bookshelves lined the right wall, a desk protruded sideways from the left wall, and a credenza stood at the wall near the door. The far wall was virtually all window. The desk had a high-backed chair, which was turned away from the desk toward the window, so that if anyone had been sitting in the chair, he or she would have been hidden.

Greenberg turned an inquiring gaze on the young woman, who pointed to the chair. Cautiously, Greenberg spun it slowly around.

Jane gasped at what rotated into view.

Holly Griffin, characteristically, looked as if she was about to say something. But she never would, because she was unquestionably dead, pinned straight through the throat to her chair with what appeared to be a metal letter opener. From where the handle protruded from her skin ran a dark stream of blood.

"Oh my God . . ." Jane whispered.

"What is it!" came a man's voice behind Jane. She turned. It was Jack Layton. Jane stepped aside just as Greenberg emerged from the room. Layton craned his neck to see what was in there, and when he did his eyes widened in horror and he put his hand in front of his mouth. "Holy . . ."

Greenberg turned to the young woman. "What's your name?"

"I'm Jilly. Holly's assistant." An eruption of tears shook her, and she began shaking again. "Holly told me she was going to her office to get a copy of Carol

Freund's jacket to give her. We had it framed for her.'' She leaned into the office and with a trembling hand pointed to the jacket, matted and framed, leaning against the wall near Holly's desk. Then she saw Holly again and shrank back.

"Why were you here?'' Greenberg asked.

"Mr. Layton was looking for her and asked me to go find her.''

"That's right,'' Layton said. He put himself between Greenberg and Jilly and looked up at Greenberg. "Who the hell are you?''

"Stanley Greenberg, Shady Hills Police Department. Just trying to help. You've called the police?''

"Yes, of course,'' Layton said impatiently. "I want you all the hell out of here, now!''

Greenberg led Jane and Jilly back down the corridor. Turning the corner, they saw two uniformed police officers emerge from one of the elevators and start toward them. As the officers approached, Greenberg pointed behind him, and the two men hurried on.

Layton ran past Greenberg, Jane, and Jilly to address the crowd that filled the corridor between the elevators and the party room.

"Ladies and gentlemen, your attention please,'' Layton yelled. "People—quiet, please!'' When finally the crowd had calmed, he continued. "There's been . . . an unfortunate accident. I'm afraid the party must end. Please leave immediately by the elevators.''

Greenberg hurried up to Layton. "You're sure that's okay?'' Greenberg asked.

"Yes, I'm sure,'' Layton answered resentfully. "I spoke to the police. Now get the hell out of here.''

"Let's go, Jane.''

"But what about Daniel and Laura?" she asked.

"I see them over there." Greenberg waved to them and got Daniel's attention. "We'll meet you at the car," Greenberg called, and Daniel nodded.

Greenberg took Jane's arm and they joined the press of people heading toward the elevators.

In Greenberg's car, speeding west along 495, all four were silent. Jane had briefly told Daniel and Laura what had happened to Holly.

"I can't believe it," Daniel said, breaking the silence. "Who would have done that?"

Laura let out a grim chuckle. "Jane, you seem to be bad luck lately. First that girl at Hydrangea House, now this. . . ."

"Laura!" Daniel said, horrified. "That's not funny."

"You're right. I'm sorry, Jane. I get like this when I'm upset."

They rode in silence for a few moments more.

"I'll drop your blouse off at the dry cleaners in the morning," Daniel murmured to Laura, "see what they can do about that stain."

Jane turned in her seat and looked at him. Laura was glaring at him in amazement.

"What did I say?" Daniel protested. "I'm just trying to maintain some semblance of normalcy here!"

"Well it didn't work!" Laura snapped at him. "Boy, have you got your priorities screwed up. A woman is murdered tonight, and you're worrying about a fifty-dollar blouse." She turned away, glared out the window at the Continental Airlines Arena. "In my condition," she muttered, "this kind of excitement I can do without." And she looked at Jane, as if blaming her for Holly's murder.

For the remainder of the ride back to Shady Hills, no one spoke again.

Jane got to work first the next morning. She heard Daniel come in, and he appeared immediately in her doorway.

"Got a minute?" he asked.

"Sure."

He sat down in front of her desk, shaking his head. "I still can't believe what happened last night. Who could have done that? Who would have wanted to kill Holly?"

Jane laughed grimly. "Everyone in publishing has wanted to kill Holly Griffin at one time or another—including me."

He looked at her and frowned, his expression making it clear he disapproved of her gallows humor. Then, shaking his head, he got up and returned to his desk.

Jane immediately felt guilty about what she'd said. She realized this was her means of coping with shock. She probably should have talked it out with someone—Greenberg, perhaps. But last night she'd been too upset to talk about it. When she'd arrived home, Nick was, of course, asleep, but Florence was awake, and when the shrewd Florence had asked Jane if something was wrong, Jane, not wanting to upset her, had said she must be coming down with a cold.

She gazed down at her desk. On top of her work pile lay the advance reading copy of *Relevant Gods.* Jane decided she had better call Carol Freund and make sure she was all right. She remembered that Carol had given her the number of a friend she would be staying with in New York for a couple of weeks. Jane found the number on a slip of paper in the work pile and dialed it. Carol answered.

"Carol, I'm so sorry we lost you last night. There was just so much confusion."

"That's okay, Jane, I understand. It was hideous. Who would have done that to Holly?"

"I don't know. Let's hope the police figure that out. You sure you're okay?"

"I'm fine, really." Carol gave a rueful chuckle. "No one ever told me publishing was like this."

After Jane hung up, it occurred to her that she should also call Jack Layton and tell him how sorry she was about Holly. She dialed his number, and his assistant put Jane through.

"It's very nice of you to call, Jane. We're all reeling here, I can tell you."

"Of course you are. Come to think of it, I'm surprised the offices are even open."

"Well—" Layton blustered, "life must go on, right?"

"Right," Jane said, shaking her head.

"In fact, Jane, I was going to call you today. Holly told me Goddess plans to do a book and that Holly steered Goddess to you for representation."

"Yes, that's right."

"Holly also said you promised to give us a first look at the project. I hope that promise still holds. We want this book, Jane. I've already assigned it to a new editor, Hamilton Kiels."

"Jumping the gun a little, aren't you, Jack? You don't even know exactly what the book is—or how much I want for it."

"If it's by Goddess, it doesn't really matter what it is. And as for price, I'm sure we can reach an agreement."

Holly was already virtually forgotten. Jane couldn't believe what she was hearing—or maybe she could. *These people are all pigs*, she told herself. "I keep all my promises, Jack. You'll have first crack at the book. But as for coming to terms, I make no guarantees."

"Fair enough, Jane. Thank you for calling."

Jane felt dirty after their conversation, and couldn't get off the phone fast enough. As soon as she hung up, her intercom came to life.

"Jane?"

"Yes, Daniel."

"Ernie Zabriskie is here to see you."

Ernie? What on earth did *he* want? "I'll be right there."

She went out to the reception area. Ernie, in a too-tight sport shirt that accentuated the roll of fat around his middle, stood at Daniel's desk. He looked up at Jane with a wan smile.

"Hello, Ernie," Jane said, making an effort not to sound too cold. "What can I do for you?"

"May I speak with you, Jane? Privately?"

"Certainly. Come on in."

She showed him into her office and indicated the visitor's chair while she shut the door.

"Now," she said, sitting at her desk, "what's up, Ernie?"

"Jane"—he looked her directly in the eyes, as if trying to be assertive—"Dara called me about your little visit to her shop yesterday."

Jane met his gaze right back. "Did she now?"

He looked down. At least he had the decency to feel ashamed.

"So?"

"You're blackmailing her, Jane. That's not right. Who are you to get involved in this? It's none of your business."

Jane felt her face growing hot. "Is that what you came to say?"

"I came to say that however you found out about this, it's not your concern, and you certainly have no right to tell Dara not to see me again. I also came to ask you not to say anything about this to Louise."

A pounding began in Jane's head. Looking at Ernie's simpering fat face, she imagined herself getting up from her desk and slapping him. She leveled a loathing look at him instead.

"Listen, you pathetic coward. Louise already knows you fool around—she just doesn't know with whom. I had no intention of telling Louise that the luscious Dara is the one. But as for this being none of my business, you're wrong. Dead wrong. Louise is my friend, Ernie, can you understand that? In fact, right now I'm far more of a friend to her than you are. And if I choose to tell Dara not to see you again—*for my friend*—or if I choose to tell Louise that Dara is your squeeze—*for my friend*—I will bloody well do so. Because what I do for my friend is none of *your* business."

He said nothing, just watched her, brows lowered.

Jane shook her head and laughed derisively. "Weak, pathetic men like you make me want to puke, you know that? Men who don't have the courage to just tell their wives it's over, that they want to play the field; men who pretend to honor their marriage vows while making fools of the people who trust them. Who *love* them. Louise *loves* you, Ernie. Do you know how fortunate you are to have a woman like Louise love you?"

He opened his mouth to respond, but she swept on.

"So tell me, Ernie, why is it that you haven't just sat Louise down, and said, 'Louise, I don't want to be married to you anymore because I don't want to be faithful the way I said I would when we exchanged our wedding vows'? What keeps you there? How do you sleep nights?"

She waited, finally willing to let him speak.

"I . . ." he began. "Louise and I . . . we have the inn. We have a life together. Louise—"

"Has money. I see. That's all it is. Your lifestyle. You don't want to give it up, but you don't want to play by the rules either."

Ernie regarded Jane with something like disbelief, then smiled a pitying little smile. "You're very old-fashioned, Jane."

She jumped up from her chair, the pounding in her head unbearable. "Get out!"

Alarmed, Ernie jumped up, too, and ran for the door.

Jane remained behind her desk, because she knew that if she went after Ernie, she'd hurt him. "Get the hell out of my office!" she ordered. "That's right, take your two-timing ass back to the inn you bought with Louise's money and live your lie so you can keep your sleazy affair going and not upset your cozy little life! *Get out!*"

But he was practically out anyway. Through the open door of her office she saw him hurry across the reception area and throw open the door. It shut with a bang.

She sat back down at her desk and put her head in

her hands, waiting for the pounding to subside. Presently she was aware of Daniel standing in the doorway.

"Are you all right?" he asked quietly.

"I'm fine," she murmured. "Just mad."

"Want to talk about it?"

"No. Can't."

"Okay." He returned to his desk.

Didn't people like Ernie realize how lucky they were to have people who loved them? Didn't they see they owed it to these people to honor their trust?

Didn't they see how precious these people who loved them were?

No, they didn't. And they wouldn't . . . until those people who loved them were gone. How did that Joni Mitchell song go? People didn't know what they had till it was gone.

Jane had known what she had in Kenneth, she'd been faithful to him, and now he was gone anyway.

She put her head back in her hands and cried.

Fourteen

Jane got out of the cab and looked up at the unassuming storefront restaurant on Carmine Street in the Village. Aldo, it was called, an Italian place Goddess liked. Goddess had called Jane yesterday and said she wanted to explore "this book thing," so they'd made a date to meet there for brunch. Goddess couldn't do lunch, because it was Wednesday, and she had to get to the theater by noon to get ready for the matinee.

The maître d' greeted Jane pleasantly. When she told him she was meeting Goddess, he positively lit up. "This way, please," he said crisply, and led her past the bar, up a few stairs, and along a railed balcony with tables along the side.

Goddess sat at the last table. She barely acknowledged Jane. A waiter came and asked if Jane wanted something to drink. She noticed that Goddess was drinking what looked like a screwdriver, but ordered only Perrier for herself.

"Well," Jane said brightly, arranging herself in her chair. Then she took a good look at Goddess and did a double take. Goddess was dressed exactly like Dorothy in *The Wizard of Oz*: a blue-and-white-checked dress with attached white bodice and short sleeves. Jane glanced under the table. Goddess's feet, in ruby slippers and little white socks, tapped the floor. Goddess's hair was of course longer than Judy Garland's hair had been in the film, so Goddess's beribboned pigtails were a yard long. It was a bizarre sight.

"Love the outfit," Jane said. "Is it for your show?"

"Nah." Goddess played with her napkin, tying it in a knot. "I always dress like this. In different themes, I mean. I like it."

"Ah," Jane said, wondering what other themes were in her repertoire.

Jane looked down and noticed something on her plate. She picked it up. It was a bottle of nail polish—Desert Sunrise, the label said.

She frowned. "I wonder what this is doing here?"

Goddess smiled like a little girl. "I put it there."

"You did?" Jane frowned. "Why?"

"It's for you."

"I—don't understand."

Goddess leaned forward. "I *took* it for you. I take things. That came from that Walgreen's down the street."

She was a shoplifter. Jane didn't know what to say. So she simply set the bottle aside. *What kind of a nutcase am I getting involved with?*

Goddess threw down her knotted napkin, apparently finished with it. She grabbed one of her long pigtails and began wrapping it around her wrist and arm. "I still can't believe what happened to Holly," she said, not looking at Jane. "I mean, I've known her practically all my life, since I was a little girl. Who would ever have done that to her?''

Jane shook her head. "We're all asking ourselves that. It's something for the police to figure out."

Goddess made a dismissive gesture and blew out her breath derisively. "The police. Bunch of idiots."

Not all of them, Jane thought, but did not respond to this. Instead she said, "It's the most horrible thing I've seen in all my years in publishing." She smiled grimly. "I guess it's one way for a company to get out of paying severance!"

Goddess looked at her sharply. "Gallows humor," she said, nodding. "It's because you're upset, and you don't want to admit it. You're acting out."

"Quite the therapist, aren't you? Have you discussed your little habit"—she touched the tip of the nail-polish bottle—"with your therapist?"

"Who said I'm in therapy?"

"You seem remarkably well educated in psychological matters."

"Maybe I read a lot. Anyway, that's what you're doing, and if I didn't understand why you're doing it, I would say it was in pretty bad taste."

Jane blinked, duly chastised. "You're right. Holly wasn't my favorite person, not by a long shot, but I would never have wished this on her."

A waiter came to the table. Jane ordered a muffin, some fruit, and a Diet Coke. Goddess ordered a bowl of croutons and a glass of water.

"Croutons?" Jane said when the waitress had gone.

"Yeah," Goddess said, her tone slightly defensive. "I like croutons. Hasn't anybody ever told you it's impolite to talk about what someone else is eating?"

Again Jane just stared at her. Now the young woman just stared off across the restaurant, her thoughts seemingly miles away. Then suddenly she turned back to Jane. "Can I ask you something?"

"Of course."

The waiter brought their drinks. Goddess waited until he was gone before continuing.

"Okay, listen to this." She leaned forward. "Have you ever dreamed of someone you've never met, then *met* that person?"

Where had this come from? Jane sat nonplussed, then shook her head. "No. Have you?"

"Yeah." Suddenly Goddess threw the pigtail she'd been playing with over her shoulder and leaned even farther across the table toward Jane. "Know what I think?" she said, smirking, as if she had a dark secret. "I think *you* killed Holly."

Jane nearly spit out her Diet Coke. Finally, she managed to say, "That's not funny, not funny at all. Talk about gallows humor!"

Goddess shrugged. "Who said I was joking?"

"I think," Jane said with forced cheerfulness, "that we should talk about your book, and whether you and I will work together."

"We'll work together," Goddess said easily. "Holly said you were the agent to go with, so you're it. Yves— Yves Golden, he's my manager—he said I should go with someone at the Morris office, or ICM. He said that if Swifty were still alive, he'd have been perfect. But I choose you."

"Well, that's very nice," Jane said, trying to hide her excitement. "I'm honored."

Goddess shrugged. "I told you, it was up to Holly."

Once again Jane felt guilty about all the things she'd thought and said about Holly Griffin.

"Very good," Jane said. "I'll have Daniel, my assistant, draw up an agreement—"

"Which you'll send to Yves. I never look at paper."

"All right. I'll need his address, phone number . . ."

"You'll get it. Now what about the book. How does this work?"

"Well, first we find you the perfect ghost—a ghost-writer, I mean."

"I know what a ghost is," Goddess said, rolling her eyes. "Go on; I'm listening."

"And the ghost—with your input, of course—puts together a dynamite proposal, which we show to Corsair first, as I promised Holly and Jack."

Goddess nodded her approval.

Jane continued, "If Corsair doesn't come up with a satisfactory offer—"

"You mean enough money?"

"Yes, partly, but the offer consists of other—"

"Yeah, yeah. Go on."

"If we don't like what Corsair offers, we auction the project."

Goddess sat quietly for a moment. Reaching into the neckline of her Dorothy dress, she withdrew a pendant and started to rub it between her fingers. Why did that pendant look familiar to Jane? Had Goddess been wearing it at Carol Freund's publication party?

Finally, Goddess said, "That all sounds fine, except for the part about the ghostwriter. *I'll* write the book."

"Dear . . ."

"Don't call me dear."

"In order to produce a top-quality proposal and book, we really need a professional—"

"I said," Goddess said slowly, her tone threatening, "I'll—write—it. Let's get something straight. You work for me. I call the shots. Got it?"

Jane controlled herself. "Very well. I'm sure your editor will be more than happy to work with you on—um—shaping the book."

"There's another thing. I want Corsair to have this book. The money doesn't matter."

Maybe not to you.

"Corsair *understands* this book," Goddess went on. "And after all, it was poor Holly who brought me to you. You should want Corsair to have the book. Where's your sense of justice?"

Jane opened her mouth to respond, but decided it was no use and said nothing.

"I want to meet with this Hamilton Kiels guy at Corsair. Jack Layton told me that's who he's assigned my book to, since Holly's . . . gone." Goddess giggled. "His nickname is Ham. Isn't that a scream?"

Jane frowned. "When did Jack tell you Hamilton was your new editor?"

"This morning. He called me. Why?"

That sleazeball. "I'll be happy to arrange a meeting. I'll need to be there—for your own protection. I should be at all meetings you have with your publisher."

"Well, I wouldn't go alone," Goddess said, as if that were obvious. "What time is it?"

Jane glanced at her watch. "Eleven-forty-five."

Goddess jumped up. "Gotta fly to the theater. Listen, can you come see me this Saturday? I want to prepare for this meeting. You gotta coach me and stuff. I've got

a pied-à-terre on the Upper East Side. Write this down,"
she said, and gave Jane an address on East Eighty-second
Street. "We'll have lunch. Okay?"

"Okay," said Jane, who in general was trying to stop
working on Saturdays but in this case would gladly make
an exception.

The waiter arrived with their food.

"What about your croutons?" Jane asked.

"Can't." Goddess reached into the bodice of her
dress and pulled out a bill, which she flung onto the
table. It was a hundred. "See you Saturday!"

"But this is too much money," Jane called after her.

Goddess was already down the stairs and crossing the
front of the restaurant. "Whatever!" she yelled up to
Jane, and hurried out the door. Through the window
Jane saw her break into a jog and disappear up the
street.

"Unusual girl," Jane muttered.

"She's a genius, an artist. She's brilliant," the waiter
said, setting down Jane's muffin and fruit. "People like
that are allowed to be unusual." He put his hands on
his hips and shook his head. "Didn't you know that?"

Jane didn't know what to say. She gathered her things
together and rose to leave.

The waiter was still talking. "That part in *Slick Monkey*
when she's running around trying to find her brother's
baby ..." He threw back his head and roared with
laughter. "Funniest thing I ever saw. I'm telling you,
she's a genius!"

"Have a nice day!" Jane called, heading down the
stairs.

"Wait!"

Jane turned.

The waiter held up a small object. "You forgot your nail polish!"

"Don't want it," Jane called to him, and hurried out.

On arriving in Shady Hills later that afternoon, Jane decided to stop in at the police station to see Greenberg. He looked genuinely delighted to see her.

"Well, this is a surprise. Sit down, sit down."

She sat in the extra chair in his tiny cinder-block office. "I've just had brunch with Goddess," she told him.

"And what was that like?"

"Umm, unusual. She's—well—how would one describe her? Blunt? Bratty? Totally unconcerned with what people say about her? A shoplifter."

"A *shoplifter?*"

"Yup. Brought me a bottle of nail polish. Desert Sunrise."

Greenberg stared at her. "She must be one of the richest people in America. Why would she shoplift?"

She looked at him in surprise. "Stanley! You know better than that. Shoplifting has nothing to do with money. People who compulsively steal like that are under terrible emotional strain."

"That's true," he said. "I took a course on shoplifting, kleptomania, pickpockets, at County College of Morris. Shoplifters aren't as interested in *what* they steal as they are in the *act* of stealing."

"That's right."

"And how did *you* become such an expert on the subject?"

She smiled. "I do a lot of reading."

He nodded, shrugged. "Just before you got here I

spoke to an old friend of mine who's a homicide detective in New York. He knows the guys who are investigating Holly Griffin's murder. They've concluded that the killer was someone acquainted with Holly who knew where her office was."

Jane snorted. Maybe Goddess was right and the New York police *were* idiots. "Not necessarily. Think about it. It could have been someone who got into the building while the party was going on, someone who wandered the corridors looking for handbags. That's quite common, you know. When I worked for Silver and Payne, my bag was stolen right out of my office that way—and I'd only stepped out to go to the ladies' room! Security at these buildings is very lax.

"So . . . the killer could have been someone there ostensibly to attend the party. He or she could have been an employee of Corsair, someone who knew Holly— a 'friend,' a boyfriend, an ex-boyfriend—or someone working at the party, like a bartender or caterer, or a complete stranger! Which means that in actuality, the police know nothing at all."

Greenberg looked taken aback. "I guess you're right."

"I haven't had a chance to ask you about your interview with Arthur. How'd it go?"

Greenberg laughed, looking at her as if she'd been presumptuous. "I wasn't aware you'd joined the Shady Hills Police Department."

"Oh, no, you don't," she said. "You're not getting away with that. It's in for a penny, in for a pound; you're not letting me into this case only partway." She grinned. "You should have known that once you showed me the cave, you were lost. Besides, *I* was the one who convinced Doris to have Arthur talk to you.''

''That's true,'' Greenberg conceded, and breathed a deep sigh. ''Arthur admitted to having walked with the young woman, to having shown her the cave, and to having gone into the village and bought her a map and some food. But he swore that after he brought her those things, he never saw her again. He also had an alibi he never mentioned to his Aunt Doris: He was having drinks with two friends at the Roadside Tavern during the hours we figure the woman died—between eight o'clock Saturday night and one o'clock Sunday morning. His story checks out.''

''I'm so relieved,'' Jane said. ''Doris will be, too.'' She had a thought. ''What about that Mike Vernell, the hiker who was staying at Hydrangea House? He left Sunday, the day the woman was found. We don't know a thing about him.''

''We're already checking him out. He lives in Pennsylvania. A widower with a grown daughter. We spoke to her. She said her father was supposed to be at the inn for another week. So apparently he departed early—and he didn't go home.''

Jane pondered this. ''Still no word on who the dead girl was?''

''No, but we're still working on it.''

''Keep checking with Mike Vernell's daughter. I think there's something there.''

''Yes, chief.''

She laughed. ''I'd better get back to the office, make a living.''

''Good idea.'' He walked her out. At the door he said quietly, ''I reserve the right to a second second date.''

"Oh?" She smiled up at him. "Why is that?"

"You have to admit the Corsair party didn't turn out quite the way we expected. How about something a little . . . calmer?"

"Sounds good to me."

"Good. I'll give it some thought and call you."

That evening, Louise called Jane and told her she wanted to suspend the Defarge Club meetings for a while. She just wasn't up to hosting them for the time being. She would be calling the others, too, she said.

Saddened by this news, Jane asked if Louise would like *her* to host the meetings for a while.

"That's up to you, Jane."

"Would you come if I did?"

"No. I'm just not in a knitting mood right now."

"Maybe we can help. If you want people to talk to, I mean."

"No, thanks, Jane. I've done as much confiding as I intend to do—to you. You know I'm devastated about Ernie—about his . . . affair. But I won't tell the others that. I'll just tell them I'm still upset that the woman was found here." And she hung up.

Jane decided she'd have to give some thought to the idea of hosting the meetings. The Defarge ladies had always met at Hydrangea House.

It just wouldn't be the same.

Fifteen

Florence speared four pancakes from the platter with her fork, deposited them on her plate, and wandered over to the kitchen table, lost in thought.

"Murder . . . death." She shook her head. "I don't think we have it like this in Trinidad."

Jane set down her coffee mug and regarded her skeptically. "Come now, Florence. Murder is everywhere; you know that as well as I do."

"Perhaps, missus, perhaps. But it certainly seems to be following *you* around lately."

Jane frowned, troubled. "That's what Laura said," she murmured.

Florence poured syrup over her pancakes and took a big bite. "Mm, missus, with pancakes you have what my dear mother calls 'the touch.'"

"Why, thank you, Florence."

From the family room came the sound of Nick calling to Winky.

"Let's not talk about the murders anymore," Jane

whispered to Florence. "Nick!" Jane called. "Come for breakfast."

"You mean Nick and Winky," Nick said, appearing in the kitchen doorway with the ball of tortoiseshell fur in his arms.

"Yes, sorry. Nick and Winky." Jane smiled.

Florence brought Nick a plateful of pancakes and poured him some milk.

"Forgetting someone?" he said innocently.

"Ah, how thoughtless of me!" Florence cried, and got another plate, onto which she dropped several pancakes. She placed the plate on the table near Nick, and Winky jumped up to examine its contents.

"Syrup, Wink?" Nick asked her.

She looked up at him and gave a tiny mew.

"Winky would like some syrup, please," he told Florence.

"Here you are," she said, handing him the bottle.

"Just a little," Jane said, remembering what she'd paid for that bottle at Pathmark.

Nick drizzled syrup onto Winky's pancakes.

"So, tell us about this Goddess, missus," Florence said, and took a sip of her coffee. "Is she as outrageous as everyone says?"

"She's pretty outrageous," Jane replied, "though I'm not sure that's quite the word I'd use. Perhaps *rude* or *bratty* would be more accurate."

"She *is* very young," Florence pointed out.

"Not that young," Jane said. "She's what—twenty-five?"

"No one knows for sure," Florence said. "That's part of her mystique."

"Mystique! Please." Jane rolled her eyes. "She's a fresh brat who needs a good spanking."

"Spanking is bad," Nick interjected. "Did you know you could be arrested for spanking me?"

"Have I ever spanked you?" Jane asked him.

"No."

"I didn't mean it literally," she went on. "What I mean is that she's obviously been spoiled her whole life, and now that she's a star, she has absolutely no limits. She says what she wants, goes where she wants, buys what she wants, and doesn't give a darn what anyone thinks of her." She laughed. "Come to think of it, I'd like to live that way!"

"Really, missus? Do you mean that?"

"Yes ..." Jane said thoughtfully, "except that if I were Goddess, I would try to respect people's feelings when I spoke. And I would get into therapy for—some of my bad habits."

"What bad habits?" Nick asked, eyes innocently wide.

Jane wouldn't tell him about the shoplifting. "Just the way she behaves," she said vaguely.

"Her dad invented the Hammer. Did you know that, Mom?"

"Yes, Carl Hamner. Rich as Croesus. That's what I was talking about."

"So much money," Florence said, pouring Nick some more milk. "I just cannot imagine it. With all that money, she doesn't have to work, doesn't have to do her songs and films and plays and things, but she still does. Why do you think that is, missus?"

"Because," Jane said, "she's a genius!"

Nick and Florence both looked at her, frowning.

Jane laughed. "That's what the waiter said after my

brunch with Goddess on Wednesday. She *is* exceptionally talented. And she must love her work, since she obviously doesn't do it for the money."

The phone rang. Florence answered it.

"Missus, it's for you. It's Daniel."

Jane took the phone, smiling. "It's Saturday, Daniel. You don't have to work today."

He laughed. "I'm not. Well, actually, this afternoon I *am* planning to read Tanya Selman's new manuscript. But I'm not calling about work. I want to ask you a favor."

"Of course! What is it?"

"Can I come over and see you?"

What on earth can it be? she wondered. "Certainly. Name your time."

"How about in half an hour?"

"You got it. I'll keep the coffee hot."

Sitting on the sofa in Jane's study off the living room, Daniel, in khaki shorts and a T-shirt, sipped coffee from his mug.

"So shoot," Jane said. "What's the favor?" She smiled. "You know I'll do it."

He set down his mug on the end table, his face growing serious. "Thanks, Jane. I think I mentioned to you that Laura has no family."

"Yes."

"So she has no mother, no aunt, no sister—no one to help her get ready for the wedding. I think she'd really like some help, but she's too proud to ask for it. So I thought, well, that it would be perfect if you would help her. You know, picking out her gown, that sort of thing. After all, you're like family to us."

"Of course. I'll be delighted to help her," Jane said. "As long as you're sure she'd really want me to."

"I'm sure she would. I haven't asked her yet, of course, because first I wanted to make sure you were willing. But you know she's extremely fond of you."

"Is she?" This was a surprise. Jane had never picked up any vibes either way from Laura.

"Absolutely," Daniel said. "And thank you, Jane. I'll speak to her." He paused, looking troubled about something. "Now I need another favor from you, Jane. Your opinion."

"You know I've always got plenty of those!"

"Thanks. You know I respect your judgment more than anyone else's." He looked down, as if unsure where to begin. "Jane," he said at last, "my father called me."

She stared at him. "Your *father*. I thought your father was dead."

"No, my father's not dead. You probably thought that because I never talk about him. But he's very much alive. For the past seven years, though, we've been . . . I guess you'd say estranged."

Jane waited.

"Anyway," Daniel said, "he called to ask to come to our wedding. He said he wanted to correct some mistakes he'd made in his relationship with me. I . . . said yes."

"I think that was the right answer. But how did he even know about the wedding?"

Daniel looked uneasy. "When I tell you who my father is, you'll understand. Jane, have you ever heard of *Onyx*, the magazine for African-Americans?"

"Of course I've heard of *Onyx*," she said with a little

laugh. "It's one of the leading magazines in the country."

"In the world, actually. My father owns it. Founded it, in fact."

Jane just stared at him, stunned. Daniel Willoughby. Everyone knew that the founder and owner of *Onyx* was Cecil Willoughby.

Jane leaned forward. "But—but Cecil Willoughby . . . he's one of the richest people in the country."

Daniel smiled, looking almost apologetic.

"Wait a minute, wait a minute," Jane said. "If Cecil Willoughby is your father, why the hell have you been toiling away for the past four and a half years as my assistant? Why have you been living in a rented apartment? Why are you—forgive me—always short of money?"

"Because," Daniel replied, "as I've told you, my father and I are not on good terms. I don't have any of his money, and I don't want it."

"Well *I* sure as hell would! What's the problem?"

"While I was in my second year at Yale, I told my father, as gently as I could, that I had no interest in taking over the running of the magazine when I graduated. That had always been the plan. My father was very hurt. He took my decision as a personal affront; I'd rejected his dream of passing along his empire to his son. Just the same, he begrudgingly offered to provide me with an income. I turned down his offer. That offended him even more. From that day on, I've had no contact with him. Obviously, however, he's had people watching over me—he's always made liberal use of private investigators—and that's how he found out about the wedding."

Jane took a deep breath and big gulp of coffee, trying to take this all in. "Wow. I think it's sweet that he's been watching over you."

"Sweet? Hah! Believe me, my father's no guardian angel. He's a tough, powerful son of a gun. How else do you think he became a multimillionaire? If he's been watching over me, it's been for his own reasons—like wanting to see if I showed any signs of giving up my chosen career to take over his. He desperately wants me to run that magazine.

"Anyway," he said, rising, "obviously you think I did the right thing by saying he could come to our wedding."

"Yes," Jane said, smiling sentimentally, "I do."

"Thanks, Jane—for agreeing to help Laura, *and* for the feedback. I'll see myself out—and I'll see you at the office Monday."

She watched him leave the room. Then she sat, mug in hand, smiling fatuously, still stunned by what he had told her, a single word rattling around in her head: *multimillionaire.*

Twenty minutes later the phone rang. Jane picked it up. It was Laura.

"Jane, that's so great of you to want to help me," Laura gushed. "You know I have no mother, so *you* can be my mother!"

"Your mother *figure*. I'm not *that* old."

Laura laughed. "You know what I mean. The first thing I need is my gown. Could you help me pick one out?"

"Sure. When were you thinking of going?"

"Well . . . how about this afternoon?"

Jane hadn't expected to be called into service so soon, but Nick would be at his friend Aaron's house for most of the day. "That would be just fine. In fact, now that I think about it, the sooner the better, what with fittings and everything. Where were you thinking of looking?"

"Well, there are several really beautiful shops in New York I'd like to try."

"Okay." Then Jane remembered her luncheon date at Goddess's pied-à-terre. "Laura, I just thought of something. I don't mean to be rude, but I've just remembered I'm having lunch with Goddess in New York this afternoon. I guess I forgot to mention it to Daniel. I almost forgot myself!"

"We could do it another day." Laura sounded disappointed.

"No, we can still go today, but would you mind terribly if I leave you on your own for a couple of hours while I go to this lunch? Then we can meet up again afterward."

"That would be fine," Laura said, brightening. "I'm sure I can find something to do."

They agreed that Jane would pick her up in about an hour and that they would drive into the city. Jane hurried upstairs and changed into a copper-colored watered-silk suit she deemed appropriate for her lunch with Goddess. She drove Nick over to Aaron's house, then headed for Daniel and Laura's apartment.

On the way, Jane reflected that she was glad to have this opportunity to get to know Daniel's fiancée better. Jane had always felt a tension between her and Laura, a tension that had only worsened when, last fall, Daniel had turned down the high-paying job offer from Silver and Payne.

Jane knew that Laura, though always supportive of

Daniel's idealistic career goals, harbored a slight resentment toward Jane. Daniel had told Jane that for years Laura had wanted a wedding, a house, a child; but they'd been unable to afford any of these things. If Daniel had taken the job at Silver and Payne, all of these things would have been possible. Well, now she was getting the wedding and the child; the house would have to come later—unless Daniel made peace with his father.

Jane's impression of Laura had always been that she was a bit shallow; yet Jane couldn't imagine the deep Daniel being in love with a shallow woman. Turning left onto Packer Road, where Daniel and Laura lived on the top floor of a two-family house, Jane resolved to get to know Laura better, to find her best qualities and learn to like her more. To make her her friend.

Jane had no sooner pulled into the driveway than Laura came bounding out of the house in jeans and an oversize T-shirt.

To Jane's surprise, Laura gave her a kiss on the cheek as she got into the car. "Thanks, Jane. Really."

Jane waved away her thanks. "It's my pleasure." She continued on Packer and got onto Route 46 East.

"Isn't this fun?" Laura said. "Girls' day out! We can gossip and everything."

"I never turn down good gossip," Jane said with gusto.

"Me, neither. Daniel hates gossip, but I bet he'd learn to like it if he had to work with boring old pharmaceuticals all day, like me."

"I see your point. Then what's my excuse?"

They both laughed.

"So," Jane said, "got anything juicy?"

"*Well . . .*" Laura's eyes gleamed devilishly as she fingered a pendant she'd worn for as long as Jane had known her. "At my company—you know, Unimed— there's been talk about Ernie Zabriskie."

Jane stiffened, but kept her smile pleasant. "Oh?"

"Whoa yeah! There's this woman I work with, Grace. Grace is friends with another woman at the company, this sleazy type who lives in Lake Hiawatha." Lake Hiawatha was right next to Shady Hills. "Turns out this woman—her name is Abby—was having an affair with Ernie, when all of a sudden he dumped her!"

Jane, disturbed at this turn in the conversation and wanting to protect Louise, pretended to be shocked. "You've got to be kidding! Pudgy little Ernie, who's so devoted to Louise?" The skunk. "No way!"

"Oh, yes way," Laura said. "Don't let that chubby exterior fool you. You, of all people, should know better than to judge a book by its cover. In fact, apparently this wasn't Ernie's first fling." She looked thoughtful. "I feel bad for Louise."

"Me, too," Jane agreed, and said nothing more about it.

Emerging from the Lincoln Tunnel, Jane drove north and parked at a Quick Park on West Forty-sixth Street between Eighth and Ninth Avenues. At the corner of Forty-sixth and Eighth, Jane called Goddess to confirm lunch.

" 'Course we're still on," Goddess said, her voice flat. "I'm looking forward to it. But you're a little early."

"I know that. I'm with my friend Laura. You met her at the Carol Freund party. Daniel's fiancée. We're doing some shopping—for her wedding gown, in fact."

"Bring her along," Goddess said.

Jane was surprised. "Are you sure? Didn't you want to talk business? Laura really doesn't mind being on her own for a few hours."

"I don't mind talking biz in front of her. Tell her she's gotta come."

Jane pressed the phone to her chest and turned to Laura. "She wants you to come to lunch."

Laura looked surprised, then pleased, her eyes widening. "Sure!"

"All right, that will be very nice. Thank you," Jane said, and hung up.

"Yipes," Laura said as they started across Eighth Avenue. "Lunch with Goddess!"

They went first to Priscilla of Boston, where Laura tried on several gowns but liked none of them. She was quite petite and had a lovely figure, and to Jane she looked smashing in everything she modeled. But Laura clearly had a certain look in mind, and wasn't prepared to rest until she'd found it.

"Okay," Laura said as they emerged from the third shop. "Next is Janine Dray up Madison. Do we have time?"

Jane checked her watch. It was just after eleven-thirty, and Goddess wasn't expecting them till one. "Sure," Jane said. "But Janine Dray . . . I mean, it's gorgeous stuff, but pricey."

Laura shrugged carelessly. "How many times does a girl get married?" And before Jane could respond with a sarcastic remark, Laura answered her own question: "Once, for this girl, and she's gonna look the way she's always dreamed of looking."

They hailed a cab and rode up Madison to the exclusive shop. Laura tried on two gowns, frowning no at each of them. Then she emerged in a breathtaking Christian Lacroix—billowy, low cut, topped with a huge hat covered with a bridal veil. She was beaming. Jane had to admit it was the most beautiful gown Laura had tried on so far.

"Isn't it heaven?" Laura breathed. "Daniel will flip."

"It's heaven, all right," Jane said. "And I'll bet the price is sky-high."

Both Laura and the saleslady frowned disapprovingly at Jane for bringing up so vulgar a subject as money.

"Well, I—" Laura looked inquiringly at the saleslady.

The woman told them the price, her tone faintly belligerent.

"Holy smoke!" Jane said with a laugh. She turned to Laura. "You want me take out a second mortgage on my house for you?"

Neither Laura nor the saleslady saw anything funny in her remark.

"I'll take it," Laura said.

Jane gaped at her. "Laura! Are you sure. Can you—"

Laura was already reaching for her bag on a nearby chair. She brought out a MasterCard. "Charge it," she told the saleslady.

Jane held her tongue. Arrangements were made for Laura to come in during the week for her first fitting. Then she and Jane left the shop.

"Laura," Jane said as soon as they got outside, "I don't mean to stick my nose into your business, but don't you think that gown is a bit beyond your budget?"

"I told you. A girl—"

"Only gets married once. If you say so." Jane checked her watch. "We'd better get over to Goddess's now.

She's on East Eighty-second between Fifth and Madison. We can walk it."

They started west, Laura leading the way. Jane, regarding her from behind, shook her head.

Goddess's pied-à-terre was a four-story town house. A uniformed maid led Jane and Laura from a stark white-marble foyer into an equally stark sitting room. The walls and ceiling were bright white, the floor was dark polished wood, and the only furniture were two immense black-and-yellow-striped sofas that reminded Jane of bumblebees, and between them a coffee table consisting of a boulder with a flattened, polished top.

"Cozy," Jane said.

"I heard that!"

They jumped and turned toward the doorway. Goddess stood in its center, arms folded. She wore a white kimono, her hair piled on the top of her head and held in place with at least half a dozen shiny black chopsticks. Suddenly she threw back her head and laughed, sauntering into the room as if she were wearing a sweatshirt and jeans. "Had you there, didn't I?" She perched on the coffee table and regarded them. "You think I give a damn what anybody thinks of this place? *I* don't even give a damn about this place."

Jane and Laura looked at her in puzzlement.

"It's very . . ." Laura began, but trailed off, apparently unsure what it was.

"It's worth millions, of course," Goddess said nonchalantly. "I bought it last year with the money I made from *Goddess at Large.*" She turned to Laura. "Did you see me in that?"

"Of course," Laura said. "Daniel and I both did. It was hysterical."

"Mm." Goddess reached under the sash of her kimono and drew out a pack of Camels. Then she pulled out a Bic lighter and lit a cigarette, drawing on it deeply. "This place used to belong to a Saudi arms dealer. He got tired of it—or his latest wife did—so they sold it to me. It's got a pool, theater, the works. Handy while I'm doing the play."

She was referring, of course, to *Goddess of Love*, her Broadway show.

"I thought maybe this place belonged to your parents," Laura said.

Goddess turned on her viciously. "Well it doesn't! My parents are not part of my life, and I don't want anything of theirs. Got that?"

"Yes," Laura said, fear in her eyes.

Goddess smiled. "Let's eat."

She led them to the back of the sitting room, where on the right there was an arched entrance to a dining room. This room was as ornate as the sitting room was spare, decorated in pure Louis XIV. Passing a massive sideboard, Jane noticed row upon row of oddly common trinkets: half a dozen Max Factor lipsticks standing like soldiers, a package of cuticle sticks, a transparent yellow-plastic pencil sharpener, a package of Silly Putty, a thimble. Undoubtedly the spoils of Goddess's pilfering.

The table was set with a lavish array of sliced cold chicken, salads, and fruit. Goddess sat at the head of the table, Jane and Laura to each side of her. The maid appeared and offered them food from the trays, then asked if they would like wine with lunch. Laura and Jane both asked for mineral water.

"So," Goddess said, smoking her cigarette and ignoring the food on her plate, "since we're on the subject of parents, tell me about yours, Laura. You gonna have them at your wedding? Got a big family?"

Laura stared at her, openmouthed. "I—I'm an orphan," she replied quietly. "The people on my side of the wedding will be just friends."

What an odd turn of conversation, Jane thought, and decided to try to steer the talk to the reason for the lunch—preparing for their meeting with Hamilton Kiels.

"Would you like to go over what we'll discuss at our meeting with Hamilton Kiels on Monday?" Jane asked Goddess.

"No." Goddess puffed, blew smoke in Jane's face.

Jane felt an overpowering urge to slap her, but restrained herself.

"But I thought that's why we were getting together," Jane pointed out politely.

"What's to discuss? We go, we schmooze, we have a meeting. I write a book. People buy it. I get richer."

Jane smiled a tiny smile. "I wish it were that easy."

"With me, babe," Goddess said, fixing Jane with a frank gaze, "it is." She picked up her fork and toyed with a slice of chicken breast, dragged half a walnut across her plate. "So what's the scoop with Holly? They find out who did her?"

"I don't believe so," Jane said.

"What a way to go." Goddess shook her head. "Pinned through the neck like some butterfly or something." She shivered. "I mean, I know she was a jerk and everything, but nobody deserves that." She looked at Jane. "Do you think she took a long time to die?"

Jane dropped her fork. It rattled loudly on the fine china. "I—I really wouldn't know. Would you mind if we talked about something else?" She looked at Laura, who was staring down at her plate as if she were about to vomit.

"Yeah, sure, whatever," Goddess said, shrugging. "Let's talk about my favorite subject—me. I got a new movie coming out. You hear about it? It's called *Adam and Eve.*"

"Actually," Jane said, grateful for the subject change, "I did read about it—in *Entertainment Weekly*, I think. They said you were brilliant."

"I am. You wanna come to a screening?" she asked them both.

Jane and Laura nodded.

"You got it. I'll tell Yves. You're gonna love the movie. There's this fabulous actress in it who plays my mother—Darlene Hunt. The studio wanted Beatrice Straight, but I said no—Straight is great, but Hunt is better for the part. And I was right. Wait till you see the two of us together. I'm telling you, an Oscar's gonna come out of that movie, and it may very well go to me."

The rest of lunch was much like this: Goddess talking about herself, about her talent, about her upcoming projects. She would leave her Broadway show during the summer to shoot a movie with Vanessa Williams called *Girlfriends.* Another film, a thriller, was in the discussion stages, with a number of leading men being considered as Goddess's opposite: Brad Pitt, Tom Cruise, Ben Stiller, John Travolta. Madonna was considering a cameo role.

Goddess was also developing a new Broadway show for herself.

"I'm gonna play all these outrageous women in history. Joan of Arc, Marie Curie, Marie Antoinette. It's gonna be a musical. There's one number—" Goddess laughed, blowing out smoke. " 'Let 'Em Eat Cake!' It's fabulous. All the songs are by Nikkee Waldman, who did *Goddess of Love*."

Jane, who would never have used the word *outrageous* to describe Joan of Arc, Marie Curie, or Marie Antoinette, found all of this conversation utterly boring. Not to mention that Goddess clearly had no intention of discussing their upcoming meeting at Corsair, which was why she had wanted Jane to come to lunch in the first place.

Later, as Jane and Laura were taking their leave, Jane pointed out that they hadn't prepared for the meeting.

"I told you," Goddess said, "don't worry about it. Goddess'll finesse it." She winked at Jane. "She always does. You be good, you two." She bowed serenely and a chopstick fell out of her hair, clattering on the foyer floor. "*Sayonara*."

And Jane and Laura found themselves back on Goddess's front steps, staring at each other.

"What just happened?" Laura asked.

"I'm not quite sure."

"I thought you and she were supposed to talk about your meeting with the publisher on Monday."

"So did I."

"Maybe she felt self-conscious talking about it in front of me."

Jane shook her head. "She said she didn't mind. Besides, I don't think Goddess feels self-conscious doing anything."

Sixteen

The receptionist looked Goddess up and down, barely able to contain her excitement, but also puzzled at Goddess's costume. Today she was Raggedy Ann, complete with fake pasted-on freckles and a red-yarn wig. She was also chewing gum.

"Goddess and Jane Stuart to see Hamilton Kiels," Jane told the young woman behind the desk, who called back to announce them and asked them to please have a seat.

Jane and Goddess sat in facing armchairs. Goddess stared up at a lighted display of Corsair's current books on the wall nearby. At last she said, "Do people really *read* that stuff?"

"Yes, certainly. In fact, the third book from the left on the top row—*Relevant Gods*—that's Carol Freund's novel that I handled. You remember the party was for Carol. It's a wonderful book. I'll give you a copy if you like."

"I don't read," Goddess said, looking bored, and

blew a huge bubble and popped it, gathering the gum back into her mouth. "That's your department."

Minutes seemed to stretch to days, and finally the door to the offices opened and Jack Layton appeared. "Jane! So good to see you."

"Good to see you, Jack," Jane said. "And you know Goddess, of course, from the . . . party."

"Yes, of course," he said enthusiastically. "I never got a chance to tell you how much I enjoyed your performance."

Goddess simply stared at him. He looked surprised and quickly turned to Jane. "So! Shall we go back and chat?"

They walked through the door and down a corridor to a conference room.

Three people, two women and a man, were already seated at the conference table. They rose as Jack, Jane, and Goddess entered, eyeing Goddess's getup.

Jack introduced Barb Goldman, Corsair's director of sales and marketing, a thin woman in her fifties with a mop of brown hair threaded with gray; and Ellen McIntyre, director of publicity and promotion. Jane had met Ellen before; Ellen and Jane and Carol Freund had had lunch to discuss publicity and promotion plans for *Relevant Gods*. Ellen was another publishing "type" that Kenneth had found amusing: the publicity director who was chronically shy and socially inept. True to form, she gave Jane and Goddess one sharp nod and sat down without putting out her hand or saying a word.

"And this gentleman," Jack said, "is Hamilton Kiels."

Kiels was a portly dark-haired man who looked to be in his early forties. He wore black-wire-rimmed glasses, a bright red bow tie on a button-down denim shirt, and, peeking out from under his blue blazer, red suspenders. The classic editor look. Kenneth used to make fun of the way editors dressed, saying they took a perverse pride in looking scruffy and disheveled. Jane wished he could see this one.

"Jane, I know, of course," he said. "I saw you at the party, Jane, and never got a chance to speak to you in all the—uh—confusion." He looked uneasy. "And you," he said to Goddess, "were just marvelous."

Goddess just stared at him. He sat down, looking uncomfortable.

"Now then," Layton said, turning to Goddess, "I want you to know we're extremely excited about the possibility of publishing your book. We're glad you wanted to meet with us today, because we'll be able to get a sense of what you intend to do with the project." He turned to Jane. "I assume you already have a ghost?"

"No," Jane replied uneasily. "You see, Goddess—"

"I'm writing the book myself," Goddess announced flatly, chomping on her gum, and proceeded to blow a bubble that grew and grew until it was bigger than her head. Suddenly she stuck her index finger into it and it popped loudly. It began to deflate, but before it could cover her face, she sucked it quickly back into her mouth with a slurping sound.

Out of the corner of her eye, Jane saw Barb and Ellen exchange glances.

"I see," Layton said. "Well, I'm sure that will be fine. Ham here is a fine editor and can help you in any way necessary."

Goddess just stared at Layton. Suddenly she giggled, and Jane heard her murmur, "Ham."

Layton went on, "The book, I understood from—uh—Holly, will be your autobiography?"

"That's right." Chomp, chomp.

"Well, that should be fascinating. And pretty straightforward. A nice hardcover, two sixteen-page photo inserts . . ." He looked at Barb. "Six-by-nine?"

She nodded.

"Wait a minute," Goddess said. "Wait a cotton-pickin' minute."

They all stared at her. Jane wondered what on earth she was going to say.

"This is *my* book," Goddess announced, sitting up straight at the table now, "and *I* decide how it looks and what goes into it. Got that? 'Cause if *you* don't, Simon & Schuster will."

Layton looked at Jane with something close to horror. Jane smiled, embarrassed, and shrugged. Layton turned back to Goddess. "Do you have some special ideas in mind for the book?" His tone was deferential.

"Sure do," Goddess replied. "First of all, I want it long—you know what I mean?"

"Mm-hmm, horizontal format," he said, nodding.

"No jacket."

"No jacket?"

"Nope. I don't see the point of them. They just fall off or tear. I want the picture—*my* picture—right on the book."

"Paper on boards," Layton said, to no one in particular.

"Whatever you call it. I got some more ideas, too. For instance"—chomp, chomp—"I want a pop-up, maybe a few pop-ups."

"Pop-ups?" Kiels repeated, looking queasy.

"Yeah, you know—like in a kids' book."

"A pop-up of what?" Layton asked pleasantly.

Goddess rolled her eyes. "Of Gloria Swanson," she said sarcastically. "*Of me*, who do you think? I've got the whole thing worked out in my head. On one page, here on the right, you got this beach scene—waves, sand, maybe a palm tree. Then you turn the page and there's me, rising out of the sea like Venus on the half shell. That's the logo for my show. We'll do cross-promotion. It'll be marv."

"Marv?" Ellen repeated. "Who's Marv?"

Jane said, "I think she means marvelous."

Ellen frowned. She looked quite alarmed.

"I got a few more ideas, too," Goddess went on. "I want a music chip in the cover, so when you open it, you get me singing a few lines from one of my songs. I haven't decided what song yet. Maybe 'Stranger Than Fiction.' "

"Well, that would certainly be appropriate," Layton said, and everyone laughed—except Goddess. Layton continued, "Jane, I think we've got a pretty good idea of what you and your client have in mind." To Goddess he said, "It all sounds absolutely terrific." And then to Kiels, Barb, and Ellen, "Doesn't it?"

The three of them bobbed their heads rapidly in unison.

"We really appreciate your coming in today," Layton said to Jane and Goddess. "Let us run some numbers, have a few discussions, and we'll give you a call, Jane, see what we can work out."

They all rose, Jane said good-bye to Barb, Ellen, and Kiels, and Layton walked Jane and Goddess to the reception area. Before Layton could thank Goddess for coming, she walked straight out the glass door to the elevator bank and pressed the DOWN button. As soon as the door had swung closed, Layton turned to Jane.

"What are you, nuts? She doesn't want a book, she wants a toy!"

"Well, why didn't you say so in the meeting, instead of kissing her ass?"

He glared at her. "It is your job to keep your client in line, to explain the realities and practicalities of publishing a book."

"Hah! Practicalities and realities are not two things Goddess worries much about. Let me save you a lot of time and trouble. If you really want this book, be prepared to do it her way. 'Cause if you won't," she said cheerily, heading out to join Goddess at the elevators, "Simon & Schuster will!"

He was still standing there, watching them, as the elevator doors slid shut.

"So that was a publishing meeting," Goddess said thoughtfully as they descended.

"Yes," Jane replied, "that was a publishing meeting."

"They don't know much, do they?"

Jane opened her mouth to respond, then thought better of it and said nothing.

"Call Greenberg," Daniel told Jane when she entered the office around noon. "It's important."

Jane called him from her office.

"Jane, I wanted you to know this from me, since you're friends with Louise," Greenberg said.

"Know what?"

"I've just had Ernie Zabriskie in for questioning in

the murder of the woman found hanging behind his inn."

For a moment Jane simply sat speechless.

"Jane?"

"I'm coming over to see you."

She hurried back out of the office and drove to the station. Greenberg looked uneasy.

"What's this all about?" Jane asked him.

He closed his office door and sat behind his desk. "I didn't tell you this before, but we found a man's handkerchief in the dead woman's pocket. We've now identified it as belonging to Ernie Zabriskie. We had him in, as I told you. He says he has no idea how it got there, says he'd never laid eyes on the girl before she was found there in the woods."

Jane was stunned to silence. She thought about Ernie and Dara, and about what Laura had told her in the car on the way to New York. Yes, Ernie was quite clearly a philanderer—but a *murderer*? Could the hanging woman have been one of Ernie's girlfriends, whom Ernie had killed for some reason? No—it just wasn't possible. Jane just couldn't see Ernie in the role of a killer. She decided to say nothing to Greenberg about Dara and the secret room. She'd spare Louise at least that embarrassment, and besides, it wasn't relevant anyway.

From the police station Jane drove directly to Hydrangea House to see Louise. Greeting Jane at the door, Louise looked worse than Jane had ever seen her look—her eyes red from crying, her face pinched and gray. They sat in the kitchen and Louise poured them coffee.

"I know all about the questioning," Louise said. She looked as if she was about to burst into tears, and hung her head over her mug. "Jane, you've got to help me.

I love Ernie. I know it's hard to believe, after all I know, all he's done, but I love him, and I know he loves me. He's made some mistakes, but we can work all that out. I can win him back, but not if he's in prison for a murder he didn't commit."

How, Jane wondered, could Louise be so sure Ernie hadn't committed the murder? But she did not voice that thought.

"Of course I'll help you in any way I can, Louise." Jane realized she'd already helped Louise by warning off Dara. "Where's Ernie?"

"Upstairs in his study. He's in shock."

"What can I do to help?" Jane asked.

"Talk to your friend, Detective Greenberg. Tell him what Ernie is like. Tell him Ernie could never do a horrible thing like that. You know Ernie, Jane; you've known him for ten years. Please, Jane."

"I agree with you, Louise. I don't think Ernie is capable of murder. I'll tell Greenberg so."

There was a message from Jack Layton waiting for Jane when she got back to her office. She rang him back and was put right through.

"What a nutcase," Layton said. "We'd like to make you an offer. A million, hard/soft," he said, referring to a deal in which the publisher bought both hardcover and paperback rights at the same time. "Standard royalties."

"A million! Jack, *you're* the nutcase. Morrow paid Whoopi Goldberg six million dollars!"

"Not a good example, Jane. The book bombed. And, uh, look at Morrow now."

He was right. Whoopi, whom most would consider a

genius on the same level as Goddess, had not succeeded as an author. And Morrow, her struggling publisher, had been swallowed up by HarperCollins.

"Irrelevant," Jane said in a tired voice. "I want five million, North America only."

"*What?* Jane, you're as crazy as this girl is. A million five, and that's it. Best I can do. You'd be a fool not to take it."

"I'm writing down your offer, Jack, to present it to my client, who I fear will want to explore other options. Keep in mind, too, that she will want to confer with her manager and probably her lawyer as well. So I may need a few days to get back to you."

"Don't you dare shop this, Jane. We have your promise that Corsair is seeing this first and exclusively."

"Seeing what? There's nothing on paper."

"Don't be cute, Jane. Present our offer to your client and call me."

"I'll present it, but I can't guarantee she'll want it. In fact, I'm pretty sure she won't."

"Present it," Layton repeated, and hung up.

Jane glared at the phone. Negotiating this deal was the last thing she needed right now. It was also, financially speaking, the first thing she needed right now, because even if by some fluke Goddess accepted Corsair's offer, Jane's commission at 15 percent would be $225,000. Not all at once, of course, since advances of that size were usually broken up into payments on signing, acceptance of manuscript, and publication, at the very least. But still, that was good money, even spread out—money Jane could definitely use.

She dialed Goddess at her pied-à-terre, and to her

surprise Goddess answered the phone. Without pream-
ble, Jane told her Layton's offer.

"Take it," Goddess said in a bored voice.

"Take it! But we haven't even negotiated."

"You just said it's the best they can do."

"I said he *said* it's the best they can do. They always
say that, but they usually don't mean it. They're testing
us. You're one of the biggest stars in the world. You're
worth far more than that. But we're probably going to
have to go to another publisher to get it. I'd like to get
something on paper and auction this project. That's
how you drive up the money."

"I don't want the money 'driven up,' " Goddess said
flatly. "I just told you to take it."

"The one-point-five million?"

"Yeah, whatever. The money doesn't matter to me."

Maybe not to you!

"I want Corsair to have this book. They . . . *get* me.
They understand where I'm coming from. Take—the—
deal. *And don't blow it*!" Goddess hung up.

"Why the arrogant little . . ." Jane muttered, and
fiercely punched Layton's number.

"We would consider four million," she told him.

"Good-bye."

"Wait! What's going on here, Jack? You know you'll
make back far more than you're offering. Why are you
lowballing me on this?"

"Because I can," he said simply. "Goddess wants this
deal, she wants it with us, and she could care less about
money. She told all this to Holly. Let's face it, Jane, the
girl's got more money than you and I will see in ten
lifetimes. So you've got zero leverage and a client who

wants to close fast. I'd say you'd better do so, or you're in serious danger of losing your client."

Jane didn't know what to say. It didn't matter, though, because Layton rushed on.

"Besides, you *owe* us this book, Jane. After all, Corsair brought Goddess to you. She was practically a gift."

"Excuse me, Jack," Jane said, fuming, "but you've contracted a common disease known as publishers' amnesia. It wasn't Corsair that brought Goddess to me; it was Holly Griffin."

"For Pete's sake," Layton said, exasperated. "Holly worked here. It's the same thing."

"I'm surprised you remember who she was. How long did it take you to move someone else into her office?"

"What, now you're insulting me? Of course I remember who she was. But life goes on. Now this is your last chance. One and a half mil, we work the rest out later. Are you taking it or not?"

"Yes," Jane said numbly.

"Thank you, Jane," Layton said sweetly, and rang off.

When Jane looked up, Daniel was hovering in her doorway with an armful of mail.

"I'm afraid I was eavesdropping," he confessed.

"No prob," she said, banging her pen on her knee in irritation. "He's insufferable."

"Jane—don't you realize you just made your biggest deal ever? A million and a half advance! I don't see Bertha getting that."

Jane looked at Daniel, brightening somewhat. "You're right. We should be celebrating, shouldn't we?"

"Absolutely."

"It's just that the advance should have been several

times that—you know that, and I know that, and Jack Layton knows that.''

Daniel shrugged. ''Doesn't matter. Your client is happy, and you got the deal, a *great* deal. I insist on taking you to lunch to celebrate.''

''You're on. Thanks,'' she said, giving him a warm smile. ''You always know the right thing to say.''

He smiled back and dropped the mail onto her desk. On top was this week's edition of *Publishers Weekly*. As Daniel left her office, she picked it up and leafed through it. Something caught her eye and she spread open the magazine to look at it.

In Memoriam
Holly Griffin
Our Dear Friend and
Respected Colleague
CORSAIR PUBLISHING

Jane could only shake her head. She threw down the magazine and dialed Goddess.

''You've got your deal,'' she said with forced cheerfulness.

''Fine. I've been thinking about it, though, and I want a different editor.''

''A different editor? Why?''

''That Kiels guy is a total nerd bomb. I want that Layton guy.''

''But he's the editorial director. He doesn't do much actual editing.''

''He does now. Besides, he's way cuter than Ham bone. I want him.''

"I can ask," Jane said, holding her head with her free hand, "but keep in mind that Hamilton Kiels is reputed to be quite a good editor—better than Holly." Jane grimaced at what she'd just said. "Sorry—I shouldn't have said that. Holly was your friend. And I should be grateful to her for recommending me to you."

"What did you just say?"

"I said I should be grateful to Holly for recommending me to you when you were looking for an agent."

There was a long silence on the line. Finally, Goddess spoke. "When the contracts come," she said distractedly, "send them to Yves. That's Yves Golden—"

"Yes, I know—your manager."

"You catch on fast."

Seventeen

It was three days later, Thursday, and it was time to leave the office for the day. Daniel poked his head into Jane's office and they bade each other good night.

From her desk, Jane could see Daniel leave the office by the front door. He stepped onto the sidewalk but, instead of heading toward his car in the municipal lot around the corner, he walked to the curb and simply stood, as if waiting. Jane frowned, curious.

It was a beautiful evening, the weakening sun casting a golden glow over the village green, its tall lush oaks, the ornate white Victorian bandstand. Daniel seemed to be admiring all this, turning his head from side to side, craning his neck a bit as if to see Center Street at the other side of the green.

Jane rose from her desk and went to the window. Just as she reached it, a black limousine pulled onto Center Street at the far end of the green and drove around it, stopping, to Jane's surprise, right in front of Daniel.

A chauffeur got out, came around to the rear passenger door, and opened it. An elderly African-American man, heavy and gray-haired, in a dark suit, slowly got out of the car. He and Daniel stood regarding each other for a moment; then Daniel stepped forward and offered the older man his hand. The older man stepped forward, took Daniel's hand, and then suddenly the two men were embracing. When they broke apart, they spoke for a few moments. Then Cecil Willoughby—for that, of course, was who it must be—ushered Daniel into the limousine. The chauffeur closed the door, got back behind the wheel, and the car pulled away from the curb.

Jane, stepping from the window, wiped a tear from her eye.

Saturday, the day of the wedding, had dawned sunny and mild, a glorious day. Jane, Nick, and Florence, arriving at Eleanor's, found tables set up on the back lawn, which sloped gently down to the millpond, on which three swans glided.

"Very beautiful," Florence breathed.

Jane scanned the crowd, from which rose laughter and happy chatter. There was Ginny; Cecil Willoughby; a red-haired young man Jane presumed was a college friend of Daniel's whom Daniel had mentioned; Rhoda Kagan; Doris; Penny, Alan, and little Rebecca; Greenberg; several young women, who must have been friends of Laura's from Unimed, with their husbands; Nell and Ann, who owned the gift shop next to Jane's office, with *their* husbands; an uncomfortable-looking Louise and Ernie.

Jane went to the punch bowl. As she filled a glass for Nick, she glanced up and saw a yellow New York City taxi pull up in front of the restaurant. "What on earth . . ."

she murmured, and her jaw dropped when she realized that the woman getting out, dressed in a tiny dashiki and a feathered African-style headdress, was Goddess.

The other guests had noticed, too, and there was a flutter of whispers as they all watched Goddess pay the driver and saunter down the lawn, smiling a broad smile. She walked up to Jane.

"Surprise. Bet you're wondering what the hell I'm doing here." Before Jane could respond, Goddess went on, "Laura invited me, kind of a last-minute thing, and here I am." She winked at Jane. "Thought I'd give all the little people a thrill."

Insufferable as ever, Jane thought, and wondered if the African getup was in Daniel's honor.

The wedding ceremony, held under a white tent, was picture-perfect. Laura was magnificent in her Christian Lacroix, Daniel heartbreakingly handsome in a tuxedo. There were lots of tears. After the ceremony, Jane managed to get Daniel alone for a moment.

"Jane, you're crying."

She dabbed at her eyes with a handkerchief. "What can I say? I'm a crier! I want to give you your gift—a little something just for you, and something for both of you." She handed him a gift-wrapped box containing the lapis desk set she'd bought him. Then she handed him an envelope containing a check.

"Thank you, Jane."

"You're welcome. Something toward the down payment on that house you and Laura want." She started to cry again. "You know I love you like a son."

"Nick's big brother!" he joked, and they both laughed. Then Daniel grew serious. "I feel the same way, Jane. Thank you for all you've done."

She made a dismissive gesture. "Speaking of sons, your father is absolutely *charming*. Good-looking man, too."

"Thanks," Daniel said, nodding thoughtfully. "Dad's always looked well. Even years ago, just after he'd started *Onyx* and was heading for a whopper of a heart attack and quadruple bypass surgery. Dad says his doctors are all surprised he's made it this long."

"Let's hope he lives a lot longer," Jane said, "especially now that you two have reconciled."

"Amen," he said.

Luncheon was served. Jane sat next to Greenberg, handsome in a navy suit. On his other side sat Nick, and then Florence, Daniel, Laura, Mr. Willoughby, and between him and Jane, Goddess. Jane, munching on her salad, noticed that Mr. Willoughby and Goddess were engaged in lighthearted conversation, Willoughby's manner almost flirtatious. Mr. Willoughby must have said something funny, because suddenly Goddess threw back her head and laughed. Then she turned to him. "In that case," she said, sounding quite serious, "why don't you have me appear on the cover of your magazine?"

This captured everyone's attention. The table grew silent.

Mr. Willoughby smiled. "Thank you for the kind offer, but unfortunately—your lovely African costume notwithstanding—all the models on the cover of *Onyx* are of true African-American background."

"But that's reverse racism!" Goddess protested, her smile fading.

Mr. Willoughby looked surprised. Before he could respond, Jane rushed in with a comment about how moving the ceremony had been. Goddess shot Jane an exasperated look, then reached down to the big jute macramé bag at her feet and reappeared with a flattish gift-wrapped box. She handed it to Laura.

"Thank you," Laura said.

"Open it," Goddess urged.

Laura looked surprised, then shrugged. "Okay," she said graciously, and unwrapped the gift. "Ah," she said, and held up an ornately framed photograph of Goddess.

"Thank you," Daniel said, and shot Jane a look when Goddess wasn't looking.

"You're so welcome," Goddess said, as if she'd given them all the riches in the world. She looked about her. "This whole middle-class marriage thing—I find it very interesting."

Jane noticed that Laura was watching Goddess with a slight frown.

Goddess swept on. "It's so . . . innocent or something. You know, in one of my music videos—the one I did for 'Always a Virgin,' I played a bride, except that my gown was pitch-black and I was barefoot."

No one seemed to know quite what to say. Jane saw Nick whisper something to Greenberg, who shushed him.

Laura threw out her hands. "Well, I admit to being totally middle-class, as you put it. Totally traditional. I mean, look at me! I'm wearing something old . . ." She held out her hand to display a large gold ring. "I've had this for years. Something new: my beautiful gown— which Jane helped me pick out. Something borrowed: this bracelet Jane lent me. And something blue: my garter! Can't show you that!" She blushed slightly.

Goddess, looking totally bored, turned to Mr. Willoughby. "What'd you give 'em for their wedding?"

Mr. Willoughby, taken aback by her bluntness, gave a little cough. "Why, I gave them their honeymoon," he said. "Three weeks in Italy."

"That's right," Daniel said, beaming. "Laura and I are leaving right after Jane and I attend the romance convention."

"Don't remind me," Jane groaned, and they all laughed.

Just then Goddess grabbed a flute of champagne at Mr. Willoughby's place and, with a grimace of disgust, spilled it onto the ground. "Yuck, there was a caterpillar in it. That must be one drunk caterpillar!"

Again everyone laughed. Mr. Willoughby thanked her, making a joke about the worm in a tequila bottle, and everyone fell to talking amongst themselves.

Later, there was dancing. Jane danced with Greenberg, and a few feet away Daniel danced with Laura. The band was playing a song Jane loved, Burt Bacharach's "Walk on By," and she lost herself in the good feeling of Greenberg's body pressed to hers as they swayed to the music.

Suddenly there was a commotion at Jane's table. Craning her neck, Jane saw Mr. Willoughby lying on the ground. "Oh my God!" she cried, and rushed over to him. His face was bright red, and he was clearly in great pain. "Call an ambulance!" Jane yelled to a waiter, who ran toward the restaurant.

Within a few moments the wail of an ambulance could be heard. It pulled to an abrupt stop on the restaurant's drive, and two paramedics jumped out.

"Over here!" Jane called to them, and a moment

later they were attending to poor Mr. Willoughby, who had not moved from where he had fallen.

Daniel came up to Jane. "It's his heart. I'm going to ride with him in the ambulance. They're taking him to St. Clare's," he said, referring to a hospital in nearby Denville.

"The poor man," Jane said. "I'll have Florence take Nick home. Stanley can drive Laura and me to the hospital."

"That would be great," Daniel said. "Thanks, Jane." And he hurried off.

Jane, wringing her hands, went in search of Florence.

Jane couldn't concentrate on the copy of *Newsweek* she had grabbed in the waiting room of St. Clare's. Nearby, Greenberg, Daniel, and Laura sat staring blankly. Daniel's father had indeed suffered a heart attack, and was in Intensive Care.

Minutes stretched to hours. When Jane thought she would lose her mind, a doctor emerged from the corridor and approached Daniel. They spoke quietly. Daniel hung his head. "I'm sorry," Jane heard the doctor say.

Laura took Daniel in her arms. The others stood in shocked silence. Then, like zombies, they all filed out of the waiting room into the sunlight, which now seemed garish and harsh.

"Daniel," Jane said, embracing him, "I'm so sorry."

"Thank you, Jane." He thought for a moment. "I'm only grateful Dad and I had patched things up, that he got to see Laura and me get married. Which, ironically, must have been too much excitement for his poor weak old heart."

"What are you going to do now?" she asked.

"I'll go back to Chicago tonight to arrange the funeral. Needless to say, the honeymoon is postponed indefinitely."

"Daniel," she said gently, "there's something I've been meaning to ask you, and I hope you'll forgive my asking it now. Why didn't you tell me who your father was?"

He shrugged. "I guess I felt it was . . . irrelevant. Who he was had nothing to do with what I planned to do with my life. Besides, he and I didn't even have a relationship when I first met you and Kenneth." He shook his head. "I never really stopped loving my father—though I didn't always approve of some of his business practices, and I didn't want any part of them."

"Well, it's all yours now," Jane remarked. "Unless you've got a mother hidden away somewhere."

"No," Daniel said with a sad smile, "she died when I was seventeen. Ovarian cancer. As for my inheritance, you're right—everything Dad had, including *Onyx*, is mine now." But clearly this thought brought him neither joy nor comfort. He kissed Jane's cheek and walked slowly away.

Jane called after him, knowing she shouldn't but unable to stop herself. "Daniel," she said hesitantly.

He turned.

"Do you still want to play agent with me?" She had to know.

He frowned at her. "How can you even ask me that? Nothing will change . . . except that now I guess I can buy Laura that big house she's always dreamed of."

"Right—with a big nursery!"

He gave a melancholy nod. "The baby—that's one thing Dad didn't live to see."

* * *

Later that afternoon, Jane called Daniel.

"Is there anything I can do for you while you and Laura are in Chicago?" she asked.

"Laura's not going," he replied. "She was insisting on it, but I told her it wasn't necessary. She didn't even know my father."

"Daniel, my love, she would be going for *you*, not your father."

"I know. That's what she said, and I appreciate it, but I told her it would actually be easier for me if I went alone. I'll arrange for the funeral, meet with my father's attorneys to start settling his estate. That should turn into a tangled mess, but I can get things started. As for your doing anything, thanks, Jane, but I can't think of anything. Well, I *can* think of one thing," he added. "The RAT convention. It's a week from today. It looks as if I won't be able to go with you after all."

Damn! "That's all right, don't even worry about it. I'll do just fine on my own. Good luck. I'll see you when you get back."

Jane was watching TV with Nick and Winky when the phone rang. Florence picked it up in the kitchen and appeared in the family room a moment later. "Missus," she said, "it is for you. Detective Greenberg."

Jane took the phone.

"This may not be the most appropriate time to ask you this," Greenberg said, "considering what happened to poor Mr. Willoughby this afternoon, but since every time I'm with you, someone seems to die, I thought I'd ask anyway: Can I take you to dinner and a movie tonight?"

Jane felt a rush of delight. "I'd love to. Just let me ask Florence if she'll baby-sit. She's officially off on the weekends. Florence," she called.

"Yes, missus," Florence replied from the kitchen.

"If you have no plans for tonight, would you be willing to watch Nick? I'll pay you, of course."

"Yes, missus, it would be my pleasure."

Jane got back on the phone. "You're on—and let's hope tonight proves the exception."

"Definitely. What kind of food are you in the mood for, and what kind of movies do you like?"

"Hmm . . . I like every kind of food, as long as it's cooked—so Japanese is iffy. As for movies, I'm game for anything . . . as long as Goddess isn't in it."

Greenberg picked her up at eight and they went to see a movie in Parsippany, a comedy about inept bank robbers.

"I needed a good laugh," Jane said in the lobby afterward. "Thank you."

For dinner they went to a storefront Italian restaurant Greenberg liked in Boonton.

"You know," he said, spearing a piece of fried calimari, "when you think about it, it *is* strange that someone has been murdered two out of the three times we've been together. The woman in the woods . . . Holly . . ."

"And the third time someone died! Poor Mr. Willoughby. It is strange," Jane agreed. "Do you think I'm bad luck?"

He smiled grimly. "Maybe it's me."

"We shouldn't talk like this. Goddess said she thought I'd killed Holly, and I nearly choked on my soda." She shrugged. "It's just bad luck—especially for the people who died! Oops, there I go again. I really have to stop with the gallows humor.''

He laughed, his dark brown eyes warm as he looked at her. "That's one of the things I like about you—your sense of humor. There's too little humor in the world today. At least in *my* world. As for this Goddess . . ." He shrugged, at a total loss. "What do you make of her?"

"What do I make of her? She's a spoiled, rich, talented, rude, arrogant brat. She's also, at the moment, my biggest client. So I guess I shouldn't talk that way about her."

"It's okay, I won't tell anyone."

"And I won't tell anyone you've let me in on the case of the hanging girl," she said, and as soon as she'd said it, she thought about Louise and Ernie, and this made her feel depressed. "Stanley . . . You don't really think Ernie could have killed that poor woman . . . do you?"

He looked at her frankly. "I don't know Ernie well enough to answer that."

"Typical cop answer."

He ignored this. "I *can* tell you that, strange as it may seem, no signs of violence were found on the woman's body—no sign of rape; no skin under her fingernails to suggest a struggle; no scrapes, scratches, or bruises anywhere on her body—except those left by the rope, of course. If it weren't for the fact that there was no branch she could have jumped from, and that there was nothing under her feet, it would appear that she committed suicide."

"But how do we know there *wasn't* something under her feet?" Jane asked. "Maybe there was, but someone came along later and removed it."

Greenberg frowned. "It's possible, I guess, but far-fetched. That means someone wanted a suicide to look like a murder. What reason would anyone have had to do that? Then there's the makeup on her face. Someone *did* that to her, Jane."

Jane shivered, though the restaurant was warm. "Let's change the subject—to another murder. Have the New York police learned anything more about Holly Griffin?"

"I spoke to my friend again. He says all they know is that Holly passed her assistant, Jilly, on the way out of the party room and told her she was going to her office to get the framed copy of that writer's book jacket."

"Carol Freund," Jane put in. "My client."

"Right. Holly said she wanted to give it to Carol. So that explains what Holly was doing in her office. But that's all they know so far. The letter opener was smeared with fingerprints, but the only ones the police can identify are Holly's."

"So in other words," Jane said, "they still know nothing." She rolled her eyes. "New York's Finest."

After dinner he drove her home and walked her to the front door, a true gentleman. There they kissed, a longer kiss than their first, and Jane felt a tingle right to her very core. She thanked him for the fun evening, and waved until he'd backed out of the driveway and driven past the holly hedge on his way down Lilac Way.

Eighteen

Jane staggered across the lobby of the Waldorf-Astoria.

It had been a long day. Presenting her workshop on the changing face of romance by herself that morning had been exhausting. Around lunchtime, in front of the hotel, two women reporters from rival TV tabloids, both of whom were professional acquaintances of Jane, got into an argument that turned into an outright brawl, complete with hair-pulling; the fracas ended when they both fell down the stairs and had to be taken away in an ambulance.

One bright moment had been the morning's keynote address by the witty Salomé Sutton, the *New York Times* best-selling author whom many called the inventor of the historical romance.

Jane opened her convention folder and checked the schedule. She grimaced. She couldn't leave yet because she had agreed to participate in two hours' worth of ten-minute one-on-one appointments with writers. Those were set to begin in half an hour. In the meantime she could catch her breath. She spied an empty chair, hurried over to it, and sank into its pillowy softness with a grateful sigh.

"Jane! Jane!"

She looked up. Bertha Stumpf bustled toward her. *Oh please, Lord, have mercy . . .*

"Jane, I've been looking for you!" Bertha was breathing heavily from the exertion of running. She gave Jane a stern look, as if Jane somehow should have known Bertha was looking for her.

"Hello, Bertha. Is something wrong?"

"No, nothing's wrong. It's just that I was at the registration desk checking on my bill when I happened to see one of the clerks hand a note to a bellhop. The clerk told the bellhop to page Jane Stuart and give her the note."

Jane sat up, looking around.

"Don't worry!" Bertha squealed. "I told them I knew you and would save them the trouble. So here it is." She produced a sealed hotel envelope and handed it to Jane.

"Thank you, Bertha, that was very thoughtful."

Bertha waited. "Aren't you going to open it?"

Jane sighed. "I suppose I should. I can't imagine who would send me a note." She was aware of Bertha's nosy gaze as she tore open the envelope and unfolded a sheet of hotel stationery. It was a handwritten note:

> Dear Ms. Stuart,
>   I was extremely impressed with your workshop this morning. In fact, I've been following your career with great interest for some time now, and wonder if you would be inter-

ested in speaking with me about the possibility of our working together. If you are, I
will be in my suite, #610, between two and
four o'clock.

                              Best wishes,
                              Salomé Sutton

"Not bad news, I hope," Bertha said, craning her
neck to read it.

You asked for it. "No, not bad news at all. Look!" Jane
handed Bertha the note.

Bertha's eyes widened in amazement. "Jane! You
could represent Salomé Sutton. That's fabulous." But
there was a glint of envy in her puffy eyes.

"Hey," Jane said, rising, "when you're hot, you're
hot!" And she *did* feel hot. First Goddess, now Salomé
Sutton. . . . A client like that could do wonders for the
agency's reputation. She turned to Bertha. "Thanks
again."

"You're welcome," Bertha said grumpily.

At that moment three women in full costume wandered past. One wore a sweeping green-velvet antebel-
lum gown. Another wore riding clothes—jodhpurs with
a black crop. The third was dressed as a harem girl, her
midriff bare. On her head was a jeweled tiara, strangely
incongruous.

"What the blazes was that?" Jane said.

"Oh," Bertha said nonchalantly, "they're on their
way to the Fashion of Passion Pageant."

"The *what?*"

"The Fashion of Passion Pageant. You dress up as the
heroine of your favorite historical romance. It's great
fun."

Jane looked Bertha up and down. "I see you're not participating."

Bertha scoffed at this idea. "I think I'm getting a bit on in years for that kind of thing—though in my slimmer days I did participate in the Pageant as Amber St. Clare from *Forever Amber*." She turned to the three women. "Now that first one, obviously, is Scarlett O'Hara. The second one . . ." She frowned. "My guess is that she's Leonora Hart, from Rona Peters's *Embrace Till Dawn*. And the third—well, Jane, my dear, you'd *better* know who that is."

"Why?" Oh, no. "Someone from one of your books?"

"No! It's Delilah Dare, the princess abducted by the sheikh in *Arabian Nights*. You know who wrote *that*, don't you?"

"No, who? You?"

"*Salomé Sutton!*" Bertha gave Jane a smug, know-it-all look. "*Arabian Nights* was the inspiration for my *Casbah*. I even *dedicated* the book to Salomé Sutton. Better do your homework," she scolded.

"Just did!" Jane said, rising. "See you later."

"Yeah," Bertha muttered, and wandered away.

Feeling suddenly energized, Jane tucked Salomé Sutton's note into her folder and hurried toward the elevators. She rode alone to the sixth floor and stepped off. A sign directly in front of her said room 610 was to the left, so she headed in that direction.

She felt a thrill of anticipation. What would she say first? "This is such an honor, Miss Sutton. . . ." "I'm such a fan of your work, Miss Sutton, especially *Arabian Nights*. . . ." "Your keynote address this morning was a pure delight, Miss Sutton. . . ."

She followed a turn in the corridor and spotted the door of number 610. Her heart beat faster.

At that moment she felt a sharp, stinging pain on the top of her head . . . heard from somewhere far away the crashing of glass. Strange dark shapes swam before her eyes, a wave of nausea rose in her throat, and then the whole world went black.

"Jane . . . Janey . . ."

She felt as if she were fighting her way up through thick dark mud. If only she could get to the top, open her eyes. If only she could stop the pounding pain in her head.

"Jane Stuart . . ."

At last she managed to open her eyes just a crack— and found herself looking into the face of Bertha Stumpf.

"Jane," Bertha said softly, "it's me, Bertha. Do you know me?"

"Of course I know you, Bertha," Jane said, and was surprised at her own slurred speech. "What happened? Where are we?" She was aware now that she was lying on a bed. From somewhere in the distance came the sound of a woman's voice paging someone over a loud-speaker.

"You're in the hospital, Jane, New York Hospital," Bertha said, wincing as if she hated telling Jane this.

"Why?" Jane asked.

Suddenly an obese nurse swung into view. "Excuse me," she said to Bertha, and took Jane's arm firmly and fastened a blood-pressure cuff around it. "You were mugged, dear."

"Mugged!"

" 'Fraid so. But you'll be fine. You have a mild concussion. And Doctor had to take some stitches."

"But why? What happened?"

Bertha appeared on the other side of the bed. "Jane," she said gently, "someone hit you over the head with a vase. Then he stole your bag."

It was hard to think straight because of the pain in her head. Then she remembered. "But . . . I was on my way to see Salomé Sutton."

Bertha shook her head, a pitying expression on her face. "It was all a ruse, Jane. I'm sorry."

Jane groaned and shut her eyes. "I should have known it was too good to be true. I feel like such a fool."

The nurse unfastened the cuff. "Not bad. How're you feeling?"

"Fuzzy."

The nurse nodded. "Doctor wants to keep you overnight for observation. Just a precaution—I'm sure you'll be fine. But you *were* hit pretty hard."

Gingerly Jane put a hand to the top of her head and felt roughness, stinging to the touch. "Ouch!"

"That wound'll hurt for a while. But you got off lucky, considering."

Jane gave a little nod.

"Because your bag had been stolen, no one would have known who you were if it hadn't been for your friend here."

Bertha nodded proudly. "I couldn't believe what I was seeing! I was still down in the lobby and all of a sudden these two gorgeous EMTs were carrying you out of the elevator on a stretcher! Now," Bertha said kindly, "who can I call for you, Jane?"

"If you'll dial my house for me, I'd like to talk to

Florence, my son's nanny." She recited the number to Bertha, who punched it out for her and handed her the phone.

"Missus! It is dark already and where are you?"

"Is it dark? I had no idea. Florence, I . . . had a little accident. I'm not hurt, not badly, but I am in the hospital and I won't be coming home till tomorrow."

"Good Lord! In the hospital! Missus!"

"Now, Florence, please. I don't want you to alarm Nick. I'm fine, really. Please just tell him I had to stay overnight in the city on business, okay?"

Just then there was a click on the line. "Mom?"

"Hello, darling," Jane said, trying as hard as she could to sound normal.

"Mom, you sound really weird. Where are you?"

"I'm still in the city. I have to stay overnight. Late meeting. I'm fine. I'll see you tomorrow, okay?"

"Okay," Nick said. "Bye, Mom."

There was another click as he hung up.

"I'm still on here, missus. What hospital are you at, in case I need you?"

"New York Hospital."

"Okay, missus, don't you worry about a thing. I'll see you tomorrow. And feel better now."

Jane handed Bertha the phone.

"Anyone else?" Bertha asked.

Jane thought a moment. "Yes," she said, and gave Bertha Greenberg's number.

She told him what had happened.

"I'll be right there," he said, and hung up before she could say another word.

Again she handed Bertha the phone, and as she did,

a wave of sleepiness overcame her. "I feel so tired all of a sudden," she said.

The nurse reappeared. "We've given you something to help you sleep, dear. Just let it work." She patted Jane's arm.

Vaguely Jane was aware of Bertha saying good night.

Sometime later she felt a hand take hers, a strong male hand that squeezed hers tight. She heard a man's voice, a familiar voice . . . a voice she liked. But she was so very tired. . . .

She opened her eyes. The hospital room was bright with sunlight. Suddenly the curtain at the right side of her bed was whipped back and a nurse, a different one from last night, approached her bed.

"And how are we feeling this morning?"

"Better," Jane said. "The cut hurts a bit, but the headache's gone."

"Good. You've got company."

Greenberg appeared at the foot of the bed. Jane's first thought was that she hoped she looked half-decent. He carried a bouquet of flowers, which he started to hand to her; then he appeared to think better of it, and said, "I'll find a vase for these."

"That was awfully sweet of you. Sweet of you to come see me, too."

"I was here last night, too, only you don't remember."

"I do . . . vaguely."

He shrugged. "Don't worry about it. The important thing is you're okay. You know," he said with a little laugh, "when I said everybody around you seems to get hurt, I didn't mean you!"

"But I'm alive," she pointed out. "I broke the rule."

"There's that gallows humor again. Now I *know* you're all right."

"What on earth happened?"

"They didn't tell you?"

"They did, but I'm not sure I remember it all."

"Someone attacked you in the corridor of the sixth floor at the Waldorf. That note supposedly from Salomé Sutton—it was just a trick to get you upstairs."

She frowned. "All that just to get my handbag?"

"Sure. Welcome to New York. Did you have anything really valuable in it?"

"No, just a little cash. Oh, my credit cards!"

"You won't be liable, but you'd better cancel them as soon as you can."

Jane shook her head in wonder. "I still can't believe anyone would go to such lengths to mug someone. And why me?"

"Who knows? You're a successful agent. Someone must have known you were attending the convention and picked you out as a target."

"I've got it!" she said. "It was some disgruntled writer I rejected. I knew one of them would come at me one day."

Greenberg laughed. "What an imagination!"

At that moment the nurse reappeared. "Doctor says you can go when you feel up to it."

"Doctor? Who is this doctor? I've never laid eyes on him."

"He's been here," the nurse said cheerfully. "Checked you all over. You were sleeping. You feeling up to getting dressed?"

"Yes."

Greenberg started for the door. "I'll go get my car

and meet you out front. They have to take you down in a wheelchair."

"All right." A little shakily, she got out of bed and began putting on her clothes, which were folded neatly on a nearby chair. As she dressed, she reflected that although she would have preferred not to be mugged at all, it was nice to have someone, someone like Stanley, to take her home.

Nineteen

For the third time, Jane held up the cover of Elaine Lawler's newest Regency romance, *Scandal's Folly*, and squinted, trying to read the back-cover copy. It was no use. The painting in the background was of an ornate tapestry in black and red, and the black lettering over it was impossible to read. She lifted the phone to call Abigail Schwartz, Elaine's editor, then changed her mind and replaced the receiver. She wasn't up to an argument now, not yet. She still didn't feel quite herself. She'd spent all of yesterday, Sunday, in bed, resting and being cared for by the wonderful, solicitous Florence. To explain the stitches on her head, they'd both told Nick that Jane had simply fallen.

She decided phone calls were out this morning, and carried a pile of manuscripts from her bookcase to her desk and began reading. These manuscripts were from prospective clients, and each was worse than the one before it. Jane wondered briefly if perhaps her state of mind was coloring her judgment, then decided it wasn't—the stuff really was that bad—and carried the manuscripts out to the reception room, placing them on the credenza to await rejection letters Daniel would write. She wondered how he was getting along in Chicago. It was lonely here without him. She returned to her office. The phone rang as she sat down.

"Jane Stuart."

"Daniel Willoughby."

"Daniel! I was just thinking about you. How's it going?"

"All right." He sounded tired. "I've buried my father and taken care of everything that can be taken care of at this point. Remind me someday to tell you about the joys of probate. I'm flying home late this afternoon."

"Good. I'm sure Laura will be pleased. I know I will."

"Thanks. How did the convention go?"

She told him about getting mugged.

"Holy smokes! Jane, you could have been killed!"

"Tell me about it."

"Cancel your credit cards."

"Did."

"You're sure you're all right? I know Laura would be more than happy to get groceries for you, whatever you need."

"Thanks, that's sweet, but Florence has been great. You just get home safe."

"Will do. See you in the morning, business as usual."

As soon as Jane hung up, the phone rang again. It was Bertha.

"Just checking to make sure you're feeling okay."

"Yes, I'm fine, Bertha. Thank you for all you've done."

"I blame myself for giving you that bogus note."

"Don't be ridiculous! You didn't know it wasn't real.

But I don't think I'll be attending any more conventions for a while."

"I can't say I blame you," Bertha said. "Now. Since you're feeling better, I need to run a plot question past you. Do you have a minute?"

Jane rolled her eyes. "Yes, Bertha."

The minute lasted an hour. Through it all, Jane listened politely, trying to be helpful. Bertha had, after all, been very good to her.

When at last Bertha was finished "brainstorming," Jane thanked her again and hung up. From the far left side of her desk she grabbed a manuscript that had been submitted to her a week ago—a suspense novel she'd begun to read and had thought showed promise. She'd read a page and a half when the phone rang again. Jane picked it up.

"Goddess here."

Jane forced a smile into her voice. "Hello, Goddess, dear."

"Don't call me dear."

"Sorry. Hello, Goddess. Am I allowed to ask how you are?"

"Funny." There was a faint chomping on the line— Goddess was either eating something or chewing gum. "You still interested in seeing my new movie? *Adam and Eve*?"

"Of course!"

"Yves has set up a private screening for you. You can bring Daniel and Laura and anybody else you want. Yves says we need word of mouth on this one."

"That sounds wonderful, Goddess, thank you. When were you thinking?"

"Tomorrow, but we're having it early because I have

to be at the theater for my show by seven-thirty. Come at four." Goddess gave Jane the address of a building owned by the studio, on Seventh Avenue.

Jane jotted it down. "I'm not sure who'll be able to come."

"That's up to you. But I hope that cute Daniel can make it. I thought it would maybe take his mind off his dad."

"Why, that's very thoughtful of you, Goddess," Jane said, surprised. "I believe you're right. I'll see what I can do."

Abruptly Goddess hung up. *Such a strange girl.* Jane sat pondering. This would be fun. A private screening of a major new film starring Goddess. . . . So glamorous. The knitting-club ladies would probably enjoy this, especially since Louise had suspended the meetings for a while.

Later that day, as Jane prepared to leave the office, Daniel called. "I'm home. Just wanted you to know."

"I'm so glad. Listen, while I have you on the line, Goddess has invited us to a private screening of *Adam and Eve,* her new movie. Would you and Laura like to come? It's tomorrow at four in the city, so I figure we'd have to leave Shady Hills by two-thirty."

"Short day."

"Sure is," Jane said, and reached to the back of her head to feel her stitches. She winced. "And I can use it. So, you game?"

"I'd love to, but I don't know about Laura. She'll be working. But I'll ask her, see if she wants to take time off."

"Gotcha. See you in the morning."

Grabbing her purse and briefcase, Jane headed out

the back door to the parking lot. On the way to her car it occurred to her that representing someone like Goddess had its perks. Tonight, from home, she'd call the Defarge ladies and invite them. She decided she'd also invite Greenberg. Though Goddess's primal dancing had been lost on him, he might enjoy *Adam and Eve*, which, as Goddess herself had said, was a traditional drama.

Opening the car door, Jane frowned. Was Goddess capable of doing *anything* traditional?

Twenty

"Hey, Mom!" Nick ran up to her as she came through the back door from the garage.

"Give me a hug, you little bug," she said, grabbing Nick and kissing the top of his head.

"Ouch! Mom, your briefcase is hitting me!"

"Ooh, sorry, honey." She set it down.

"Mom, all the kids at school say you're going to be a movie star. Are you?"

"A movie star!" She laughed. "How silly. Of course not. I'm representing one, though. Goddess. That must be what they're talking about. But I wonder how they heard?"

"Ashley Klein's dad works for a company that promotes movies, whatever that means. He read about you in *Variety*."

"Ah." She'd have to get a copy of that.

"So you're representing Goddess," Nick said thoughtfully. "Cool. She's bigger than Madonna."

Florence appeared from the family room. "Hello, missus. And how was your day?"

"Great, Florence, thanks."

"Your head is better?"

"Much."

"Good. Young man," Florence said to Nick, "I was about to beat you in chess, and we also have some cleaning up to do in there."

"Oh, yeah," Nick said, and ran back to the family room.

"What smells so good?" Jane asked.

"Meat loaf—Trinidad-style. It is my great-grandmother's recipe. I hope you like it."

"I'm sure I will. I've liked all your other recipes."

"It's not quite ready. You're home a bit early. We'll finish our game and clean up."

"Sounds good." Jane followed Florence into the family room and sank into the big leather armchair.

Winky lay asleep in the corner of the sofa. Seeing Jane, she jumped up and ran over to her, climbing into her lap and curling back up. Jane stroked her soft fur.

Across the room, Nick had already tossed most of his army men into their clear-plastic bin. He finished that task, then turned to the chess game waiting on the coffee table.

Florence sat on the sofa and concentrated on the board. "It was my move, correct?" she asked Nick.

He walked over on his knees. "Correct." He turned to Jane. "Mom, what are you doing here?"

She looked at him in puzzlement. "I live here."

"No, I mean why are you sitting in here with us? Usually you're in your office reading your manuscripts or something."

Jane had made a point of sitting down in the room

with them, feeling she hadn't been spending enough time with Nick.

"I want to spend more time with you," she told him honestly. "Anything wrong with that?"

"No," he said, shrugging, and watched Florence move her knight. Suddenly he sat up straight. "Ooh! What time is it?"

"Five minutes to four," Jane told him.

"Yikes. Florence, would it be okay with you if we continue this game later? I don't want to miss *CyberWarriors*. It's on at four."

"No problem," Florence said with a smile. "I'll go check on my meat loaf."

Nick grabbed the remote from the sofa, switched on the TV, and began running quickly through the channels.

Jane hated when he did that.

"Honey, could you just punch in the channel you want?"

At that moment, for a fraction of a second, there was an image of Goddess singing.

"Wait," Jane said. "Can you go back to that, please? That was Goddess."

"Mom," Nick whined, "I don't want to miss *CyberWarriors*."

"Come on, come on," she urged him quickly, and with a grimace he clicked back a few channels until Goddess was once more on the screen.

"It's MTV," Nick said, sounding bored. "One of her music videos. This is old."

"Old? How old could it be? Goddess hasn't been around that long."

"At least a year," Nick said.

"Ah. Old."

Goddess did look a little different—but then, she looked different every time Jane saw her. At this moment, Goddess, looking a bit like Tarzan's Jane in a skimpy kind of bikini made of pale green leaves, was walking down a path through a dark forest of trees, singing, "To-o-ouch me once," followed by a heavy drumbeat and Goddess's deep panting, and then again, "To-o-ouch me once. . . ."

As she walked along and sang, she ran her hands caressingly up the trunks of the trees, which Jane suddenly realized were the bare legs of what must have been exceptionally tall men.

"Good heavens," Jane said, watching with a combination of fascination and dismay. Goddess's leg-stroking was becoming more and more suggestive, her hands roaming higher and higher on the leg trees.

"But don't you da-are touch again," Goddess warned, the camera suddenly close up on her face, her pouting doll lips, and then just as quickly the camera pulled back to show an arm reach down and caress one of Goddess's breasts. She slapped the arm's hand and it withdrew. Goddess wandered on along the forest path. "To-o-ouch me once!" she belted out again.

At this vehement command, Winky awoke in Jane's lap, sat up sharply, and ran to the TV screen. She stared hard at Goddess's image and suddenly opened her mouth wide, her back and tail bristling, and let out a long, loud hiss.

"Winky, get away from there," Nick said, waving her away. Winky got down from the TV and walked slowly away, her gaze fixed on the screen. "She sure didn't look like that at Daniel and Laura's wedding," Nick commented.

"No, that she didn't," Jane said.

At that moment Florence entered the room. "I know this song," she said happily. "This is our very own Goddess. I first heard this when I was taking care of little Kerry in Randolph. Missus," she said pensively, "I was just checking on my meat loaf and I'm just wondering if I—aye-aye-aye!" She had turned to look at the TV screen. Her eyes bulged. Goddess was slapping off two breast-caressing tree hands at once. "Missus, do you think we"—she tilted her head toward Nick—"should be watching such things?"

"No, of course not," Jane said, shaking herself from her hypnotic state. "Nick, it's four o'clock anyway. You'd better put on your *CyberWarriors*."

"Fine with me," Nick said, shrugging, and clicked the remote. The bright colors of animated rocket pilots filled the screen.

Jane, aware that quality time with Nick was not possible when *CyberWarriors* was on, got up and went into the kitchen. Florence stood at the sink, cutting up string beans. She shook her head disapprovingly.

"It makes you wonder, doesn't it, missus? That that young woman—no, that child—should have been allowed to do such things. I ask you—where were her parents? Her father, isn't he that big rich sneaker man? 'Do it or else'?"

Jane laughed. " 'Go ahead and do it.' Yes, that's him. Carl Hamner. Goddess doesn't like to talk about her parents. When Laura and I had lunch with Goddess, and Laura said she thought Goddess's house belonged to her parents, Goddess became furious and made it clear she and her parents have no relationship."

"Maybe she realized what a bad job of bringing her up they did," Florence muttered, opening the oven door a crack to check on her meat loaf.

"Somehow," Jane said thoughtfully, "I don't think that was it."

Later that evening, from her study off the living room, Jane put aside the manuscript she was reading to call her friends and invite them to Goddess's screening. She called Daniel first.

"I asked Laura, and she says she'd love to. She'll take a half day off from work."

"Great. We can drive in together—you and Laura with me and Greenberg, if he'll come."

"Don't count on him," Daniel said with a laugh. "I don't think he 'gets' Goddess."

Jane called Greenberg next.

"Gee, Jane, I'm not sure that's really my kind of thing, though it's really thoughtful of you to think of me."

"It's a *movie*," Jane said. "No weird dancing, no thumping music . . . no leg trees."

"What?"

"Never mind. Please, Stanley, I'd love you to be there with me. Can't you leave work a little early, take half a day off or however the police do it?"

"All right," he relented, "I'm sure I can work something out." They agreed they'd drive in with Daniel and Laura.

Jane had no trouble at all convincing Ginny and Rhoda to come. Penny, for whom Jane hadn't held out much hope, said immediately that she couldn't possibly leave Alan and Rebecca alone on a school night. Doris declined, saying she was just too upset about Arthur, and Louise said she couldn't possibly have a good time at such a thing, what with all her troubles regarding Ernie. Jane said she understood.

The building that contained the screening room looked like any other office building on that stretch of Seventh Avenue. Jane, Greenberg, Daniel, and Laura had driven into the city in Greenberg's car, which he'd parked at the Quick Park, at Jane's suggestion. Then they'd cabbed over to the address Goddess had given Jane. As they got out of the cab, Ginny and Rhoda appeared from around the corner.

Inside the building, a security guard directed them to the tenth floor.

"Isn't this exciting?" Ginny said on the elevator.

"I wish the others had come," Rhoda said, half to herself.

Stepping off the elevator, they found themselves in a corridor with a glass wall at one end. On the glass was lettered CINEMA STAR STUDIOS. They went through a glass door and were greeted by a receptionist at a plain desk.

"I'll tell Goddess you're here," she said, and went down a corridor and around a corner out of sight.

Goddess appeared a moment later. Jane blinked. Today Goddess was dressed as a medieval lady, in a wispy gown and cone-shaped headdress.

"Love it!" Rhoda said.

Goddess chomped on gum. "Damsel in distress, right?" She gave a bored laugh. "Follow me."

She led them down the same corridor in the other direction, opened a door on the left, and ushered everyone inside. The room was smallish, with perhaps ten rows of seats like those in a movie theater, except that these seats were not connected, instead set about a foot apart, and there was plenty of leg room between the rows. The room's entire front wall was a screen about a third the size of a normal movie-theater screen. At the back of the room was a window through which the film would be projected.

"Sit down," Goddess instructed them, and started for the door.

"Won't you be staying?" Jane asked.

Goddess gave Jane a scandalized look. "I *never* watch my own films. Never. I'll be hanging out in the room next door." She pointed. "One door up. Oh, and bathrooms are a few doors farther down, on the right."

So the six of them sat in a row. The young woman who had greeted them appeared in the doorway. "Everybody ready?" They all said yes, and she switched off the light and closed the door. The room was pitch-black. After a moment, the screen burst to life, a vivid aerial view of lush New England countryside in the autumn—a lake, a covered bridge, a church—accompanied by lush orchestral music as the credits began to roll.

Cinema Star Studios
presents

Goddess

Ben Affleck

"Ooh, I didn't know he was in this!" Rhoda burst out. "I have such a case of the hots for that man."
Everyone shushed her.

Darlene Hunt

ADAM AND EVE

Jane found the film totally engrossing. It was, as Goddess had said, a surprisingly traditional story about a mother (Darlene Hunt) and her drug-addicted daughter, Eve (Goddess), who decided to come home from New York City and pull herself together to help her mother, who was dying. Affleck was superb as Goddess's brother, Adam, a successful attorney who had never left the small Vermont town, and who resented Goddess because, despite all he'd done for his mother, despite his having been there for her all these years, when his mother learned she was dying, it was Goddess she asked for.

In one scene, Affleck confronted Goddess with his hurt and resentment, and Jane fished in her purse for tissues to wipe away the tears running down her cheeks. From down the row, Jane heard someone sniffle and thought it sounded like Ginny. At the height of the scene's moving confrontation, there was a faint sound at the end of the row, then a crack of light appeared as someone opened the door.

What an odd time to go to the bathroom, Jane thought, then shrugged to herself. *When you gotta go, you gotta go.*

After a little over an hour and a half, the film ended, and the receptionist reappeared and switched on the light.

"I hope you all enjoyed the film," she said, sounding as if she said this often.

"Magnificent," Jane said to Greenberg. "She really is a genius, don't you think?"

Greenberg looked impressed. "I gotta admit, she did a great job. Had me teary-eyed a few times there."

"Let's go congratulate her," Laura said, and Daniel, who clearly had also enjoyed the film, nodded in agreement.

The receptionist smiled, and said, "She's just down here," and indicated the same room Goddess had, one door farther along the corridor.

They all filed out of the screening room, Jane leading the way. She knocked on the next door. There was no response, so she knocked harder.

Jane frowned in puzzlement and turned to the others. The receptionist was still standing nearby. "I'm sure she's in there. I think it's okay if you just go in."

Though she didn't really like that idea, Jane turned the knob and slowly pushed open the door. "Goddess?"

She pushed the door farther, glanced around the room, a small lounge with sofas and chairs, and pushed the door all the way open.

"She's gone!" Jane said.

"Gone?" Ginny said.

"Maybe she just went to the ladies' room," Rhoda said.

"No," the receptionist said. "I was just in there."

She smiled, apparently unconcerned, and checked her watch. "She must have had to get over to the theater for her show."

"But wouldn't you have seen her leave?" Ginny asked.

"Not necessarily. There's another door at the back of the lounge." She smiled at them all. "I'll tell her thanks for you."

"Strange behavior," Daniel murmured. "Though not for Goddess, I guess."

"Sh-h-h," Jane whispered. "Let's not be rude." She turned from the doorway, and as she did she noticed something. Goddess's cone-shaped headdress sat in the center of the sofa. "She left part of her ... costume."

The receptionist laughed, unconcerned. "Must have been in a hurry."

"Mmm," Jane said thoughtfully, and without knowing why, suddenly recalled something Goddess had said: *Damsel in distress.*

Twenty-one

But Goddess had not gone to the theater from the screening.

"For all her craziness, she's never missed a performance," Yves Golden told Jane when he called her office the next morning. "She's a total professional. I can't find her anywhere. I've tried all her friends, the crew at the show. No one has any idea. She's—vanished! I just thought you might have some idea where she is."

"I'm truly sorry," Jane said, also concerned, and then had a thought. "Could she have been hurt? Have you tried the hospitals, the police?"

"Done that. No sign of her."

"You know Goddess's world far better than I do, but if anything occurs to me, I'll call you. And please call me if you hear from her."

But Wednesday passed and no one did hear from Goddess. On TV and in the newspapers, it was reported that she had disappeared after last being seen at a private screening of her upcoming film release, *Adam and Eve.* Until she reappeared, performances of her one-woman show, *Goddess of Love*, were canceled, and tickets were being refunded.

Driving home late that afternoon, Jane switched on the radio to hear the news.

"One of our brightest stars didn't shine last night," the announcer began. "Goddess, the singer and actress known for her high shock factor, surprised a packed Broadway theater last night by not appearing for her one-woman show, *Goddess of Love*. The performer, whose actual name is Katherine Hamner and who is the only child of Carl Hamner, the shoe giant, was last seen at a small private screening of her new film, *Adam and Eve*."

Arriving home, Jane called Yves Golden.

"I'm pulling my hair out," he told her. "I've tried everyone I can think of—the people she'll be working with at that publishing house, Corset or whatever it's called. Strange bunch," he added.

"Corsair," Jane corrected him absently. "What about her parents?" she asked, remembering the radio announcement. "Have you called them?"

Golden made a dismissive sound. "They wouldn't know anything. She shut them out of her life years ago. Please, if you hear anything, call me—anytime." And he proceeded to give her his home and cell-phone numbers.

Next Jane called Greenberg. "I'm really getting scared," she told him. "Something must have happened to her. Everyone agrees this just isn't like her."

"Really?" he said, surprised. "I'd have said it's exactly like her."

"Goddess is eccentric, not irresponsible. There's a difference."

"Goddess at large . . ." he said thoughtfully.

"What?"

"That was one of her movies, wasn't it? And she disappears, right?"

"Right . . . So?"

"I don't know. Where did she go in the movie?"

Jane sighed. "Obviously you didn't see it. Her boyfriend finds her masquerading as a flight attendant on a jet to Rome."

"Well, there you are! Maybe she's left the country."

"Maybe. . . . I suppose anything's possible. But she doesn't own any property overseas, as far as I know, and if she has friends overseas, Golden has tried them."

"Has he tried her parents?"

"No. No point. They've been estranged for years, he says."

"Brothers or sisters?"

"She's an only child."

"Oh. Jane, the girl could be *anywhere*. Or on her *way* to anywhere. Give her a little time. She'll pop up somewhere."

"Oh, you're no help," Jane muttered, said good-bye, and hung up.

A moment later the phone rang. It was Greenberg again.

"Jane, I had a thought. If it were up to me, I'd get in touch with Goddess's parents anyway. They may know something. It's worth a try. What have you got to lose?"

Jane pondered this idea. "Nothing, I suppose. Though it's a long shot. But I'll try it. You're right, I've got nothing to lose—if they'll even see me."

As soon as she'd hung up, the phone rang again.

She laughed as she picked it up. "Another idea? I knew it made sense to date a cop."

"Jane? This is Jack Layton. What are you talking about?"

She felt herself blush. "Oh, hello, Jack. How did you get my home number?"

"It was in Holly's Rolodex."

Jane didn't recall ever having given Holly her home number. Holly must simply have looked it up; Jane was, after all, listed in the phone book. That would have been just like Holly.

"Listen, Jane, what are you going to do about this Goddess mess?"

"What am *I* going to do? What are you talking about? We're all doing our best to find her."

"You'd *better* find her. I've got a million and a half riding on this kook. If she doesn't come through with her pop-ups and music chips, I'm holding you personally responsible."

Jane felt her anger rising to the boiling point. "Listen, you hypocritical jerk. You've got nothing riding on this project. I haven't even received the contracts yet, let alone your million and a half. So get off that track. And watch how you speak to me—and how you refer to my client—or I'll see to it that you don't get this book at all. Got it?"

"Find her," Layton seethed, and the line went dead.

"Daniel," Jane called through to the reception room the next morning, "would you please place a call for me?"

He appeared in her doorway, his face perplexed. "Would I what?"

"Place a call. You know—'Please hold for Jane Stuart.' "

"Since when do I place your calls?"

"I just thought it would be a good idea this once."

"Why, who are we calling?"

"Carl Hamner."

"*Carl Hamner?* The sneaker man?"

"Yes. And Goddess's father."

"Oh, yeah, that's right. And you think that if I place the call for you—"

"I'll have a better chance of getting through. His office is in New York."

"Okay," Daniel said, shrugging good-naturedly. "I'll buzz you when I have him on the line."

She waited, watching the phone. After a few moments the intercom lit up. "Jane, I've gotten as far as his personal assistant, a Mrs. Dunlap. I have a feeling that's as far as we're going to get. Do you want to pick up?"

"Yes," Jane said, and lifted the receiver. "Hello, Mrs. Dunlap."

"What is this about, please, Mrs. Stuart?" The woman's voice was cold, all business.

"I'm a literary agent," Jane began. "I'm representing Mr. Hamner's daughter—"

"Mrs. Stuart," Mrs. Dunlap interrupted. "What does this have to do with Mr. Hamner?"

Jane wasn't quite sure what to say. "I . . . You're aware that his daughter has disappeared?"

There was a brief silence on the line. "Yes, we're all aware of that. So?"

"So I would really like to speak to Mr. Hamner about her. Please, could you ask him if he'll see me? Just a brief meeting?"

"You may relay anything you wish to say to Mr. Hamner through me. I will be sure he gets your message."

"I do have things to say to Mr. Hamner," Jane said, "but I can only say them to him. Personally. Things about his daughter. Please. Ask him."

Mrs. Dunlap let out a loud sigh of exasperation. "Hold."

Jane did hold—for two minutes, by her watch—and then Mrs. Dunlap came back on. "Mrs. Stuart, Mr. Hamner would like to speak to you. Hold."

There was a click, ringing, and someone picked up.

"What do you want?" came a man's gruff voice.

"Mr. Hamner?"

"Yes."

"Mr. Hamner, I've been working with your daughter on a book project. I'm a literary agent."

"I know all that—Dunlap just told me. What do you *want?*"

"I want to come in and talk to you about your daughter's disappearance."

"How well do you know Katherine?" he asked.

"Pretty well, I'd say," Jane said, not really sure if this was true.

"Then you know that her mother and I don't see her anymore." There was a touch of sadness in his voice.

"Yes, I do know that. Please, Mr. Hamner, may I come in and see you?"

"Come at one," he said, and hung up.

Carl Hamner had the largest office Jane had ever seen—almost like a small apartment in one vast space—yet Hamner himself was a small man, smaller than he appeared in his photographs. He was almost completely bald, with a round face and large, deep brown eyes that held a touch of sadness. From what she could see of him behind the immense slab of marble that was his desk, he was trim. He wore a blue-and-white-striped dress shirt, a navy tie, and no jacket.

"So you're here," he said before Mrs. Dunlap had even reached the door. "What was it you couldn't have said on the phone?"

"Mr. Hamner, I just felt that if I could talk to you about your daughter—"

His face grew red. "But I *told* you, I don't know where she is. My wife and I have neither seen nor spoken with Katherine for nearly seven years."

Jane sensed pain in his words. "I've come to care for your daughter in the short time I've been working with her. She's a troubled girl, but I'm sure you know that. I'm worried about her, what she might do."

"I know all about my daughter's problems—which, by the way, are none of your business."

Suddenly it occurred to Jane that perhaps Hamner was keeping tabs on Goddess, the way Cecil Willoughby had kept tabs on Daniel. Was this something rich, powerful men routinely did?

Hamner went on, "But there's nothing I can do about those problems, or about her disappearance."

"I just thought that if we put our heads together . . ."

He shook his head impatiently. "This is a waste of time. I've been trying to tell you, Katherine is out of our lives."

"Of her own accord?" Jane asked gently.

"*Of course* of her own accord!" Hamner snapped. "Viveca and I love Katherine, love her dearly. We always have. Katherine knows that. And believe it or not, we are extremely proud of her accomplishments. Hell, we even thought *Doing It* was funny," he said with a rueful laugh, "and she was making fun of us!"

His slim shoulders rose and fell. "We would give anything to see her, to have her back in our lives. But she rejected us and our way of life years ago. Which is ironic, wouldn't you say, since from what I understand, her net worth is rapidly approaching mine."

"Like father, like daughter," Jane mused, and to her surprise, Hamner looked at her sharply.

He gave her a quick half smile. "I'm afraid I can't take any credit for her talents. Katherine was adopted."

Jane just looked at him, thinking about this revelation. She was surprised—surprised at the fact itself, surprised that he would share it with her—but at the same time not so surprised. Perhaps it helped to explain Goddess's rejection of Carl and Viveca Hamner's lifestyle and fortune: They weren't even her real parents.

"Thank you for your time, Mr. Hamner. If you think of any place your daughter might be where Yves Golden might not have looked . . ."

He shook his head. "I really wish I could help. My wife and I are as worried about her as anyone. Remember—for all her act, she is, after all, just a girl."

Jane checked in with Daniel from a pay phone in the lobby of the Hamner Global Building.

"Greenberg called for you," Daniel told her. "He says call him right away. It's urgent."

She dialed Greenberg.

"We've identified the woman hanging in the woods,"

he said. "She lived in a mental institution in Sharon, Connecticut."

"Connecticut!"

"That's right. I'm going there tomorrow to speak with the director of the place. You can come along if you like—I'd enjoy your company—though you realize—"

"I know, we'd be breaking all the rules," Jane said with a laugh. "That's what I like about you, you mad noncomformist."

"Hmm. Can't say I've ever been called that before. Pick you up at your house tomorrow morning at eight?"

"I'll be ready."

It was eleven the next morning when they found Whiteson Institute, a sprawling white mansion at the top of a rolling green lawn surrounded by lush forest.

"I've done a little research on this place," Greenberg said, turning in through the gate. "It's more than sixty years old. Once a private residence. Now it's a facility for moderately to severely retarded people."

He parked in a small lot at the side of the building, and they went in through the front door into a cool dark foyer. At a reception window to the right, Greenberg announced them, and the young man behind the desk buzzed them through a door beside the window and showed them into the office of the Institute's director.

"Donald Brant," he said, shaking their hands. He was a plumpish man of medium height—not unlike Ernie Zabriskie in shape, it occurred to Jane—though Brant was better-looking, with regular, finely cut features and stylishly cut black hair. He invited them to sit in armchairs facing his desk, then sat down.

"Thank you for coming." He looked sad. "I'm grateful to you for helping us find out what happened to Hannah."

"Hannah?" Jane said. "That was her name?"

"That's right."

"And her last name?" Jane asked.

Greenberg shot her a look that said, "Be quiet."

But Brant took no notice. "No one knows Hannah's last name. At least, no one here does. Come to think of it, no one knew much about Hannah."

"Well, what *can* you tell us about her?" Greenberg asked.

"She was moderately retarded," Brant said. "She had the mental capacity of a fourteen-year-old."

"Where did she come from?" Greenberg asked.

"That's just the thing," Brant said, smiling gently. "We don't know. For as long as anyone can remember, Hannah has lived here. The person who's worked here the longest, one of our nurses, has been here sixteen years, and she recalls that when she started working here, Hannah was already here, a girl of about two."

"But *how* did she get here?" Jane asked.

"Again, we don't know. There is no record of who brought Hannah to the Institute. Our theory is that she was brought here by her unwed mother who didn't want her. Over the years, we've tried several times to find out where Hannah came from, but"—he threw his hands out—"we've come up empty." Brant shook his head. "Whoever brought her here, we'll never know for certain."

He leaned back in his chair. "Thirteen years ago, before I came here, there was a fire at the Institute— a bad fire—and a number of patients' files were destroyed. Hannah's file may have been among them.

Or perhaps the file was misplaced, or even taken—
though I can't imagine why anyone would have taken
it." He shrugged. "The oddest thing is that there *is* a
file with Hannah's name on it, but it's empty."

"Empty?" Greenberg said.

"Yes." Brant narrowed his eyes. "I *can* tell you one
thing, though. What very few people here at the Institute
know is that aside from the regular patient files, which
are kept in a room behind that office you passed coming
in, there is a special place where we keep files of an
especially 'sensitive' nature."

Jane shook her head. "I don't understand."

"Often—more often than most people realize—our
patients come from wealthy, influential families, or are
relatives of celebrities who don't want it known that
they have people here. After it was discovered that the
woman you found was our Hannah, it occurred to me
to check this special file, just in case there was something
there on her. We'd never thought of doing this before—
I don't think anyone ever imagined that Hannah would
fit into the 'sensitive' category—but I thought it was
worth checking. To my surprise, there *was* a file marked
simply 'Hannah,' and there was something in it."

He opened the lap drawer of his desk and drew out
a yellowed newspaper clipping. "This. Careful," he said,
handing it to Greenberg. "As you can see by the date,
it's nineteen years old."

Greenberg held the clipping between him and Jane
so they could both read it. The clipping, which contained no newspaper's name, bore a story whose headline read: SENTENCED SOCIALITE COMMITS SUI-
CIDE.

Jane began to read. The story told of a scandal, a

murder, right here in Sharon, involving one of the town's most prominent couples, Anthony and Rosamond Oppenheim. Anthony, the article said, had made his fortune in hotels. Rosamond, before marrying Anthony, had been a respected stage actress.

According to the article, one day a servant in the Oppenheim mansion found Anthony Oppenheim dying. He had been poisoned, and his death was slow and agonizing. Rosamond Oppenheim, the beautiful socialite, was found guilty of murdering her husband. There had been rumors in the Oppenheims' circle that Anthony had been having an affair and had demanded a divorce from Rosamond; that Rosamond had poisoned Anthony in a possessive rage—for it was widely known that she loved Anthony fiercely. A friend of Rosamond was anonymously quoted as saying that if Rosamond couldn't have Anthony, no one would.

Rosamond Oppenheim was sentenced to life in prison. However, before she could begin to serve her sentence, she shot herself, presumably out of grief and guilt and at the unbearable prospect of spending the rest of her life behind bars.

The story finished by saying that the Oppenheims had two daughters: Agnes, thirteen; and Elaine, five. Their fate was unknown, since the Oppenheims had no family to take the girls in.

Jane looked up at Brant as Greenberg handed back the clipping. "Was one of the Oppenheim girls Hannah?" she asked.

"No," Greenberg broke in, "that wouldn't make any sense. Hannah was about eighteen. The Oppenheims' daughters would be thirty-one and twenty-three now."

"Then what could this story have to do with Hannah?" Jane asked. "Why do you think it was in her file?"

Brant shook his head. "More that we don't know. But there must have been some connection, or else why would the clipping have been in Hannah's file?"

"It could have gotten in there by mistake," Jane suggested.

"Possible," Brant said, "but highly unlikely. Few people besides myself even have access to those files. They go for years without even being opened."

Greenberg asked, "Do you have any idea what she was doing in Shady Hills? She told someone she met there that she planned to meet someone in town."

Brant shook his head. "I have no idea who she could have been referring to."

"But how did she get there?" Jane asked.

"That I think I can tell you." Brant looked pleased to be able to tell them *something*. "When the weather is nice, our patients have outdoor time. Hannah's was every morning at ten. On the day she disappeared, she simply waited for her outdoor time, walked into the woods, found a space in the chain-link fence that encircles the Institute's property, and left! As for how she got to your town, I can only imagine she got rides from people—hitchhiked.

"As to why—to that question we have no answers. I wish I knew. I was very fond of Hannah. She was a sweet, trusting girl, easy to get along with. The Institute has been experimenting with smaller group homes here in Sharon, and we had planned to try Hannah in one of them." Brant's eyes grew moist and he shook his head. "I can't imagine what kind of evil person would have wanted to hurt such an innocent soul."

They sat silently for a moment.

Then Jane had an idea. "Where did the Oppenheims live?"

"Right here in Sharon," Brant replied, looking puzzled. "It says so right here in the article."

"Yes, I know, but *where* in Sharon?"

Greenberg was looking at her strangely, as if wondering why she was asking that.

"The Oppenheim estate is at the other end of town," Brant said. "It's right at the edge of the golf course." He looked at Greenberg. "But you won't find any clues there. The place has been abandoned since the scandal—that's almost twenty years ago."

They thanked Brant for his time and went out into the sunshine, painfully bright after the Institute's shadowy gloom.

They rode in silence along the streets that would take them back to the highway.

Abruptly Jane sat up straight, looking out the window. "This must be the golf course he mentioned."

"Must be," Greenberg said cheerfully.

"Stop the car."

"What? Why?"

"I want to find the Oppenheim estate."

"There's no point. It's deserted, abandoned. Besides, it has nothing to do with Hannah."

"I know all that, but I want to see it anyway."

Greenberg rolled his eyes, but he didn't say no. They had to ask for directions twice, despite being so near the golf course, but eventually they did find the estate, which was accessible by means of an overgrown drive through woods. They came out onto a lawn grown high with weeds, beyond which stood a massive Georgian-style mansion, four imposing floors of brick, with several clusters of tall chimneys reaching to the sky. Unquestionably the house had been magnificent once, but now it looked as if it might crumble at any moment, or be strangled by the ivy that had crept up its walls and taken over.

Greenberg pulled the car to a stop.

"I want to walk around," Jane said, and got out.

Greenberg got out, too. "We're wasting our time," he said plaintively.

She ignored him, wandering deeper into the estate.

It was hard to tell what had been what, with all the weeds and shrubbery that now grew everywhere. The air had grown hot and dry. As Jane tramped slowly through the brush, the loud keening and chittering of cicadas in the woods around the estate gave the whole place a sad, lonely feeling.

Behind the house she found what had been the swimming pool—not very large but deep, dust-dry, weeds and small trees pushing up through wide fissures in the concrete of the sides and bottom.

She glanced up at the house. Not a single window remained intact; most were gaping holes, others retained jagged shards of filthy glass.

She released a deep sigh. Why had she wanted to come here, to see this place? She herself did not even know.

"I'm ready to leave now," she told Greenberg, who started back toward the car. Jane tromped after him.

"Can't say I see the point of that," he said, getting behind the wheel and switching the air-conditioning on full blast. It had grown quite warm.

"Does there have to be a point to everything?" Jane asked pleasantly. "I was curious, that's all."

He shrugged, doing a K-turn and heading back toward the drive through the woods. Jane gazed out at the house, the overgrown lawn, the dark surrounding wall of trees.

Something whitish among the trees caught her eye.

"Stop."

He braked. "Now what?"

"Look," she said, pointing, "just beyond that row of pines. There's a little house or something."

"Probably a garage or guesthouse." He took his foot off the brake.

"No, wait. I want to get out for a minute."

He opened his mouth as if to protest, then seemed to think better of it and smiled. "Fine. But this time I'll wait in here where it's nice and cool, if you don't mind."

"No, not at all," she said, ignoring his sarcastic tone because she wanted to see what that little white building was. She got out and walked around the pines, the structure coming into view. It was a cottage, not a garage; perhaps a small caretaker's cottage. Oddly, it didn't look as forlorn as the big house. The lawn, though scruffy, appeared to have been cut in the recent past, and there were curtains in the windows at either side of the front door. Jane walked up a crude flagstone path and knocked on the front door. It opened immediately. Jane jumped.

"What is it?" It was a middle-aged woman, skinny, with limp brown hair and a yellowish, unhealthy-looking face. She wore a beige-cotton housedress and grimy terry scuffs. "I saw you come up. Saw you snooping around, for that matter. What is it?'' she asked again, her tone resentful.

''I—I'm sorry to bother you,'' Jane said in her most charming manner. ''I wonder if I might ask you a question.''

''Don't know till you ask it.''

''Did you know the Oppenheims, the people who once lived in the big house?''

The woman looked Jane up and down appraisingly. ''What do you want to know for? Who are you?''

''My name is Jane Stuart. I'm not from around here. I'm from New Jersey, actually. But I'm trying to track down someone who knew the Oppenheims, and I wondered if perhaps you knew them.''

''Well, *I* didn't,'' the woman said, ''but my father did, for all the good it did him.'' Her expression was one of disgust; she looked as if she would have spit in different company.

''Your father, he was the Oppenheims' . . .''

''He was their caretaker.''

''And he's passed away?'' Jane asked gently.

''No, he ain't passed away, but he might as well have. He's in a nursing home at the other end o' town. The *poor* part of town. What'do you wanna know for?'' she asked again.

''As I said, I'm trying to find someone who knew the Oppenheims.'' Jane tried to hide her excitement. ''It's regarding a young woman who disappeared recently from Whiteson Institute.''

The woman looked at Jane as if she were crazy. ''What the hell's my dad got to do with Whiteson? I think you came to the wrong place, lady.'' She started to close the door.

"No, please, wait!"

The door stopped. The woman tapped one scuff.

"Do you think I could speak to your father? I promise I won't bother or upset him."

The woman considered this for a moment. "You can do as you please," she said uncaringly. "I don't see what one thing's got to do with the other, but if you want to talk to my dad, you're welcome to try." A sly little smile curled her lips, as if there was something she hadn't told Jane.

"Try?" Jane echoed.

The woman nodded. "For one thing, he's eighty-three. For another, he's got Alzheimer's—bad. It's a wonder he's still alive. He goes 'in and out,' you might say. It's the Sunnymead Rest Home. Like I said, other end o' town. Have fun."

"And his name?" Jane asked quickly before the door could shut all the way.

"Mangano," the woman said. "Victor Mangano. I'd tell you to give him my love, but most days he doesn't even know who I am." And the door shut completely.

Jane walked thoughtfully back to the car. When she got in, Greenberg still had the air-conditioning on full blast, which felt good against her face, and he was listening to country music on the radio.

"You like that?" she asked him in a scandalized tone.

"Well, yeah, some of it?" he answered defensively. "What does that mean—that there's no future for us?"

She laughed and switched off the radio.

"Hey!"

"Sorry, I should have asked. May I turn off the radio? I want to talk to you."

"Yes." He waited, smiling patiently.

"There's one more place I would like to go, please. It's called the Sunnymead Rest Home. It's at the other end of town. I don't know exactly where, but I'm sure we can find it."

Wordlessly, Greenberg put the car in gear and started through the tunnel of trees.

"Victor?" the nurse said cheerfully, pushing open the door to the old man's room. "Victor, some friends of yours are here to see you."

Greenberg had taken issue with Jane's wanting to lie about who they were, but Jane had insisted that unless they said they were old friends of Mangano's, they probably wouldn't get in to see him.

"Victor?" the nurse repeated, but the white-haired, withered old man in the chair facing the blank TV screen did not move.

Jane looked around the tiny room. Its walls were covered with crucifixes and other religious artifacts.

The nurse beckoned to Jane and Greenberg to come closer. "See, Victor, two old friends of yours came here specially to see you."

Suddenly, as if awakening from a trance, the old man turned to Jane and smiled a lovely smile, his pale blue eyes rheumy, like those of a loving old dog.

The nurse approached Jane. "He loves having visitors," she whispered. "His daughter—well, I'm sure you know her—she doesn't come as often as she might. It upsets her that he doesn't know who she is most of the time. But I still think she owes him visits. He is, after all, her father." She turned to the old man. "Now, Victor, aren't you going to say hello to your friends?"

And to Jane, "Don't be upset if he doesn't recognize you—he rarely does."

Mangano's sweet expression didn't change. He said nothing.

"We've just been to see your daughter," Jane said, and out of the corner of her eye she saw the nurse frown in slight puzzlement. *Your daughter*, Jane realized, was not how someone who knew Mangano would have referred to her; someone who really knew Mangano would have used her name. But Jane didn't know her name.

The old man's face darkened at the mention of his daughter. The smile vanished, replaced by a distasteful sneer. "She never brings me candy," he said, and turned to the nurse. "She never brings me candy." He turned back to Jane and Greenberg, who had come up beside her. "Did you bring me candy?"

"Now, Victor," the nurse said, stepping a little closer, "you know you're not allowed candy." She turned to Jane and, shielding her mouth, said, "He's diabetic."

Jane nodded her understanding. "Victor, I'm afraid I don't have candy. I've just come to talk to you." She waited until she was sure she had his complete attention. "About Hannah."

At the sound of the name, Victor Mangano's face changed dramatically. He shot Jane a sharp, shrewd look. "It wasn't her fault!" he shouted at her.

Jane jumped, startled at the old man's outburst. Beside her, Greenberg leaned closer, his face intent.

"It wasn't whose fault?" Jane asked ever so gently, but he didn't seem to hear her. He just kept staring at her, his eyes narrowed to wet slits.

"Victor . . ." Jane went on. "The file, Victor. Why did you take all the papers out?"

Greenberg turned to Jane and gave her a baffled look, but Jane ignored him, for the old man clearly knew exactly what Jane was talking about. The look with which he now regarded her was the look of someone who has been found out.

"Because," he said, now sounding completely lucid— as if they'd been having a perfectly ordinary conversation, "I couldn't let them blame Hannah for what happened. The children," he said, leaning toward Jane earnestly, "the poor children. It's never *their* fault."

"No, it isn't," Jane agreed. "So you emptied the file so no one would know."

The old man looked down guiltily.

"You moonlighted at Whiteson?" Jane said. "Extra work cleaning, tidying up . . ."

"Please!" Mangano burst out again. "Please don't tell Mr. Anthony. Mr. Anthony would be mad as hell if he knew. He'd probably fire me. But it was *good* I worked there nights," the old man insisted, "or how would I have gotten to the file? How could I have kept people from knowing what happened?"

Jane leaned closer. "*What* happened?" she asked, urging him, but to her dismay he visibly sank back into his former state, simply staring.

"What about Agnes?" Jane persisted.

"Jane," Greenberg said quietly beside her, "I think we should go."

"No," Jane said. "Victor, what about Agnes? Was it *her* fault?"

Once again Mangano looked at her sharply, his look

a knowing one. "We tried to help her, too," he said, his eyes somewhere far away. "But she ran away."

"And Elaine?" Jane asked.

Mangano's face softened. "The little one," he said tenderly. Suddenly he turned on Greenberg. "Did *you* bring me any candy?"

The nurse stepped forward. "I think that's enough visiting," she said with forced cheerfulness.

Reluctantly, Jane followed Greenberg and the nurse out of the room.

"You lied to me," the nurse whispered fiercely when they were all out in the corridor. "You're not friends of his. You don't even know him. I oughta call the police."

"We are the police," Greenberg said, surprising Jane, and he showed the nurse his badge—quickly enough, Jane noticed, that she would not have realized just what police he was referring to.

"I'm sorry," the nurse said, respectful now. "You should have just told me at the beginning."

"No problem," Greenberg said solemnly.

"Does anyone ever visit him?" Jane asked.

The nurse seemed surprised by this question. "No . . . except for Jenny—that's his daughter. But she only comes once in a while, like I told you."

They thanked her and left.

"Well, you seemed to push a few buttons there," Greenberg said, guiding the car down I-80, "but all in all, I don't think those last two detours did us any good."

"On the contrary," Jane said. She saw Greenberg turn to her, waiting for her to elaborate, but she didn't.

Instead she said, "I wonder if Arthur realized that Hannah was mentally retarded."

Greenberg looked surprised at this sudden change of subject, but went along with it. "I already thought of that," he said. "As soon as I found out Hannah's identity, I spoke again to Arthur—who, don't forget, is himself mildly retarded. I asked him if he noticed anything 'different' about the girl. He said she acted 'kind of girlish,' but he thought she was just teasing him."

"Teasing him how? Sexually? Or making fun of him?"

"I asked him that, too. He didn't know. Or if he did have any idea, he wouldn't say."

Jane gazed out at the passing trees. "What earthly reason could Hannah have had for going to Shady Hills?" she wondered aloud, her heart breaking for this poor young woman.

They rode in silence for some time, and then Greenberg, lost in thought, gave a little laugh. "I have to compliment you on your interrogation skills."

Jane laughed, too. "I'm no detective."

"But you are. It was you, don't forget, who figured out what happened to your nanny, Marlene."

Troubled at the memory, Jane nodded in concession.

Greenberg said, "That was when you were seeing Roger Haines."

"Yes." Another troubling memory. Roger had been her agency's biggest author. The failure of that relationship had taught her the folly of becoming romantically involved with clients.

"You said you saw Roger and me at Whipped Cream, arguing." She laughed ruefully. "We did that a lot."

"I'm glad you're not seeing him anymore." Greenberg stared straight ahead as he drove. "That day you came to the police station to talk to me about Marlene, I . . . knew you were someone special."

"Thank you," she said softly.

"Tell me about your husband," he said gently.

"Kenneth," she said, gazing out the window at a jagged outcropping of rock at the side of the highway but seeing Kenneth's handsome face. "He was a wonderful man. I know people say that all the time, but Kenneth really was. He was bright, fun, generous, loving . . . yet he had no idea he was any of these.

"One day about two and a half years ago he went into New York for a meeting with a couple of editors, and after the meeting he was hit by a truck. I . . . I couldn't believe it when they told me. I said, 'But I just saw him,' which was, of course, a ridiculous thing to say."

"No, it wasn't," Greenberg said, and reached over and gently covered Jane's hand on the seat with his own.

"It hurts so bad," he said, "that you don't think it will ever stop. You don't see how you can go on."

She looked at him.

Gazing straight ahead at the road, he said, "When I moved to Shady Hills I met a woman—Veronica, her name was—though she liked to be called Ronni. She worked as a hostess at Eleanor's. Maybe you remember her."

"Yes, I do."

"We had so much in common. We got engaged, set the wedding a year away so we could do it up right, get our families all involved." He laughed at the memory, moisture in his eyes. "Then one day when we were . . . when we were making love, I felt something in one of her breasts. A lump. She said it was nothing, but I convinced her to see a doctor.

"Anyway," he said with a sigh, "the doctors removed the lump, and it was malignant. She went through chemo and radiation, and she was sick as a dog all during it, but then it was over and she was her old self again—almost. There was always this nagging doubt, always this reminder that she would never be completely out of the woods. Always her appointments for tests to make sure it was really gone."

"And was it?" Jane asked, already knowing the answer.

"No. After one of those sets of tests, they told her the cancer had metastasized, that they hadn't gotten all of it. You know the story. The next two years were the longest two years of my life. When she died, she was in my arms, kissing me. She was twenty-six."

Jane hated to take her hand out from under his, but she had to fish in her bag for tissues, and finding them, she wiped at her eyes.

"I'm so sorry," she said. "I'm so sorry." And she put her hand back on his, and they rode like that for a long time, saying nothing.

They stopped at a diner in Paterson Greenberg liked for a late lunch.

"What will happen now?" Jane asked, her club sandwich untouched before her.

Greenberg shrugged regretfully. "I'm afraid I'm probably going to have to arrest Ernie Zabriskie."

Jane's jaw fell and she shook her head vehemently. "But you can't! Stanley, I'm telling you, it's not just because I'm so fond of Louise and this would positively destroy her. It's that I know Ernie. He's no angel, believe me, but I know in my heart he's no killer, either. He couldn't have murdered Hannah.''

"Then who did?" Greenberg asked simply.

Jane had no answer.

She still had no answer late that night as she lay in bed and drifted into a fitful half sleep in which bits of information, troubling things people had said, echoed and connected, combining to form a message: that the answer to who was responsible for hanging Hannah had been presented to her. It was simply up to her to see it.

In the first hours of the morning she sat up, her eyes open wide, her subconscious now before her. And then she shut them again, for now she *had* seen the answer; now she knew the truth about who had killed poor Hannah.

And that truth was too painful to bear.

Twenty-two

Jane's head pounded and it was too hot in her room. She'd slept badly, had never really fallen completely asleep. She rolled over and stared at the ceiling, pondering what to do with the burden of her terrible knowledge.

At that moment, Winky shot into the room and across the wooden floor, her feet scampering so fast they skidded on the area rug. She jumped onto the bed, landing smack in the middle of Jane's belly, and just as quickly bounded off again, rocketing to the dresser, darting to the window, and then back to the door and out to the hallway.

"Winky!" came Florence's voice. "Come back, my girl! I'm sorry, I will not use it again!"

Frowning, Jane got out of bed, put on her robe, and went out to the hall to see what was going on. Winky was nowhere in sight, but Florence stood at the bottom of the stairs. She wore a pretty violet dress that Jane knew was one of Florence's church dresses. Florence belonged to the same church as Jane and Nick—St. John's Episcopal Church on Renton Avenue—though Jane wasn't as conscientious about attending services as Florence was.

"I'm so sorry, missus, it is all my fault. I forgot about the hand cream. I should have just thrown it out when you told me what the vet said, but I do like it, and my mother sent it to me."

Jane was about to tell her it was all right, that she should just put the hand cream away somewhere where she wouldn't use it accidentally, but Florence had already turned toward the kitchen. "I will throw it away right now, missus. I will do it just now."

Watching Florence bustling across the foyer toward the kitchen, Jane abruptly stopped. "You're going to church . . ." she said, more thinking aloud than speaking to Florence.

Florence turned, smiling. "Yes, missus."

"And the church bazaar is today, isn't it?"

"Yes," Florence said, her eyes wide, "and you'd better not forget that, or a certain little someone"—she tilted her head toward the family room—"will be greatly disappointed."

"You're going?"

"Absolutely. I have made six of my coconut cakes to donate to the bake sale."

"How nice," Jane said vaguely.

Florence continued to the kitchen, and Jane walked down the stairs and followed. As Jane entered the kitchen, Nick appeared from the family room. "I'm hungry. Can I have some cereal?"

"*May* I have some cereal." Jane got out the Cheerios and milk. "Florence," she said, getting down a bowl from the cupboard and pouring the cereal into it, "I meant to thank you for taking care of Nick yesterday while I was in Connecticut. Don't let me forget to pay you extra for that."

"Will do, missus." Florence smiled appreciatively. Then her face grew troubled. "Have the police come any closer to finding who killed that poor woman?" Then she remembered Nick was sitting there and covered her mouth with her hand.

"Florence, it's no big deal," Nick said casually, his mouth full of Cheerios. Some milk ran down his chin and suddenly Winky appeared on the chair beside him. "Here, Wink, lick this off," he said, leaning toward her, and she happily obliged, her tongue flicking his chin. He giggled.

Both women watched in horror.

Jane stepped forward. "Winky!"

The cat scampered off the chair and out of the room.

"Nicholas! Don't you ever let me see you doing that again. And what do you mean, it's no big deal? A person *died.*"

He shrugged. "I know it, Mom. I found her, remember?"

"I do remember," she said, troubled at the memory. "All the more reason why you of all people should take this matter a little more seriously." She realized that by the end of this speech she was yelling and that she was breathing hard. Nick stared at her, brows lowered.

"Mom, you don't have to get so upset about it."

"Missus?" Florence approached her. "Are you . . . all right?"

"Yes, I'm fine. I— Never mind." Jane gave Nick a last disapproving look, then turned to Florence. "In answer to your question, yes, I'm pleased to tell you that the police have found a very important clue, something the murderer left behind at the place where the young woman was living." She watched Florence closely as she spoke.

Florence was watching her, too. "A clue? What clue is that?"

"I really can't say."

"I had not heard that the police had found the place where the young woman was living," Florence said.

"Oh, yes," Jane said, knowing she was overstepping her authority—and betraying Greenberg's confidence—by revealing this. "They've found a vital clue to the killer's identity."

"Really?" Florence said.

"Wow," Nick said. "Do you know where this place is, Mom?"

"No," Jane replied, "not exactly. But I do know that for now, everything must be left exactly as it was found, in order not to disturb the evidence."

"Well." Florence, looking preoccupied, grabbed her purse from the counter. "On that note, I must run to Mass. I will see you both at the bazaar, yes?"

"Yes." Jane, smiling, watched her leave. "Nick, how would you like to play at Aaron's this morning?"

"Okay," he said with a shrug, and headed for the family room.

"Good." Jane found Aaron's number in the little directory she kept by the phone and dialed. Aaron's mother, a consistently bouncy woman named Eloise, answered.

"How are you, Jane? Gorgeous day."

"Yes, it is indeed. Eloise, I was wondering if you could

do me a favor. There's something I have to do this morning—kind of an emergency—and Florence has gone to church. Could Nick play with Aaron at your house?"

"Of course! We just love Nicholas. Aaron!" she hollered. "Nick's coming over."

"Cool!" came Aaron's response in the background.

"Great," Jane said. "Thanks."

"No prob! In fact, Jane, I was planning to take Aaron to the bazaar around lunchtime and would be thrilled to take Nick, too."

"Even better. I'm going too, after my errands. I'll meet up with you there."

"Perfect. Jane, I hope everything's all right. . . ."

"Fine," Jane assured her. "Just something I've got to do."

Jane hung up, her smile vanishing, and looked around the kitchen thoughtfully. She walked to the sink and opened the cupboards on each side. Then, shaking her head, she knelt down and opened the cabinet under the sink. There she rummaged among bottles of dishwashing liquid and piles of sponges, still not finding what she was looking for. She stood up again.

"Nick," she called. "Do you know where Florence keeps her hand cream?"

He appeared in the doorway. "The *bad* hand cream? She said she was going to throw it away."

"And did she?"

"Yeah, I saw her toss it in here." He crossed to the wastebasket and lifted off the lid. "See?" he said, pointing to the white glass jar lying atop the trash.

"Good," she said, and smiled. "Just making sure. You know how crazy it makes poor Wink."

He nodded, looking a little confused, and returned to the TV.

The minute he was out of sight, Jane grabbed the jar from the trash. Too late she realized that Winky was standing only a few feet away; seeing the jar, she let out a yowl and shot from the room.

Jane picked up her bag from the counter, opened it, and dropped the jar of hand cream inside. She thought for a moment, then returned to the cabinet under the sink and withdrew a pair of yellow latex dishwashing gloves. She dropped them into her bag, too, and placed the bag back on the floor by the door.

She walked into the family room. "Brush your teeth and comb your hair, sweetie, while I take a fast shower and get dressed. Then I'll drive you to Aaron's."

Jane pulled up in front of Aaron's house.

"Have fun. I'll see you at the bazaar."

Before closing the car door, Nick paused and peered in at her. "Mom, do you know you're acting really weird?"

Why was she always so transparent? Or was it only with Nick? She gave him a wide-eyed smile, all innocence. "Why, what do you mean, darling?"

"Mom," he said, looking at her shrewdly, "where are you going now?"

"I told you, to do errands."

"What errands?"

Her patience was running out. Besides, she had to get done what she had to get done. "That's my business," she said, all attempts at innocence abandoned. "Now please close the door. I'd walk you up to the house, but I'm in a hurry. I won't leave till you go in."

"Okay!" he said, slammed the door, and ran up the front path to the house. When Eloise had opened the door and waved, Jane drove off.

Grimly determined, she drove down Oakmont Avenue and onto Packer Road, which she followed into the village center. Here she turned onto Plunkett Lane. She passed the gate to Hydrangea House and kept on going. Finally, the road ended at Hadley Pond. She stopped, grabbed her bag, and got out.

It was a beautiful warm Sunday morning, the kind of morning when people might be walking in the woods or fishing in the pond. She hoped not. She found the beginning of the path between the two pines and started along it, watching for people, listening. She saw no one, heard only the singing of the birds in the high canopy of foliage.

She still had seen no one when she reached the wall of rock, squeezed between the bushes, and stooped to enter the cave.

In the daytime it was easy to see without artificial light. Nothing appeared to have been touched since Greenberg had brought her there. With a grim sigh, she knelt and opened her bag. She withdrew the latex gloves and put them on. Then she took out Florence's jar of hand cream, twisted open the lid, and scooped out a dollop of the white cream with two gloved fingers.

She began directly to her left, with a wax-paper wrapper that might once have contained a sandwich. Very carefully, she smeared the paper with a thin layer of hand cream. Then she replaced the wrapper exactly where she had found it.

She repeated this process with every item in the cave, moving methodically around clockwise so as not to miss anything; each item received a thin layer of hand cream and was replaced. Though Jane guessed that the whole process had taken more than twenty minutes, when she was finished she was confident she had overlooked nothing—not the Coke cans, the bits of plastic wrap and aluminum foil. The last item to which she applied the hand cream was Louise's Irish Chain quilt. That took longer, of course, because it was large, and Jane didn't want to miss any part of it.

This done, she took one last look around the cave, frowned at the thought of what would now undoubtedly happen, and hurried out, looking all around to make sure she was still alone before starting back along the path to her car.

At the corner of Plunkett Lane and Packer Road, Jane pulled up to a trash receptacle, got out, and discarded the gloves and the hand cream. Then she drove home.

When she entered the house, the light on the answering machine was blinking. It was Greenberg.

"Jane." He sounded angry. "Call me. Immediately."

She did.

"What the hell do you think you're doing?" he demanded.

"What do you mean?"

"Telling people we've found a 'vital clue' to the killer's identity in the cave. We agreed you wouldn't even tell anyone I'd *shown* you that cave. What vital clue? People all over town are buzzing about it."

She smiled; it was working. "First of all, Stanley, I never said it was a cave; I said only 'the place where the woman was living in the woods.' Only the killer knows it's a cave. And as for there being a vital clue, there is one—now."

"What is that supposed to mean?"

She decided simply not to answer that question.

"Jane, I don't understand this. What," he repeated, "do you think you're doing?"

"Flushing out a murderer," she said softly, then added quickly, "I'll see you at the bazaar."

She had no sooner hung up than the phone rang. It was Daniel.

"You going to the bazaar?" he asked brightly. "Laura and I are heading over now."

"Good. Yes, I'm going."

"Any word from Goddess?"

"No," Jane answered fretfully, and told him about her meeting with Carl Hamner, Goddess's father.

"On another front, though," she said, "the murder of the girl in the woods may very well be close to being solved."

"Oh?"

"Yes. Apparently the police have found a vital clue the killer left where the girl was living in the woods. Ooh, I'd better get cleaned up. See you at the church."

She did wash her face, applied a little makeup, made sure there were no leaves in her hair, washed her hands to make sure they bore no traces of the hand cream. Then, shortly before noon, she went in search of Winky.

"There you are, Wink," she said, finding the cat curled up in the middle of her bed. Gently she scooped her up and carried her downstairs; then, to the dismay of Winky, who never went outside, Jane carried her out to the car and deposited her on the backseat.

"Mwaaaah!" Winky protested in bafflement as Jane pulled out onto Lilac Way and down the hill, taking Grange Road to Packer and then onto Renton Avenue.

Halfway down the street on the right, the church came into view. The bazaar was already bustling—rows of colorful booths with multicolored flags fluttering in the breeze, people talking and laughing as they walked up and down the aisles.

Jane drove into the church parking lot and found an empty space toward the back. Getting out, she picked up Winky and, holding her firmly so that she couldn't run away, headed for the bazaar on the church's front lawn. She received several surprised looks and puzzled smiles from people who had never seen her with Winky before.

"Mom!"

She turned and found Nick in front of her.

"What are you doing with Wink?"

Jane smiled. "I decided she needed some of this gorgeous air. Don't you think she's cooped up too much?"

He looked at her strangely. "Told you you were acting weird. Come on," he said to Aaron, who was just behind him, and the two boys ran off together.

Then Jane noticed Eloise standing nearby, smiling her too-sweet smile. "Hello, Jane. How did your errands go?"

"Fine, thank you, Eloise. And thanks again for taking Nick."

"No prob! He's a complete pleasure." Up to this point Eloise had clearly been trying to ignore Winky. Now she looked at her, puzzlement in her eyes. "Do you . . . often take your cat out like this?"

"No, this is the first time," Jane said.

"Ah," Eloise said, and when no more information was forthcoming she started to back away. "See you later!"

"Yes, see you!" Jane called to her, and started down one of the bazaar's aisles, a long row of booths offering games of skill and chance, snacks and beverages, and homemade craft items.

"Okay, Wink," Jane whispered into the cat's mottled ear. "It's time to catch a killer."

Twenty-three

Who in Shady Hills didn't attend the annual church bazaar? Jane wondered. It seemed the whole village had turned out for this, a favorite event.

Thumping dance music blared from a tall speaker that had been set up to the right of the church stairs, and with a pang of chagrin Jane realized that the commanding voice of the singer was that of Goddess. "Don't ever be afraid to fly-y-y-y!" came her vibrant tones.

This only hardened Jane's resolve. She made her way down the aisle, stroking Winky's soft fur. By then Winky seemed to have become accustomed to being outside, and sat, quite calm and contented, in Jane's arms.

"Hello, Jane," came Rhoda's voice from behind, and Jane turned. Ginny was with her. "Jane . . ." Rhoda eyed Winky warily. "Why are you carrying that cat?"

"This is *my* cat," Jane said.

Rhoda rolled her eyes. "Well, *obviously*. But what are you doing with him here?"

"Her."

Ginny laughed. "Forget it, Rhoda. Jane's in one of her kooky moods."

Jane threw back her head and laughed. "That's it. One of my kooky moods." Suddenly she thrust Winky at the two women, who drew back slightly in surprise. "Pat her," Jane invited them. Now looking at Jane as if she were slightly mad, Rhoda and Ginny each gave Winky a tentative stroke.

"Kooky mood is right," Rhoda muttered, grabbing Ginny by the arm and pulling her away. "See you later, Jane."

"Yes, later!" Jane said, and moved on.

Two aisles over, she spotted Doris with Arthur. Doris was examining a hand-painted glass cake plate, while Arthur stood very still beside her, smiling placidly.

Then Jane saw Daniel and Laura in the next aisle, near a beverage booth. They looked up, saw her, and waved cheerily. Jane moved on, stopping to browse at a table displaying handmade silver jewelry. Just as she realized she thought it was all quite ugly, she also realized she recognized it as the work of Rob, Ginny's boyfriend. Jane looked up and found herself looking into his pale gray eyes. He was smirking.

"Hi, Jane. What's with the cat?" he said, his head bobbing in that annoying way he had, his ponytail jiggling.

"What's with the cat? She's my cat," Jane said, realizing she sounded inane but not caring. In past years she'd always bought something from Rob, for Ginny's sake, but this time she didn't think she would. Ginny and Rob were on the rocks, and besides, Jane had something important to do. "See ya!"

She walked on and came face to face with Daniel. He

carried two tall cardboard drink cups. He saw Winky and opened his mouth to speak, but Jane beat him to it.

"I'm thinking of making her an indoor/outdoor cat. Why don't you pat her?"

"Jane," he said, looking at her strangely, "I *can't* pat her—I've got my hands full of drinks. One of which is for you, by the way."

"How thoughtful. Which one?"

"This one, of course." He handed her the cup filled with the dark fizzing beverage. "Your favorite—Diet Coke. I'm having this strawberry papaya swizzle."

"And welcome to it," she said, taking her Diet Coke. "How much do I owe you?"

"Don't be silly," he said.

"Thanks. Now pat Winky."

He studied her a moment. "Okay." And he dutifully stroked Winky's fuzzy head. She gave a little purr and closed her eyes.

"She always has liked you," Jane said, and took a little sip of her drink, grateful for the refreshingly cold carbonation on this day that had grown quite warm.

Daniel continued to pet Winky. "I thought you'd sworn you'd never let her go outside. Wild animals and all that."

She shrugged and gave a little smile. "I decided that didn't seem quite fair. Why should she be deprived of this?" She indicated the lovely day around them. "And she's got her claws. I think she'd do surprisingly well defending herself in the wild, wouldn't you, Wink?" And she squeezed the cat affectionately, giving her a little shake. "You always *want* to go outside, don't you, Wink?" She looked at Daniel. "This is a trial run."

"Ah," he said, and they walked together to the end of the aisle. Three aisles over, close to the church, Jane was surprised to see Louise and Ernie, perusing what appeared to be a display of embroidered linens. In the next aisle over, Laura was now at a game booth, throwing back her head and laughing as she tossed colored plastic rings at tiers of goldfish bowls.

"Let's go cheer her on," Daniel suggested playfully.

"Great idea." Jane followed him.

But when they reached the end of their aisle, Jane was overcome by a wave of dizziness. "Oh," she said, wobbling a little.

Daniel looked at her, his face concerned. "Are you all right?"

The dizziness, to her surprise, didn't stop; it kept coming, the bazaar beginning to rise and fall sickeningly around her. She steadied herself on Daniel's arm.

"Jane, what is it? Are you sick?"

Then, mercifully, the world righted itself again. "That was so strange," she said, making an effort to hold on to a now-squirming Winky. "I didn't get much sleep last night. I'm just plain overtired."

He nodded, watching her carefully. "And a lot has happened lately. It's inevitable that you would feel the strain. I know *I* have been."

"I'm sure it's all of the above."

"Would you like to go inside the church and sit for a few minutes?"

"That won't be necessary." But then the spinning began again, worse this time. "Actually, yes, I think that would be a good idea."

Daniel took her arm and led her toward the old white building. They walked up the four steps and Daniel pulled on one of the doors. When it held fast, he tried the other, but it too appeared to be locked.

"Locked," came a man's voice behind them, and they turned to see the Reverend Lockridge himself smiling up at them. "Hello, Jane . . . Daniel. We always keep the church locked during the bazaar," he explained. "But if you need the facilities, we've got several Porta-Johns set up behind the building."

The spinning grew faster. Even the music, another Goddess dance tune, seemed to spin with the bazaar, the looming white church. Jane suddenly felt a wave of nausea rise in her throat and literally prayed she wouldn't vomit in front of the Reverend Lockridge.

But he had moved on and was already deep in conversation with an elderly couple.

"Daniel," she said, still holding his arm, "I think I'll just sit in my car for a minute, take it easy. That's all I need." A thought occurred to her. "I hope I'm not coming down with something. She started down the steps, Daniel assisting her. "Would you do me a favor?" she asked him. "Nick might look for me and not know where I am. Would you find him and let him know I'm just in the car and will be right back?"

"Of course, Jane. I'll walk you to your car."

"No, no, I'll be fine. Just find Nick. Thanks."

She gulped down the rest of her Diet Coke, tossed the cup in a trash can, and tottered to her car at the back of the parking lot. Carefully she deposited Winky in the backseat. Then she got into the front passenger seat, knowing it reclined farther than the driver's seat. She closed the door, opened her window a crack, and lay back, closing her eyes. Even with them closed, she couldn't stop the nauseating spinning.

"What on earth is the matter with me?" she muttered to herself, but just as she did she became aware that the spinning was mercifully subsiding, giving way to a warm, enveloping darkness.

Twenty-four

"Jane . . . ? Jane . . . ?"

A familiar voice, gentle, solicitous.

So hard to open my eyes . . . to rise out of this darkness.

"Jane, drink this. It will make you feel better."

Vaguely she felt something with a hard rim being pressed to her lips.

"Come on now."

Finally, with a supreme effort, Jane was able to open her eyes.

She was still in her car, still in the front passenger seat. But she was no longer in the parking lot of St. John's. Outside the car window, not four feet away, stood a wall of grass—thick green stalks, easily six or seven feet tall, like cornstalks without the corn, densely packed and swaying slightly in the breeze.

She looked to her left. In the driver's seat sat Laura. She was smiling at Jane, a gentle smile, the kind of smile one gives someone who's coming out of an illness or awakening from unconsciousness, as Jane realized she had just done.

"Laura," Jane said groggily. "Where are we? What happened? What's going on?" She tried to sit up, but the grogginess was still thick in her head and she gave up, relaxing once more into the seat.

"You gave me quite a scare," Laura said. "You fainted." She raised a cup, a large cardboard one like the ones at the bazaar. "Please, Jane, have a drink of this. It will make you feel much better." She brought it closer to Jane's face.

"Where are we?" Jane asked again.

"In the Meadowlands, in Secaucus. We're not far from Unimed, the company where I work." Laura looked about them. "I know this area well." She concentrated again on Jane. "Really, Jane, you've been ill. You're still not yourself. If you'll just drink this"—she raised the cup, her expression earnest—"you'll feel well again."

Jane watched Laura closely. "The way your father did?"

Laura's look of solicitous concern abruptly vanished. "So you do know," she said flatly.

"Yes." Jane's voice was sad, and now it was her turn to show sympathy.

"Don't look at me like that," Laura said contemptuously, "with such . . . pity. You don't pity me. You don't even like me, any more than I like you."

"Why'd you do it, Laura?" Jane asked softly. "Why'd you poison your father?" She was taking a chance here, for this was only a theory, but she knew immediately from Laura's reaction that her theory was correct.

Laura was breathing rapidly, clearly about to cry. Then her face contorted almost grotesquely. "So you've got it all figured out, haven't you. Our very own Miss

Marple, isn't that what *People* called you? Damn them," she muttered viciously.

"Your name is really Agnes, isn't it," Jane said calmly. "Agnes Oppenheim."

Laura spoke as if she hadn't heard Jane. "I loved him." A large tear welled in one of her eyes, and Jane watched it roll down her cheek until Laura swiped at it with her hand, the hand that bore the ring.... "He called me the most beautiful girl in the world...." Laura's eyes unfocused, seeing the past. "And Daddy had met the world's most beautiful women."

"Of course he had," Jane said. "Anthony Oppenheim owned luxury hotels around the world."

"That's right," Laura said eagerly, as if a girl of thirteen again. "He took me to a lot of them. London, Paris, Rome, Madrid. . . . We had some of our best times in those places."

"Until you realized you were expecting his child."

Laura nodded, her gaze lowered to the console between their seats. "I waited until we were back in Sharon—Sharon, Connecticut—to tell him. I waited for a special moment, when Mother was out with Elaine. I thought he'd be so pleased." She met Jane's gaze, her eyes wide with horror. "He said it was impossible, that I was too young. But I *wasn't* too young, I hadn't been too young for two years! I explained this to him. I explained that I had always avoided him when I had my period because he wanted me pure, his beautiful little girl. But I *wasn't* a little girl, I was a young woman, and I was pregnant."

"He wanted you to get an abortion, didn't he," Jane said.

"Yes." Laura's face reflected the disbelief it must have

reflected at that horrible moment so many years ago. "We had a terrible fight. He said awful things to me. He said he wasn't about to give up everything he'd worked for and be a figure of shame around the world because of some kid. 'Some kid'! But I told him I wanted the baby, *our* baby. I loved the baby, loved *Daddy*. It was part of us both.

"But he wouldn't listen. Even as I was talking to him, pleading with him, he picked up the phone beside the bed and started calling someone. I looked shocked, then he smiled at me and said of course this was all terribly upsetting and I needed time to accept what had to be."

Laura's eyes came back into focus, fixing sharply on Jane's face. "I knew what had to be. I knew what it all came down to."

"Either you or the baby," Jane said hollowly.

"That's right. You know what I decided."

"How did you do it, Laura?"

Laura smiled, her gaze darting to the cup in her hand. "There's poison everywhere if you know where to look. For Daddy I felt rat poison was appropriate. We had lots in the gardener's shed. Daddy always had the same cocktail every evening, something called an imperial. The night after we fought, I told him I'd get his drink for him, and I added an extra ingredient."

She frowned, remembering. "Oh, it was awful. Daddy on the floor, holding his stomach, vomiting, pleading with me to call a doctor. It was a shame, it broke my heart, because I loved him, loved him more than anyone in the world. But he'd sealed his own fate, hadn't he?" she said simply.

"I just left him there on the floor. It must have been

a good twenty minutes before Christine—she was one of our maids—found him and screamed. I was surprised he was still alive. The ambulance came, but he died in it."

"And everyone blamed your mother," Jane said.

"Well, I had to set her up for it, didn't I?" Laura asked, as if this were obvious. "What would have been the point of killing Daddy if I'd gotten blamed and hadn't been allowed to keep our baby? *The baby* was the one I'd done it for!"

"Your mother, Rosamond, was convicted."

"Yes. I'd made sure of that. I put some of the poison in a little plastic bag at the bottom of one of her dresser drawers." Laura looked vaguely regretful. "She loved Daddy, too, or at least she *said* she did, and her grief, combined with the thought of having to be locked away in prison the rest of her life . . . well . . ." She shook her head. "Before the police could come for her so that she could start serving her sentence, she took one of Daddy's guns and blew her head off."

"Don't you also think," Jane suggested gently, "that the truth—that *you'd* murdered your father—was too much for her to bear?"

"Oh, she never figured it out, I'm sure of that. She got me alone once and said she was sure Victor, our groundskeeper, had done it, and had I seen him in Daddy's room, and to please think hard. . . ."

"That was ironic," Jane said. "I mean, that your mother would suspect Victor. Since it was Victor Mangano and his wife who would take you in."

Laura looked distressed at this memory. "Neither of my parents had any family. The Manganos volunteered to take me in, but they had two children of their own and said they couldn't take Elaine too. So Elaine was put up for adoption." She gave an empty laugh. "The Manganos thought they were doing me such a favor. I could stay right there with people I knew. Yeah," she said with a disdainful chuckle, "*in the caretaker's cottage.* From the window of my room there I could see the window of my old room in the big house. . . .

"I wished I was Elaine. . . ."

"Who was adopted by Carl and Viveca Hamner, who named her Katherine."

Laura laughed. "Later to become Goddess!" She shook her head. "I shouldn't be surprised, I suppose. Our mother had been an actress—before she married Daddy. She was quite talented, actually, did a lot of stage work in New York. I guess Elaine inherited her talent. I'd say she's quite an actress in her own right."

"I'd say you were, too," Jane said solemnly.

Laura just stared at her for a moment. "Elaine grew to hate the Hamners," she said thoughtfully. "I see now why her films and music are so angry. She even rejected the name they gave her."

"And you hated the Manganos, too, didn't you?"

"No, not that way. I didn't hate *them.* It wasn't their fault they were poor. But I hated being poor. Funny, isn't it? Elaine was only five when all this happened, young enough not to remember what her life had been like. If the Manganos had taken her instead of me, she wouldn't have known the difference. I loved the life I'd been living—the beautiful big house, traveling around the world with Daddy to all those fabulous places. . . ."

Jane said, "But the Manganos' taking you in turned out to be fortuitous for you, didn't it?"

"Yes," Laura said uneasily. "When Hannah was only

a few months old, it was clear there was something wrong with her. Victor told me it wasn't my fault, that he knew what Daddy had done to me and that this was God's way of meting out punishment. 'The sins of the fathers,' Victor said. He was very religious."

Jane nodded, remembering his room at the nursing home.

"Victor moonlighted as a janitor at a place called Whiteson Institute. Finally he and his wife convinced me Hannah needed special care. They were right. Hannah was unbelievably difficult; it would have been hard for a grown woman to take care of her, let alone a girl of fourteen! And Victor's wife said she had her hands full with her two, a boy and a girl, and me.

"When Hannah had just turned two, Victor came to me one day and said he'd arranged with the people who ran Whiteson for them to take Hannah in. He never told me this, but his wife made sure I knew he was paying for Hannah's care by working there." Laura looked down into the cup in her hand. "I suppose it was all for the best. Now Hannah could be cared for by professionals, and Victor could keep an eye on her for me."

And, Jane thought, as a janitor with full run of the Insitute, he could empty Hannah's file so no one would know her shameful, scandalous origin. But he didn't know there was another file—the file for "highly sensitive" materials—into which the director had placed a newspaper story about the Oppenheim scandal.

"Having Hannah at Whiteson worked for you, too," Jane said. "Now you could leave town without worrying about her."

"That's right." Laura's face was impassive. "I had

to get away. Victor, with all his brimstone and Bible-thumping, sour Mrs. Mangano, always the martyr—I couldn't stand it anymore. But I couldn't leave yet, I was too young. I went to high school in Sharon. I used the Manganos' last name so no one would know who I was—before then I'd always gone to private schools." She frowned, remembering. "Two or three times Victor took me to the Institute to see Hannah, but I told him I couldn't go anymore. The older she got, the clearer it was that something was terribly wrong with her. That was another reason I just had to get away."

"So you left," Jane said. "You enrolled at Yale."

Laura let out a derisive laugh. "You need money to go to college. I didn't have any, remember?"

Jane looked at her in puzzlement. "But why was that? With both your parents dead, their fortune would have gone to you and Elaine."

"We were children, Jane. The money was put in 'trust' for us." Laura laughed again, a sharp bitter sound. " 'Trust'—that's a good one. *Millions* of dollars. Elaine and I were supposed to get it when we turned eighteen. Well, my father's business judgment wasn't always as good as it should have been, and his lawyer, who administered the trust, had gone through it all by the time I was old enough to claim my share. I considered suing him, but for what purpose? I looked into all my options, believe me."

"Oh, I believe you," Jane said. "So you had nothing. Then how did you pay for Yale?"

"It took me five years to save enough money, five years of working two jobs at a time in towns you've never heard of in Connecticut, Massachusetts. . . . Once I was in college, I got financial aid and kept working. I'm older than you and Daniel think, Jane. Five years older. When Daniel entered Yale at eighteen, I was twenty-three. I'm thirty-one now, but I've always looked younger than my age. So has Elaine."

She gazed out the car window at the high walls of grass flanking the narrow road. "I enrolled as Laura Dennison."

"And you met Daniel."

Laura's smile was sly. "Met? You might say that. I've always been a good researcher. I started checking out my classmates, and bingo! Daniel Willoughby, son of Cecil Willoughby and heir to the *Onyx* magazine empire. So I made it my business to 'meet' Daniel." She smiled. "And I liked him! I thought he was sweet. Better yet, his father had just had a heart attack that nearly killed him. He had quadruple bypass surgery. I figured it was only a matter of time before he kicked."

"But that fortune was of no use to you unless you were married to Daniel," Jane interjected.

"That's right." Laura suddenly looked weary. "And oh how I worked at him—all through school." She shook her head. "Daniel was stronger-willed than I'd thought. I got him to agree to live together, I even convinced him we should get engaged, but I couldn't get him to actually *marry* me. And all the while, old Cecil refused to die. Worse than that, he was getting better!"

Laura looked back at Jane, shrugged. "So I bided my time. After college, Daniel got his job with you and Kenneth, so we moved to Shady Hills, that godforsaken gossip cesspool of a town. And I . . . I got my job at Unimed. I figured the pharmaceuticals industry was just right for me." She gave Jane a deadly smile. "I've always had a keen interest in . . . chemicals."

Suddenly Laura seemed to deflate, her thin shoulders dropping. "Years passed," she said despondently. "Daniel still wouldn't set a wedding date. His father refused to die. And all the while, his empire grew, he got richer and richer, while Daniel and I struggled to get by because he was too proud to take a penny from his father."

Jane said, "You must have hated me when Daniel turned down that job offer from Silver and Payne last fall to stay with me. That job would have paid three times what I pay him."

Laura shrugged. "That kind of money doesn't make a difference, Jane, not when you're from the world I'm from. And as for hating you—I hate you anyway. I always have."

Jane blinked. "Why?"

"Because you—and Kenneth, too, when he was alive—you encouraged Daniel to nurture his stupid little dream of 'becoming an agent.'" Laura's voice dripped with ridicule. "If it hadn't been for you two, Daniel would have gone to work for his father. All those years—wasted."

"Yes, all those years," Jane echoed, "during which your daughter was growing up."

"Mm. I didn't know Victor had shown her pictures of me, the sentimental fool. He would never have given them to her, of course, because if anyone at the Institute had found them, they would have figured out where Hannah came from. And he never told her who I was."

"But then *People* ran its story on me," Jane said. "On all of us."

"That's right. Hannah told me she couldn't believe her eyes. She decided the moment she saw the photo of me that she would meet me, no matter what it took. So one day while she was out for her walk around the Institute, she went out into the woods and slipped through a tear in the chain link fence. She hitched rides all the way to Shady Hills. All she had with her was that article from *People*.

"When she got here she met Arthur, Doris's nephew. She told him she needed a secret place to live until she was ready to reveal her 'wonderful surprise.' He brought her food, a map of town."

"But someone found her in the cave," Jane said.

Laura nodded. "Some hiker staying at the inn. Hannah begged him not to tell anyone she was there. He finally agreed, even brought her a blanket."

Louise's antique Irish Chain quilt, Jane thought, the first thing he saw to grab at the inn.

She shook her head thoughtfully. "Hannah wasn't the only person to be taken aback by your photo in *People*. Goddess—Elaine, if you like—saw it, too, and though she didn't recognize you—she'd been only five when you were separated—"

"She recognized my pendant," Laura finished, fingering it at her clavicle. "I never take mine off. Daddy gave one to each of us when we were babies."

Jane nodded. "So using the pretext of wanting to write a book, Goddess approached her only friend who worked in publishing, Holly Griffin, and asked Holly to introduce Goddess to me. Through me, Goddess could get to Daniel, and to you. It wasn't Holly who brought Goddess to me, as Holly claimed. It was Goddess who *asked* Holly to introduce Goddess to me.

"And Goddess's plan worked. At Carol Freund's publication party, Goddess came face-to-face with you, had an opportunity to examine your pendant more closely than she could have done in the *People* photo."

"I recognized her immediately." Laura looked stunned even as she recalled that moment. "I—I couldn't believe my eyes. My little sister Elaine was—*Goddess*! I couldn't tell whether she recognized me, too. Later she told me that the Hamners had told her everything about her past. I didn't know that then, but I had to assume the worst. I had to assume she knew enough to tell the world who I really was."

Jane smiled ruefully, shaking her head. "And then poor, foolish, big-mouthed Holly, always wanting to be seen as an insider, made the mistake of telling everyone that Goddess had already told Holly everything—and thereby sealed her fate."

"The idiot," Laura said. "I followed her back to her office while Elaine was singing. Holly looked surprised to see me. I told her I was intrigued with publishing because of Daniel's being an agent. We chatted for a moment. When she bent down to pick up the framed book jacket for Carol, I took her letter opener. I came around her desk, pretending to admire the view. Then I just spun around and stuck the letter opener right through her neck. It was harder than I'd thought it would be," she said, looking uncomfortable; then she giggled. "She kind of . . . wiggled on it, like a bug pinned to a board."

Jane recoiled. "That must have been difficult for you, stabbing her. After all, your first method had been poison."

Laura laughed. " 'First method'! You talk as if I'm some kind of serial killer."

"You are."

Laura shrugged indifferently. "The point is—no pun intended—that I couldn't let Holly get in the way of all I'd worked so hard for, waited so many years for."

"Some of Holly's blood spattered on your blouse, didn't it," Jane said. "That's why you spilled tomato juice on yourself at the bar—to cover the bloodstain."

"Oh, you are good." Laura giggled. "The poor bartender! Who knows what he must have thought. He saw me do it to myself but didn't dare contradict me."

"So that was one down," Jane said. "I was next, wasn't I?"

Laura nodded. "I didn't know how much Elaine knew, didn't know how much of what she knew she'd told you. I couldn't take any chances. I knew Daniel wouldn't want me to go to Chicago with him for his father's funeral. I followed you to the Waldorf . . ."

". . . gave the desk clerk that phony note from Salomé Sutton, and bashed me over the head with a vase. But I didn't die."

"No," Laura said pensively, then brightened. "That's why we get second chances."

"Hannah had no second chance," Jane said, and Laura's face grew serious. "She'd located you, hadn't she, and approached you?"

"That's right. She actually came to our house, *rang our bell.* Thank God Daniel wasn't home yet. She was so happy. I was horrified."

"You thought you'd rid yourself of her eighteen years ago." Jane shook her head in wonder. "Years ago you chose the life of this child over that of your father. Now . . ."

"I couldn't afford to have her jeopardize my plans." Laura spoke as if her words made perfect sense. "Besides, I hadn't seen her since she was a little girl. She was a stranger to me."

"You told her you'd meet her later in the cave, didn't you?"

"Yes. She took me there so I'd be able to find her. She said I was beautiful. She must have noticed I was wearing makeup, because she asked me to bring some when I came back to the cave."

"Which would be that night. You slipped Daniel something to knock him out, right?"

"That's right, my own little Mickey Finn. I just dissolved some sleeping pills I'd taken from work in his coffee."

"So Daniel thought you were in bed with him all night. He was your alibi."

"Right again."

"But you slipped out of bed and went to the cave to meet Hannah as planned."

"Mm. She was so excited. She wanted so badly to look pretty for her introduction to the people of Shady Hills. You should have seen her trying to put on the makeup I'd brought. She'd never worn makeup before. She made herself look like a clown."

"You wouldn't help her."

"What would have been the point? She was about to die."

"What did you give her to make her cooperate?"

"Would you recognize the name if I told you? It was a hallucinogen. I put it in a Coke I'd brought her. Then it was easy. I led her through the woods to a tree behind the inn, hauled her up, and tied the rope to another tree."

Jane regarded her with horror. "And to pin the murder on Ernie, you stuffed one of his handkerchiefs into the pocket of Hannah's dress."

Laura gave a simple nod.

"You took it from the clothesline behind the inn," Jane said, and Laura nodded again.

"And when we went to New York to pick out your wedding dress, you told me you'd heard gossip about Ernie having extramarital affairs."

"I really had heard it," Laura said.

"I believe you," Jane said, thinking of Dara.

"In fact, hearing the gossip was what made me decide to frame Ernie in the first place. I wanted the cops to think she was one of his girlfriends."

Jane sat thoughtfully, pondering this horror. "So you returned home, where Daniel was still sound asleep."

Laura smiled slyly. "Not so sound asleep that I couldn't get him to make love to me."

"Ah," Jane said, eyes widening, "so it was then that he made love to you without protection."

Laura looked sickened. "He *told* you about that? You two have a twisted relationship, you know that?"

Jane ignored this remark. "If I'd known that was when it happened, I could have told him it was too soon for a home pregnancy test to be reliable."

"But you didn't know." Laura laughed disdainfully. "Men. They really are so naive about such things. The important point is that he believed me."

"So drugging him served a dual purpose. It gave you an alibi—how could you have been in the woods behind the inn hanging Hannah when you were in bed with

Daniel all night?—and it allowed you to announce believably that you were pregnant.''

"You got it," Laura said brightly.

"But you weren't, were you."

"No. But how else could I get him to marry me? You know how traditional he is. I knew that if he believed I was pregnant, he'd finally agree to set a wedding date.''

Jane nodded. "Hannah's appearance in Shady Hills had unnerved you, given you a new sense of urgency." She shook her head, remembering. "But even as cold-hearted a murderer as you had a trace of conscience. Daniel said you cried off and on after Hannah's body was discovered. You were crying at the realization of what you'd done. You'd murdered your own daughter.''

For several moments the two women sat silently, Laura staring vacantly out the windshield at the gently waving grass.

Jane broke the silence. "But marrying Daniel wouldn't have done you any good if his father was still alive.''

"That's right," Laura said. "And as far as I was concerned, he couldn't die a moment too soon."

"What better place to kill him than at your own wedding?''

Laura said nothing, watching Jane.

"You called Daniel's father and told him about the wedding, didn't you?''

"That's right.''

"What did you say to him—that Daniel would be upset if he knew you'd called, so you'd rather keep it your little secret?''

"Right again.''

"And at the wedding you slipped a poison into Cecil

Willoughby's champagne, a poison you knew would cause him to collapse as if his heart had finally given out. After all, everyone knew he had a bad heart. He'd already cheated death for years. It was only a matter of time. And you knew no one would request an autopsy if he appeared to have died of a heart attack.

"But your sister—Goddess—saw you slip the drug into Mr. Willoughby's glass—that's why she suddenly spilled it onto the ground, pretending she'd seen a caterpillar in it." Jane shook her head. "But she only postponed Mr. Willoughby's murder. You managed to slip the poison into his drink again later. I'm curious about where you carry your poisons, Laura. My guess is it's in that big ring you always wear."

Laura held up the ring, gold with a filigreed dome top. "*Very* good," she said, flipping open the lid to reveal a compartment inside.

"Just like Lucrezia Borgia. . . ."

"What?"

"Never mind. . . . So now poor Mr. Willoughby was dead, and you were Mrs. Daniel Willoughby, the wife of a millionaire." Jane shook her head. "But it still wasn't to be smooth sailing for you. You must have suspected that Goddess had seen you slip the poison into Mr. Willoughby's drink, and during the private screening of *Adam and Eve*, you sneaked out and went to speak to Goddess in the lounge down the corridor. Goddess must then have told you she knew you were sisters and that she knew you had murdered Mr. Willoughby."

"She threatened me," Laura said. "She said she'd tell the police what I'd done if I didn't disappear. She said she was giving me a chance because we were sisters, because blood is thicker than water." She snorted. "I told her I had no intention of 'disappearing,' and that if she said a word to anyone about what she *thought* she knew, I'd kill her, too."

"Which you intended to do at a later date anyway."

"Yes . . . but that wasn't the time."

"Goddess must have sensed your plans for her, because it was *she* who disappeared, afraid for her life."

"Right," Laura said. "I'll find her eventually. But in the meantime I have another problem. You, Jane. I'm curious . . . How'd you figure it all out?"

Jane frowned in thought. "Goddess made a strange comment to me, a comment about dreaming of someone and then meeting the person she'd dreamed about.

"Last night, while I was trying to sleep, I remembered this comment. Suddenly all the pieces came together for me. Goddess was five when you and she were separated—too young to remember you clearly, but old enough to have residual memories that came to her in her dreams. It was you she was referring to. Without realizing what she herself was saying, she was revealing that she knew you.

"Goddess didn't dream about you and then meet you. She vaguely remembered you, *thought* she was dreaming about someone she'd never met, and *then* she met you again. It was only a matter of time before she realized who you were.

"It gave me terrible pain—on poor Daniel's behalf— to believe my theory possible, but I was pretty sure of it. I just had to be certain. If I was right and you were a killer, I would still be a target for you. So I decided to flush you out before you could get me."

Laura looked amused. "And how were you going to do that?"

"I went to the cave in the woods and smeared everything in it with a hand cream that contains a chemical that drives my cat Winky crazy. Then I called Daniel and told him the police had found a clue the killer had left at the place where the murdered woman was living. I knew he would share this information with you. If I was right about you, you would visit the cave before going to the church bazaar."

"Right you are. I told Daniel I had an errand to run and that I'd meet him at the church."

Jane nodded. "I intended to hold Winky, my 'murderer detector,' close to you to see if she reacted. If she did react, I would know it was you who had been in the cave, searching the objects there.

"It hadn't occurred to me that you already had plans for me. You'd slipped something into the Diet Coke Daniel brought me, hadn't you? It made me so dizzy I had to sit for a few minutes in the car. Then I passed out."

Laura nodded. "I saw you go to your car. I told Daniel I was tired—in my condition—and would meet him at home."

"You got into my car and drove us here."

"Yes," Laura said, pleased. "Your final resting place." She gazed out into the tall grass. "It could be years before they find you." Swiftly she reached into the back pocket of her jeans and produced a switchblade. Expertly she flicked it open, its six-inch blade gleaming in the sunlight. She held it a few inches from Jane's neck. "Now, as you know, *Miss Marple*, I much prefer poison to stabbing. But you also know I'll stab you if I have to. So you choose. The knife, or"—she lowered her gaze to the cup in her hand—"the drink."

"Another of your potions?"

Laura nodded. "It will work quickly. Why not take the easy way out?"

Jane didn't want to take either way out.

At that moment she remembered Winky in the back-seat.

"Winky," she called, and the cat seemed to appear from nowhere, jumping onto Jane's lap and nuzzling her face, oblivious to the blade at Jane's neck.

Laura let out a little cry of surprise. "I didn't know she was in the car."

Jane had an idea. "Laura, I think I will choose the drink."

"Smart choice," Laura said and, smiling sweetly, brought the cup to Jane's lips.

Suddenly Winky bristled and let out a wild yowl, lashing out at Laura's hand that held the cup. The liquid in it splashed into Laura's face. Laura let out a cry of horror.

Seizing her moment, Jane opened the car door and, still holding Winky, scrambled out. But Jane realized she was still a little groggy and couldn't move as fast as she wanted to. Laura, wiping hard at her face and mouth with her T-shirt, had also gotten out. She ran around the car toward Jane.

"Winky, run!" Jane cried, and the cat jumped from her arms and ran into the tall grass an instant before Laura came around the back of the car. Her face the very picture of loathing, she brandished the knife and with a fierce grunt lunged at Jane. The knife went into Jane's side, but not all the way because Jane jumped back, even as she felt the sting of the blade. She spun around and dashed headlong into the sea of grass, knowing it was her only hope of escape.

Running through the tall heavy stalks was like running through mud in a nightmare. As Jane rushed forward, madly parting the grass before her, she heard rustling behind her and knew Laura was gaining on her.

"Jane, come back here," Laura said fiercely. "Jane!"

Jane kept running. She felt the ground begin to slope gently upward.

"Jane, you come here," Laura commanded again, but her voice was different now—tired, weaker.

And then all at once the tall grass ended, and before Jane was trim green grass that rose on a steep embankment about eight feet high.

Suddenly, not five feet to the right of where Jane stood, Winky shot out of the tall grass. She looked straight at Jane, let out an exceptionally loud meow, and ran up the embankment. Halfway up, she stopped, looking behind her, waiting; then Laura burst from the grass, and apparently not seeing Jane, stumbled up the embankment after the cat.

Now Jane was aware of a whooshing sound, and in that instant she realized what lay at the top of the embankment: one of the highways that crisscrossed the Meadowlands.

Laura was about three-quarters of the way up the embankment. Winky stood at the very top.

"Winky!" Jane cried out, wanting to stop the cat from running out into traffic; but Winky kept going.

Laura, looking dazed, her skin a sickly white, glanced quickly at Winky, then down at Jane. For a moment she simply wavered, as if unsure whom to pursue, Jane or

Winky. Then suddenly she made a horrible choking sound, her face contorting, and collapsed out of sight onto the highway.

Jane ran up the embankment. Halfway up she heard the long insistent blare of a car horn, then the sickening screech of brakes; it seemed to go on forever.

Panting hard, Jane finally gained the top. Before her, a dark-colored car stood slanted across the highway's nearest lane. Laura lay beneath the closest front tire, one arm outstretched as if in supplication, a river of dark red running from her crushed head.

"Oh!" Jane cried out, clasping a hand over her mouth, and looked away.

Then she noticed a tiny movement far across the wide highway. There, at the road's edge, sat Winky—solemn as a statue, unharmed, her face inscrutable.

It was a few hours later. Jane sat in one of Greenberg's visitor's chairs, Daniel in the other. He was perfectly still, his face expressionless, as if all that Jane had told him he could simply not take in . . . as if it were all a bad dream.

"It was the issue of adoption—of learning from Carl Hamner that Goddess was adopted and had rejected her adoptive parents—that first got me thinking," Jane said. "Do children put up for adoption always end up in happy situations? How do they react to these situations? This line of thought enabled me to put together the many pieces of a rather complicated puzzle into a theory." She looked at Daniel, her heart breaking for him. "A theory I was later deeply saddened to learn was correct."

"Why didn't you come to me?" Greenberg demanded.

She gave him a skeptical look. "Would you—would anyone—have believed such a far-fetched story?"

"No," he admitted, "I suppose not."

"So I had to find out on my own."

"And almost got yourself killed," Daniel said hollowly.

She cast sad eyes on him. "I'm so sorry, Daniel. When Winky bristled at the smell of the cream on Laura's hand, the poison splashed into her mouth. I hadn't meant for that to happen; I only wanted to distract her so Winky and I could get out of the car." She shook her head, remembering. "If she hadn't been killed by the car on Route Three, her own poison would have done her in."

The room was silent, everyone looking at the floor. When Jane glanced up, a tear was running down Daniel's cheek.

"You asked me if I loved her. I did," he said.

Jane took him in her arms, held him tight. "I know," she said. "I know."

And you, you poor, trusting, innocent man—how long will it take you to realize that you would probably have been Laura's next victim?

Twenty-five

It was one week later. Sitting at her desk trying to read Bertha Stumpf's *Casbah*, Jane grimaced and gazed out the window. At that moment a white stretch limousine pulled up to the curb. Jane remembered Cecil Willoughby's limo, but it wasn't poor Mr. Willoughby who got out, of course.

It was Goddess. Jane jumped up and ran out to the reception room.

Goddess burst through the door, all smiles. Today she was dressed like a matador. She looked at Daniel, then at Jane. "I'm baaaack!" she cried.

Jane grabbed the girl and hugged her. "Thank God you're all right." She drew back and looked at her. "I'm so sorry about your sister."

Goddess chomped on her gum. "Yeah, thanks. But she wasn't really my sister, not *really*." She looked into Jane's eyes. "Blood isn't always thicker than water." She turned to Daniel. "I'm sorry about Laura."

"Thank you."

Goddess chomped again, looked around the agency.

"Cute. Well, I guess I'm ready to start my book now. And thanks to you, Miss Marple, I've got a hell of a lot to put in it." She winked at Jane. "Maybe we won't even need that pop-up idea you hated."

Jane opened her mouth to protest; then they both burst out laughing.

Abruptly, Goddess's expression turned to one of regret. "First, though, I'm going to see Mommy and Daddy. I figure life's too short to let this kind of thing go on. Where's the bathroom? I wanna check my hair."

"Right next to my office," Jane said, pointing.

Goddess hopped off.

Jane turned to Daniel. He gave her a little smile.

A moment later, Goddess reappeared. "Okay, kids, gotta fly. Love ya! Oh," she said, pausing at the door, "don't forget to send those contracts to Yves." And she was gone. Through the window they saw the white limo slide away.

Jane shook her head and laughed. "And I thought Bertha was bad!"

Daniel actually laughed, a good sign.

"Take you to lunch?" Jane ventured.

Daniel looked down shyly. "Thanks, but I'm having lunch with Ginny today. Did you know she broke up with Rob?"

"Yes, she told me," Jane said thoughtfully, and worked to keep her face serious. Daniel and Ginny . . . What a wonderful thought.

"Did you also know that Ginny is a whiz with computers?" Daniel asked. "She's going to help me with this confounded program we bought."

"Perfect," Jane said, and returned to her office, ready to confront Bertha's manuscript once more.

Looking down at her desk, she discovered something that hadn't been there before: a gift-wrapped box. Jane pulled off the bow and lifted off the lid.

Inside were several items. A new CD—by Goddess, of course. *What We Need,* it was called. On the front was a photo of Goddess done up as Marilyn Monroe. Jane laughed and set it aside.

Beneath it were two orchestra tickets to *Goddess of Love.* She'd take Stanley, she decided, and then laughed at the thought of that.

The last item in the box was a bottle of deep red nail polish. Sitting down, Jane examined the label. Eternally Yours.

With a little chuckle, she unscrewed the top and began brushing the polish onto her nails. A thought occurred to her.

"Daniel!" she called out to him.

"Yes?" came his voice through the intercom.

"If *People* magazine calls . . . hang up."

Please turn the page for
an exciting sneak peek
of Evan Marshall's
newest Jane Stuart and Winky mystery
STABBING STEPHANIE
coming in June 2001!

Lillian Strohman's house, which was built of pale stone and resembled a castle, made Puffy's look like a cottage. A wide drive made of paving stones climbed the slope of an immense lawn and passed beneath an arched porte cochere in the house itself.

When they were halfway up the drive, Florence said, "Una asked us to come around to the back door, so we should go through here." She pointed to the archway. "There's a place to park in the back."

"Why does she want us to come to the back?"

"Because that's the door to the kitchen, and she's working in there right now. Or she might be in the laundry room, but that's right off the kitchen. She didn't want us coming to the front door, all public—you know."

Jane drove through the porte cochere, and they emerged onto a wide paved area behind the house.

As they got out of the car, Florence said, "Sometimes Una doesn't hear the doorbell when she's in the laundry room, because the washer and dryer make a lot of noise, so she said she would leave the door unlocked for us."

"Okay." Approaching the kitchen door, Jane noticed that some construction work was in progress. The ground between the paved area and the door itself had been torn up—chunks of concrete lay off to one side—and a wooden frame had been put in place, the kind of frame used to contain poured concrete. The floor of this frame consisted of exposed earth as well as large amounts of white dust from the broken-up concrete.

"Oh," Florence said, seeing this mess and remembering, "Una said to watch where we walk. Mrs. Strohman is having this part replaced."

"So I see," Jane said, irritated that no boards had been put down between the concrete that was still intact and the door. Carefully she and Florence picked their way across. Jane's feet sank into the earth and concrete dust; she could see white powder collecting on her shoes.

The door had a window in it, but it was covered with a shirred white curtain, so they couldn't see into the kitchen. Jane turned the knob and the door opened. She was about to enter the house when Florence placed her hand on Jane's.

"Missus, I'm thinking it would be best if I go in first and speak to Una, tell her again that you're okay. Would that be all right? It will only take a minute or two."

"Yes, if you think so," Jane said, and stood aside so Florence could go in. With a nervous smile, Florence stepped into the kitchen, which Jane could see was large but old-fashioned, as many of the kitchens in these old mansions were. Florence left the door ajar.

Jane turned away from the door and gazed up at the house. From here it was clear that the building was a jumble of levels at various heights; she could easily see how a burglar might have climbed up and used the roof of one level to gain access to Lillian Strohman's bedroom.

"Missus!"

Jane jumped. It was Florence, shrieking in terror, shrieking as Jane had never heard her shriek. Jane spun around and pushed open the door. It nearly hit Florence, who had been running toward it. Her face was twisted in terror and tears streamed down her cheeks.

"Missus—" Panting, she leaned on Jane, apparently unable to say any more.

Jane's heart pounded. "What is it? Florence, what happened?"

"Missus," Florence gasped. "It's Una. She's ... dead!"

ABOUT THE AUTHOR

Like his sleuth Jane Stuart, EVAN MARSHALL heads his own literary agency. A former book editor and packager, he has contributed articles on writing and publishing to numerous magazines and is the author of *Eye Language* and *The Marshall Plan for Novel Writing*. He lives and works in Pine Brook, New Jersey, where he is at work on the next Jane Stuart mystery. Evan loves to hear from readers, and you can email him at: *evanmarshall@thenovelist. com*